THIS IS HOW YOU DIE

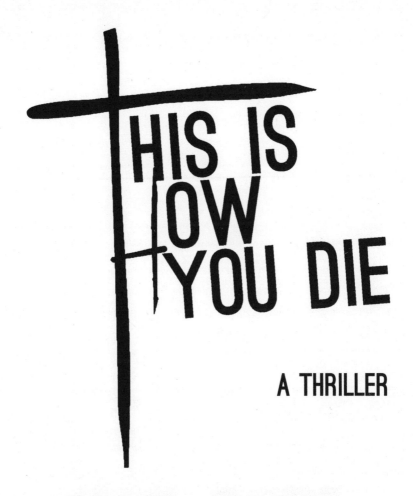

THIS IS HOW YOU DIE

A THRILLER

DAVID JESTER

Skyhorse Publishing

Skyhorse Publishing books may be purchased in bulk at special discounts for sales promotion, corporate gifts, fund-raising, or educational purposes. Special editions can also be created to specifications. For details, contact the Special Sales Department, Skyhorse Publishing, 307 West 36th Street, 11th Floor, New York, NY 10018 or info@skyhorsepublishing.com.

Skyhorse® and Skyhorse Publishing® are registered trademarks of Skyhorse Publishing, Inc.®, a Delaware corporation.

Visit our website at www.skyhorsepublishing.com.

10 9 8 7 6 5 4 3 2 1

Library of Congress Cataloging-in-Publication Data is available on file.

Cover design by Lilith_C (lilithcgraphics)

Print ISBN: 978-1-940456-76-8
Ebook ISBN: 978-1-940456-77-5

Printed in the United States of America

To my father, my very first beta reader and the first to believe in me.

PART 1

1

School was out. The children were set free upon the world, swarming out of iron gates like animals let loose from a zoo. A variety of species. A variety of noises.

"Hey, Catherine! Nice ass." The mating call of the pimpled buffoon, jostling his way through the herd to get to his orange-tinted mate.

On the main street of Whitegate, where scarce shops nestled inside rows of boarded-up businesses like glistening crowns on yellowed dentures, the voices of excited schoolchildren beefed up the afternoon air with boisterous calls, shrill whistles, and high-pitched laughter.

In the alleyways and alcoves, the highways and byways of small-town life, sly cigarettes and hastily rolled joints were hurriedly smoked. Between gleeful puffs of toxic joy, little faces lit up the dim gloom. First graders, third graders, sixth graders; first-time smokers, long-time smokers, part-time smokers—all eager for their own dose of disease before going home to questioning parents, home-cooked meals, and two hours of condescending television.

I was doing what I did every Friday afternoon: I was getting the shit kicked out of me by the school bully, Darren Henderson. He first started beating me in elementary school and had stuck with it throughout the years. He was committed to it and he clearly enjoyed it, so who was I to break with tradition?

Every boot in my chest shocked the air out of my lungs. Every punt into my back, from his brother-in-torture Barry Barlow, was

1

like a dagger through my spine. Every laugh a hazy taunt to my ringing ears.

It was hard to tune them out, but I did. I went to my safe place—a room of brilliant white. The floors were a fluffy carpet of the purest color, soft and yielding underfoot. Nothing on the walls; nothing on the ceiling. No distractions, no clutter, just pure white. And there, at my feet, curled into a helpless, sobbing ball of self-loathing, was Darren Henderson. After enjoying his torment, I grabbed him by his fringe and yanked him to his feet. The taut hair pulled his flesh, ripping it from its follicles like Velcro. I stared into his misty eyes, soaking up the sorrow, despair, and fear that swam through the hazel orbs.

I cut his throat with the serrated side of a hunting knife. I excavated his chest with a single thrust, plunging until the razor-sharp tip shaved his spine. I hacked off his limbs with the blunt edge of the blade and I pricked his legs like a pin cushion. Then, after long and enjoyable moments of extreme torture, I sat back and bathed in the crimson room of my creation.

His friend wasn't involved in my fantasies; he was just a pawn. A worthless prick who only did what he did because his psychopathic boyfriend told him to do it. He would have his comeuppance without my assistance, right around the time he finally tells Darren he thinks he's in love with him and wants him to be his "first." Suicide through dejection and melancholy, or murder through attempted mutual masturbation with an aggressively heterosexual alpha-bully.

Eventually they grew tired—their legs fully exercised for the day—and they stopped pummeling me. Their finish, their *pièce de résistance,* was, as usual, thick slabs of viscous phlegm gathered through thirty seconds of throat-clearing and propelled at my face.

I watched them go through blurry eyes, almost skipping with joy as they hopped through the iron gates to join their friends.

I had no friends. I didn't really like anyone in the school, and certainly no one who liked me.

While I waited for the coast to clear, apathetic about the gelatinous glob running down my cheek, a wind kicked up and dried my eyes, the tears having fallen through pain rather than misery. A single sheet from a week-old newspaper, discarded on the cold and damp streets, lifted in the breeze and swept into my face, where it plastered itself, the phlegm acting as an adhesive.

I sat up, the sheet stuck to my face. The movement was excruciating; my back, stomach, ribs, and shoulders screamed out in agony. I peeled the paper from my face, drawn to the smudged words on its front.

The Butcher Strikes Again.

A serial killer that had stalked the streets of this county and the next. A legend, five years in the making. A couple of victims had been teenagers not much older than Darren Henderson, kids who were abducted, brutally murdered, and then butchered. Their limbs had practically been torn from their bodies.

I straightened out a few wrinkles in the paper, using my lap as support.

". . . 27-year-old nurse . . . in her own home . . . reportedly hanged with her own . . ."

The rest was indecipherable but I already knew the story, as did everyone else in the country. His most recent victim worked as an emergency room nurse at the local hospital, a place where the inept found employment and the funeral homes found business. She had worked for an exhausting thirty straight hours and had gone home, informing her colleagues and friends that she would probably sleep for the next two days. The Butcher had followed, murdered her in her sleep, and then worked his own tireless shift, spending the night and the next morning tearing her to pieces. Her friends discovered her decaying body three days later, hanging from a light fixture in her bedroom, the macabre scarf of her large intestine strung around her neck.

The newspaper article brought a smile to my face, a flicker of delight that twitched through the agony. I was thrilled to live in times of a legend. A killer with more infamy and respect than Jack the Ripper, and deservedly so. Here was a man who had butchered more than fourteen young men and women without preference. A man who killed purely for the joy of killing.

In years to come, he would be remembered. Even if they caught him tomorrow, next week, or next month, bringing an end to his spree, his reign of terror, these five years of reverence and fear, would never be forgotten.

I rose to my feet with a smile on my face. In my head, I was back in my happy place, only now I had company to help me murder the delinquent who had made my schooldays a living hell.

————

School was over for the Easter holidays. Spring break—two weeks without the misery of being surrounded by tedious people who hated me, and who I viewed with similar contempt.

As I strolled along the pavement, the noise of my fellow pupils faded to a mere background holler. The remaining few were making their way to houses on the edge of Whitegate, the rest having already boarded the buses and cars that would take them home. One of those buses passed my house, stopping just a few feet from the rusty gate that snaked down a gravel path to my doorway, but I preferred to walk. The thirty minutes it took to trudge through the streets and fields to my home was usually enough to force the endorphins into numbing the pain.

It didn't matter if I returned home in this state, because I was going back to an empty house. In the past, I had hidden my distress from my father, despite his apathy to my regular beatings, but his indifferent demeanor wouldn't be there to greet my distress. He had taken a short working holiday, keeping up with an erratic schedule that saw him take sporadic flights from our homestead, sometimes for a week or two at a time.

"Don't be throwing any parties," he often mocked before his excursions. "But if you do, leave some booze for me!"

Ever the joker, never the comedian. I kept up appearances. I smiled and nodded when I thought it was necessary. But despite being drawn from the same vein, we were completely different people.

My father was a pleasant man, a friendly man. He wasn't overpowering, rarely spoke out of turn, and never interrupted anyone. He was a man seemingly trained in social etiquette and a man who made it his goal in life to please everyone he encountered. He had his moments, of course, moments of vicious anger that seemed to flare up out of nowhere and for no discernible reason, but I was usually the only one to witness them, and I rarely minded. If anything, I was relieved to see him angry; it was comforting to know that he was human and not a machine hell bent on pleasing the entire fucking human race.

My mother also saw him angry, and one of my earliest memories was of a fight between them. Her face a picture of regret and fear; his the flared red of an archetypal psychopath.

He beat her to within an inch of her life and seemed to enjoy himself. I watched him tear the fear from her frail face and then mock her sobbed pleas. When he saw me sitting wide-eyed on the bottom step, his face a snarling, frothy mess of madness—mine an ambivalent collage of fear and confusion—something changed inside him. In an instant, he reverted to the innocent man everyone knew and loved. He helped my mother to her feet, apologized more times than was necessary, made her a cup of coffee, and then spent the day doting on her. He didn't acknowledge me until the following morning. The incident wasn't mentioned.

My mother left a year after that. I was eight at the time. She never said good-bye; never gave me a reason. She didn't even leave a note. I didn't blame myself; I didn't blame my father. I blamed her. If either of us had meant anything to her, regardless of what we had done, she would have at least said good-bye.

5

"Good afternoon, Herman!"

A little old lady popped her head out from behind a bush she had been pruning. I smiled at her, watching her wrinkled features morph into something that also resembled a smile. Her skin, worn like a tanned sheet over a science-class skeleton, looked like a piece of balled-up paper someone had frantically tried to straighten out.

"Afternoon, Mrs. Jones, how are you today?"

"Well, you know." She put her hands on her hips, exhaled deeply.

I prepared myself for a long lecture. A boring story about a boring day from a person I gave less than two fucks about. She said something about her cat. It had either died or had given birth; I wasn't really paying attention and it didn't matter. She referred to the cat by name, despite the fact that I had never even seen it, let alone did I know its fucking name. I did my best to pretend I was interested in what she had to say. I had seen my father do something similar on a number of occasions. I knew he couldn't really be interested in some of the shit people said to him, it wasn't possible, but not only did he stand and listen, he did so with enthusiasm.

I tried to be like him. Despite my apathy to his existence and my hatred of his social acceptance, a part of me respected his ability to conform to the mundane protocols of a tedious society without the slightest modicum of visible resentment.

"Well?" Mrs. Jones said, seemingly not for the first time.

My efforts were futile. She already looked annoyed. I let my smile fade, allowing a natural look of disinterest to take over.

"You haven't been listening to a word I've said, have you?"

I was a little offended that she was angry. If anything, she should be embarrassed that her story had sent me into a fucking trance. That's the problem with neighbors—they force themselves to adhere to the pathetic principles of small talk in an effort to be nice and neighborly, when the nicest thing they could do is shut the fuck up and let everyone get on with their day. I don't want to hear about your fucking cat and I don't care if it's going to get warmer, wetter, or windier later in the week; if I did I would check the forecast instead of relying on some dimwit who stops me in the street because they live near me and thinks that gives them the right to interrupt my peace with their banal bullshit.

I tried my best to suppress my rising anger. I cleared my throat and averted my eyes from hers when a thought of ripping them out of her cardboard skull and stuffing them between her accusing lips entered my mind.

"I'm sorry," I said with an apologetic shake of my head.

She sounded a disapproving *tut tut* noise, her head shaking from side to side like a lopsided Nodding Dog, her bony hands pressed to her hips all the while. "You're nothing like your father," she said with a sneer.

I nodded and hung my head. "Tell me about it," I muttered when she was out of earshot.

I slumped down the path to my front door and tried the key in the lock, but it didn't turn. It took me a few more tries before I realized the door was already unlocked. I figured my dad had canceled or delayed his trip, and that his blank expression would be waiting for me on the other side of the door. He would be ready to ignore my distress and gloss over my wounds by making me a cup of tea and watching television in silence for the rest of the night, punctuating the sitcom laugh-tracks, soap opera exaggerations, and newsroom gloom with small talk and sexism.

I found my father in the middle of the living room floor. His expression was blank, but it wasn't aimed at me. He was lying flat-out, staring through lifeless eyes at the dusty light fixture that hung from the yellowed ceiling like an abscess on jaundiced skin. His left arm was elevated, casually flopped onto the brown leather sofa; his head was resting against the cold laminate floor. A small trickle of blood had leaked out from underneath his head, drying and darkening on the wood like congealed varnish.

The front door was still open, my left hand on its edge, my right still grasping the keys. I didn't know how I was supposed to react, what I was supposed to do.

A strong stench hung in the air, something I had never encountered before fused with plenty of smells that I had. My father was a clean freak, and when he wasn't scrubbing or dusting, he was bleaching the surfaces and the floor. The pungent smell of bleach and scented polish had become impregnated with the smell of feces. The odor faced me like a wall as I finally found the courage to move forward, leaving the door open.

My heart was pounding and my legs were trembling, but I made it over to my father's body. I knelt down on unsafe legs, stretched a wobbly arm, and touched the flesh around his neck. He was cold and I couldn't find a pulse.

I looked into the face of my father. Eyes that had previously shone with utter contentment and flared with demonic rage were now blank and void of life. The blood that had pooled on the floor came from a small cut at the base of his head. There was no blood anywhere else. No cuts, no obvious signs of injury. All of my medical know-how came from TV shows, but any idiot could spot if someone had been bludgeoned to death or not, and he hadn't.

I sat by his side, staring blankly for what could have been minutes but may have been hours.

2

The flashing lights and the pace of the ambulance seemed a little redundant as it screeched to a stop outside my house. My father was dead—I told them as much over the phone—no amount of haste was going to save him.

The paramedics spoke in dulcet tones and went about their macabre business in relative silence, bagging his body and carrying it to the back of the ambulance. They said it was most likely a heart attack, which I had already suspected. Years of bottled-up anger, a lazy lifestyle, and a bad diet had finally caught up with him. The paramedics had a practiced look of pity, but they didn't really seem to know what to do with me. I was too old to console by getting on one knee, patting me on the shoulder, and telling me everything would be all right. I was too cold and indifferent for a hug.

"Where is your mother?" one of them asked when my father's body had been carted away like a broken appliance.

I shrugged. I had been asking myself the same question for years.

"Is she alive?" he pushed.

A little insensitive, but I understood his intentions.

"She doesn't live here anymore."

He nodded slowly and fired an inquisitive glance at his partner, standing idle by the back of the ambulance.

"Someone will be here for you soon. Is there anyone who can look after you?" he asked with a furtive glance down the street.

A few neighbors had appeared to watch the unfolding drama, their heads popping out of open windows and through hedges like predators sensing prey. The heads that were close enough to hear the raised voice of the paramedic ducked out of sight.

"I'll be fine."

He gave me a creased smile, a half nod, and then he disappeared. The lights on the ambulance turned off, the speed minimal as they carried the deceased cargo to the hospital.

Ten minutes later, two police officers came to the house. They began by offering their deepest regrets and sympathies, and then they invited themselves in and asked me questions.

They asked about the cut above my eye, sustained during Darren's earlier attack. They asked which school I went to, their fine-tuned observational skills failing to notice the large crest on the school uniform I was wearing. They asked how long my journey to and from school was; if I walked, if I took the bus, if there was ever any variation in whether I did or did not.

I lost my patience but I answered their questions, despite none of them being relevant. They also asked if I had anyone else to look after me, and at that I shrugged.

"Grandparents?"

I had one surviving grandparent. She was a borderline invalid who relied on a succession of caregivers just to take a shit in the morning.

I shook my head.

"Any family friends or godparents we can leave you with in the meantime?"

My father had plenty of friends, but I didn't like any of them and none of them liked me.

"No."

"No one at all?"

I looked into his eyes and sighed inwardly. There was one person—a despicable, worthless human being. He seemed to like me and he certainly liked my father, but I didn't like him. Nor did I respect him.

"My father's brother," I said regretfully.

The police officer's eyebrows rose in confusion. "You mean your uncle?"

"If you prefer to call him that." I didn't. I didn't want to think of him as *my* anything, but I had to acknowledge that, as the only surviving member of the family who still had control of his bladder, and one who my father—for whatever reason—respected, he was my guardian.

I gave them his number and they said they would get in touch. They repeatedly offered to put me up for a night or two at a hostel, to get me out of a house where the floor was still stained with the blood of my dead father and the air was still warm with his dying breath, but I refused. I didn't want to go anywhere.

In any other town, and with any other police force, they might have taken me to get the support I refused. At the very least they would have waited to ensure that I was safe in the company of social services. But in Whitegate, where the police rarely went out of their way to uphold the law and were often the ones breaking it, things worked a little differently. Still, at least they pretended to care.

———

The police were gone for an hour before I finally stood and took my eyes off the blood-stained floor. I made myself a cup of tea, which I drank standing over the sink, staring into the back garden.

The grass was perfectly manicured, tended by my father's own hands. He was out there most nights, planting, seeding, or harvesting from his small vegetable patch, pruning and picking at the flowers that ran an aesthetically pleasing border around the meadow green grass, or enjoying the heat and the fruits of his labor while sipping a beer on the deck.

I drained the contents of the cup and traced my father's last steps through the house. At the top of the stairs, the door to his office was open, an office that he locked when he wasn't inside and sometimes even when he was, an office where he spent the majority of his time, hiding away in the darkness, while I studied the stream of flickering blue light that whispered underneath the door like an spectral cipher.

"Every man needs a room to himself," he told me once. I had my bedroom, which he made a point of never entering, and he had his office. "The rest of the house is for both of us."

It felt a little treacherous entering his office, but I was intrigued. I had only been in on a few occasions over the years and had never been invited. It had looked very plain on those occasions, just like any office of a man who really doesn't need an office.

I crossed the threshold with a sense of achievement and took in the sights I had previously been reprimanded for witnessing. There was nothing grand about the office, nothing out of the ordinary. Far from the bachelor pad I would have expected it to be, the office had no visible bottles of alcohol sitting proud and half empty. No porn magazines stacked high beside a box of tissues. No football memorabilia or framed pictures of overpriced and unachievable cars. It was simple, boring. The room was tiny. The smallest room in our semi-detached house. The window was tucked away in the corner, small, dusted and covered with a thick curtain that blocked out any light and any intrusive eyes. Against the back wall was a short desk, on top of which sat a computer with a screen so heavy it bent the wooden desk. Many times I had heard him tapping away at the keyboard. I never asked him what he was writing and he never volunteered to tell me. In a time before the Internet became a social norm and an accepted technology for what seemed like every single household on the planet, and long before chat and instant messaging became popular, I could only assume he was keeping a diary, typing out notes for his job, or maybe even writing a novel.

The swivel chair in front of the desk sank with a pleasant sigh when I sat down. Reams of paper gathered dust in the corner. Pens cluttered up the desk. Sticky notes scrawled with illegible words were strewn about. Junk mail sat unopened. Two empty pop bottles lay under the bottom of the desk.

The desk unit, a cheap and weighty construction, was supported by four heavy drawers, two on either side. I was disappointed to find the first of these empty. There was a bottle of whiskey in the second, and it was half-empty. It cheered me up to see that. At least there was some sense of normality in what my father had been doing here. The whiskey looked expensive and old. A crystal tumbler had been turned upside down over its top and a few drips had leaked from the glass and dried on the bottle. He had drunk from it recently. Maybe it was the last thing he had done.

There was also a picture in the drawer, creased, worn. I picked it up and straightened it out. It had been taken ten years ago on a sun-drenched holiday to the south of Spain. Mine and my mother's first trip abroad. Our only family holiday, discounting the miserable rainy summer in Scarborough I spent with my father a year after she left.

In the picture, I was sitting happily between my parents, their arms sloped over my tiny shoulders, our eyes, alive with happiness, staring into the camera, caught in mid-laugh. The picture had been taken by a fellow tourist, a stranger whose face I can't even remember, yet one that had been part of the happiest moment of my life.

In the third drawer was a Polaroid camera and a few cartridges. I picked up the heavy camera and felt its weight. This hadn't been the camera he had used all those years ago—that had been disposable, cheap; those pictures needed developing. I took my picture, expecting the camera to fail. It startled me when it flashed.

A little photo jutted out, a blurred picture of my nonchalant expression in transition. I stared at the little image without emotion. I shook it a little and blew on it, actions I had seen on television but never performed myself. The photo was clear before long. The camera definitely worked.

I put it on the desk and rummaged in the drawer some more, but there was little else of interest. I tried to open the final drawer but it resisted with a shudder. Like the others, there was a lock in the top right corner, a small pinhole mechanism, but unlike the others, this one had been engaged.

The lock was there for the illusion of safety more than anything else, something to make the home-office user think their junk was worth securing. I gripped the handle with both hands and pulled. The small slip of metal holding the drawer in place bent and snapped with a pathetic whine before the drawer sprang open.

There were a few floppy disks inside, along with a small ring-box. My dad still wore the ring my mother had given him when they shared their vows; he hadn't seen the need to take it off. He hadn't had any serious relationships since, certainly nothing worthy of a ring and a proposal. I opened the box to discover a small key, nestled into the grove where a ring would usually go. Not sure what my father's cryptic plan was, I took out the key, pocketed it, and dropped the empty box back into the drawer.

I wasn't interested in the floppy disks just yet; my curiosity could wait. It had been a long day. I slammed the bottom drawer, watched the wooden frame bounce against the broken lock, and then removed the whiskey from the top drawer. Using the glass my father had probably held that afternoon, I poured myself a large measure. I had only drunk on two previous occasions and both of those had been with my father. When I was thirteen, we had shared a beer during one of the England football team's many failings. I didn't like football and I don't think he did either, but he had been caught up in the moment down at the pub, his friends cheering behind him.

The second time was just last year. My fifteenth birthday. Trying to make up for the lack of a party—something I didn't want and had no friends to invite to—he took me out for the day, culminating in a pub lunch and a couple of pints. He practically had to carry me home after my second pint, but the day hadn't been all that bad.

My first few sips of the expensive whiskey were hard to swallow and made me gag and cough simultaneously, but after that it became easier. I could feel the fluid tracing a line of warmth to my stomach, the aches and pains of the beating and everything else fading away under the amber glow.

I finished the glass within twenty minutes, already intoxicated. I put the bottle back in the drawer, reclined in the chair with my feet up on the desk, and fell into a much appreciated sleep.

———

I woke with a start, the chair turning and twirling at my sudden movement.

I checked my watch. I had been asleep for four hours. The sun had already dipped over a graying horizon, leaving nothing more than an afterglow to light the skies. There was a sour taste in my mouth and a pain above my right eye. I cleared my throat, clawing and coughing until a sticky block of saliva dislodged itself.

Downstairs, I took a long drink of water and swallowed two aspirin. I stood over the sink and stared out of the back window, feeling the last dregs of water creeping down my esophagus and into my stomach, lubricating the path the alcohol had scorched.

I wondered what the key was for, what sort of treasures my father thought it necessary to hide. It wasn't for a door, a car, or a safety deposit box; those keys would be smaller, newer. This was old and looked like it belonged to a trunk or an old box, but what could possibly be worth locking away? It could have been money, but unless he was avoiding taxes or stockpiling blood money, there was no need for him to hide it. His wife was gone, he had no long-term relationship or an obligatory joint bank account to accompany it. I didn't have access to his bank account either, so if he was hiding money, he was hiding it from himself.

For a moment I wondered if he had a gun. Then it dawned on me, breaking through the pain of my headache. What if the box held the secrets to my mother's disappearance? My father had never really talked about her, vaguely stating that she moved away and probably wasn't coming back. He didn't blame me for it and I didn't blame myself, but I had always wondered.

I took the key out of my pocket. It was thick and looked like it would unlock the front gates to a manor house. I gripped it in my palm, the steel digging into my flesh.

I began my search in his office. I took apart the drawers and checked behind them. There was a lot of dust, even some scraps of paper from candy wrappers that had wormed their way into the abyss (more proof of his normalcy), but there was nothing that required a key. Nothing under the desk and nothing hidden discreetly away among the things in or around it. Nothing on the windowsill, where the thick curtain acted as a safe itself.

I checked the attic, a musty place where I rarely ventured. The light fizzled and popped when I turned it on, giving off a faint burning smell as the intense heat scorched the accumulation of dust that had coated the bulb. There were signs of life up there, droppings from small animals, feathers from trapped and desperate birds. A couple of boxes of old clothes; a box of Christmas decorations; a box of old vinyl records; two jackets, out of fashion long before I was born and probably long before my father was born; a tattered foosball table, lumped into a carrier bag with a set of toy soldiers and a broken toy keyboard.

I searched for a few hours but found nothing. The attic was joined on both sides by the neighbors' roof spaces. A small cinder block wall separated them, but anyone with a touch of guile and a modicum of desire could get over it. If they so desired, they could hop from the attic at the end of the street all the way to ours. Because of that, it seemed improbable my father would hide something valuable up there. It didn't matter if it was locked or not—if someone stole the box, it was still lost to him. I pushed on regardless. By the time I had finished, scouring every inch of the roof space, I was drained and ready for another nap.

Dejected, I made my way to the kitchen, rifling through the fridge to find anything flat and innocuous I could stick between two slices of bread and call dinner. I made do with slices of watery ham and cheese that was past its use-by date.

As I bit into the sandwich, I found myself looking out of the window again. There was a small spotlight in the back garden, pinned to the back wall. Its radiant glow lit up the garden like a football field whenever the light was activated by movement; mostly moths and mice. It served its purpose whenever my father ventured out in the twilight hours to putter around his own square of nature.

I surveyed his hard work as I ate, crumbs showering into the sink, wedges of insipid fare fighting their way down my throat. He had toiled for years in the garden, working his fingers to their muddy stumps, coating his clothes and skin with caked mud and sweat. It all seemed pointless now that he was no longer around to maintain it. I wasn't a gardener, I didn't know where to begin. In my hands, the garden would die an unjust and disheveled death.

At the head of the garden, bordered by a tall fence that marked the end of my father's patch of paradise, rested a row of blooming flowers, their magnificence caught in the glare of the security light. He had spent many hours making sure the garden bloomed in one shade or another, and now the seeds of summer were ripe.

The yard was so well manicured and maintained that a small bald patch in its center stood out like a disfiguring scar on a beautiful face.

My mouth stopped mid-chew. For someone who had meticulously planted and arranged a flower bed, it seemed anomalous to leave a small patch of dirt untended. The soil looked ready to plant, like the vegetable patch that had recently yielded a promising batch of carrots and was now awaiting seeding.

I swallowed the moist bread and cheese and retrieved a small trowel that my dad kept under the sink. I turned off the security light, making sure no nosy neighbors could see me. Kneeling in the mud, careful not to disturb the flowers, I hastily dug.

After less than two minutes of digging, a foot deep in the ground, the trowel crunched against solid steel. I rolled up my sleeves and reached inside the earth until my fingers brushed against the surface of a box. It was thick, solid, and heavy, despite its fairly diminutive size.

Lugging it across the garden with the support of my stomach, I carried it into the house and plonked it down on the kitchen counter. It braced the surface with a heavy clunk and I just managed to pull my fingers out from underneath before it crushed them. A small worm had attached itself to the side, embedded in a clump of mud that clung to the steel like a scab. It flopped onto the counter, took a minute to gather its bearings, and then wiggled a slow path toward the sink.

The key fit the box like a rusted glove. I heard a grating sound of defiance when it turned and a rusted groan when it opened.

I'm not sure what I expected when I looked inside. I prepared myself for a surprise, but when I peeled open the lid and peered in, I felt the contents of my stomach rush to my throat. I moved my head away from the box just in time as a torrent of liquid vomit sprayed across the kitchen surface, bathing the worm and everything else in a bath of regurgitated sandwich and hydrochloric acid, scented with the musty tones of single-malt whiskey.

3

The box was filled with manila envelopes, all of which had been scrawled with a single name and sealed. The seal on the top envelope, marked with the name Sandra and penned in my father's neat hand, had broken and the contents had spilled out.

The first sight to greet me was a Polaroid picture of a woman. She was young, blonde, pretty, naked, and dead. She was lying stretched out on a carpet that had been dyed red with her blood. Her stomach sliced open, her innards popping out through the bisected flesh. Her large intestine stroked up her body like an alien tentacle, toward breasts that had been violently mutilated. Her nipples sliced off.

I wasn't squeamish, but I hadn't expected to see what I had. I had never witnessed anything so grotesque, so violent, not even in films. My stomach hadn't been prepared.

I took a few deep breaths, braced myself, and looked back inside the box, fighting away nausea as I rifled through more of the pictures. A lot of them showed her after death, before and during mutilation. The rest were of her when she was alive, spied through the eyes of a voyeuristic lens. Snaps of her shopping; answering the door to a delivery man; having coffee with a friend; looking forlornly out a restaurant window. I'd seen this woman before.

I tipped out the envelope, spilling the contents into the box. A picture of her laughing with friends; one of her behind a desk; on the phone; eating dinner. Then, flopping out like the prize from a box of cereal, was a tiny, laminated slip.

It looked like a pair of buttons, neatly encased in their factory-sealed strip. I picked them up and studied them. They were small, off-colored, almost brown. I turned them over in my hand and then placed them to one side. Only when I looked back in the box, back at the picture of mutilation staring at me from the steel base, did I realize the two small buttons were the woman's nipples. I gagged a little as the acid in my throat threatened to release again, but I managed to keep it down.

My heart was fluttering, tapping a round of palpitations the likes of which I had never experienced. But none of it was out of fear. It was astonishment, muddled with a touch of pride and respect. Was my father The Butcher? Was it possible that the happy, friendly man who had guided me through my miserable life was the most vicious killer in recent history?

I ran back into the living room and practically dove onto the couch. Under the seat I found a newspaper, ruffled, creased and ripped in places. I grabbed at it roughly and erratically flicked through the pages until I found what I sought: pages four to eight, a detailed analysis of The Butcher's victims. There, smiling happily from her passport photo, was victim number twelve, Sandra Goldstein. The same blonde whose disembodied nipples I had just held.

I took the newspaper to the kitchen, laid it out on the counter. I opened more of the envelopes, checking off the macabre sights inside against the pictures of the victims in the newspaper. One victim after another—this one's throat had been slit; that one's fingers and toes had been amputated; this man's testicles had been removed; this woman's scalp had been sliced off.

It was a sordid collection of sickness, and one that I had taken great delight in reading about over the last few years. The thought had never crossed my mind that my own father had been the source. Even as I searched through his disturbing deeds, I found the idea hard to digest.

The paper confirmed everything in the photos and with each collection came another prize. A lock of hair, neatly encased in laminate; folds of skin still clinging to hair follicles; a piece of skin, dried, preserved, and stored in multiple pieces of plastic wrap; a finger; a toe; a testicle.

I dropped them back in the box and leaned against the counter, exhausted. I was breathing heavily, my eyes wide. As hard as it was to believe my father was a notorious serial killer, it was an invigorating discovery. I respected him for it. No more was he just a friendly, happy-go-lucky idiot who ran with the crowd and wanted to be a part of it. He was a vicious killer, a man who probably hated the world more than I did.

But what did that mean? Why did I struggle to fit in and he didn't? If anything, he should have had a harder time than I had. He had desires to murder, to mutilate, to destroy. He was a beast, a vicious demon who spent his days destroying life. How did he manage to fit in when all the while he—like me—was dreaming about ripping the throats of the very people he was befriending?

Was he like me? Did he feel the way I did?

I hovered back over the box. Alongside the envelopes were some floppy disks. I took these upstairs, making sure I locked the box first.

I booted up my father's computer. There was little of interest on there. A few card games, a puzzle game, a word processor. No files hidden in the open. I slid in one of the floppy disks. With my heart pounding in delightful anticipation and my hand trembling over the mouse, I opened up the most recent of two files.

Eliza Rowntree. A pretty little thing, no more than eighteen. Popular, friendly, athletic. Stunning body. Amazing eyes. Perfect skin.

I strangled her with my bare hands. The best way for her to go. I had to feel every inch of her depart. Watch the fear in her eyes and sense the stench of desperation on her breath.

I took my time destroying her.

I used a scalpel to carve out her eyes. So beautiful. I took a lock of her hair and a piece of her skin. She was my favorite victim.

I couldn't imagine my father writing what I had just read. It read like the diary of a madman, so succinct, so brutal. I read the second document; it was longer, more precise, detailing everything that Eliza did. Her weekly schedule, her daily routine. It even mentioned the dates of her menstrual cycle and when her parents usually visited. It was dated two months before the entry on her murder. Two months of methodical stalking before he had killed her.

The other disks described other murders and other victims. It wasn't enough for me. I wanted to know *why* my father had done it, *why* he had chosen his victims. I found a suggestion of what I was looking for on a disk created five years ago, around the time of the first Butcher murder.

I wanted more. I didn't get enough with him. It was gratifying, it was fun, but it could have been better.

I hunted down my first female victim. A prostitute. Skinny. Probably a drug addict. Her lips were chafed. Eyes sunken. Despite her evident drawbacks, she was pretty. She would do.

I took her to the woods. I suggested we get out of the car, as I didn't want to mess up the interior with our bodily fluids. She didn't object. She took off her knickers. Pinned herself nonchalantly up against a tree. Waited casually, chewing gum.

I felt disgusted. She wasn't even looking at me. Her pin-pricked pupils were staring at everything but me, despite the fact that she was half naked and waiting for me to fuck her.

I persevered nevertheless. I pinned her throat to the tree. She didn't object at first, assuming I was just kinky. She was probably working out how much extra to charge me when the realization dawned.

I closed my hand around her throat, so tight I could feel the gum slide down as she swallowed and prepared to scream. I clasped my free hand around her diseased lips. Squeezed until the blood drained from her face.

With my free hand, I worked open my zipper. I was excited and eager, but my penis wasn't. I left it dangling. Waiting.

I ripped off her top, exposing an exquisite pair of breasts. Big, firm, smooth. I stared at them. Sunk my face into them. There was no movement. No erection.

I thrust myself up against her, feeling her dry clitoris against the skin of my flaccid penis. A few pubic hairs, missed by the razor, brushed against my foreskin as I pumped myself back and forward.

She screamed underneath the flesh of my palm. She bit my hand. I pulled it away in surprise and she freed herself. Kicking her heels into the undergrowth, disappearing into the forest.

I followed her. Stalking around in the darkness, my pants still open, my eyes refusing to leave the grayness ahead of me. I enjoyed the chase. Striding through the fields. Avoiding the noisy leaves and twigs underfoot. Listening to the distant skips and stumbles as she struggled to run and hide.

I reached a dead end. A wall of foliage. I pinned my ears to the air, heard her thick breaths, the perspiring sounds of an addict and a smoker. She was waiting behind a tree. Hiding. Petrified and breathless.

I took her in my grasp for the second time. She was crying. Bawling her eyes out. Pleading and sobbing with every breath. I squeezed tighter and tighter until her eyes bulged. Her screams stopped. I used both of my hands to wring the life out of her like a wet towel.

She slumped. Lifeless and breathless in the still night air.
I was fully erect. I let her body drop. Eager for more.
I dismissed the thought of having sex with her. She disgusted
me as much dead as she did alive, but when I began to manipu-
late her body, I felt something I have never felt before. It was a
fulfillment and an excitement topped only by squeezing the last
dregs of life out of her.
I finished her off with the tools in my boot. A pair of pliers
for her bones. A scalpel for her flesh. I let the rain wash away the
blood from my hands and face. It was reckless. It was risky. But
it was fun. In the future, I will be more careful.

Every killing had been documented. All twelve murders over the last five years, along with a few that hadn't been attributed to The Butcher. I took great pleasure in reading about them, amazed that the image of The Butcher in my mind, an image created through years of avid reading and daydreaming, had now morphed into that of my father. It seemed illogical that he could have done such a thing, and yet he had.

I finished reading the macabre material, packed everything back in the box, and buried it back in the garden. I kept the key for myself, depositing it in my underwear drawer.

I didn't know why my dad did what he did—why he started or why he continued—but it didn't matter. He had done it. He had created a legend. He had created a God. Everyone feared him, everyone respected him, everyone revered him. And now what? Felled by something natural, something he couldn't control . . . probably a heart attack, the cruelest and most primal of physiological failures. This wasn't how great men died. It didn't seem right. It wasn't fair.

The press anticipated his killings with giddy glee—each succession of slaughter another front page for their newspaper and another twenty-minute slot for their prime-time news show. Everyone awaited news of his next victim, every emaciated prostitute who had little choice but to stand on the streets and sell her body for a fix; every trembling teenager forced to walk home alone; every otherwise physically capable adult who imposed their company on others to avoid being alone.

And now what? Their fear would grow, stagnate, and then, eventually, die. The Butcher would retire to the pages of history. An interesting segment in a book of unsolved crimes. His legend, borne of fear, reverence, and spectacular brutality, would fade with an anti-climactic whimper.

It was obvious what I had to do. I would like to say that I deliberated over it for a few days and maybe even suffered a series of sleepless nights. That would make sense, after all. But there was no deliberation, no sleepless nights. I had made my mind up before I had even realized the full extent of what my father had created.

I had to take over. I had to continue my father's legend. I had to become The Butcher.

4

—

Barry Barlow. One of the most feared and despised kids in my school. A friend and a brother-in-thuggish-arms to Darren Henderson, the bully who had tortured my educational existence since its lowly inception.

He wasn't the sharpest tool in the shed. People said that he and Darren Henderson were two peas in a pod, but the truth was that Barry was as connected to Darren as a genital wart was to a sexually transmitted infection. He was the bum-fluff to his penis, the hangnail to his broken finger. But, as useless as he was, there was no denying that he and Darren were close, which was the first stumbling block I encountered when I decided to murder Darren Henderson.

It was a no-brainer really. The Butcher had killed teenagers—albeit not exclusively—and he had killed within a few miles of the area. No one would bat an eyelid if Darren happened to be the next victim. It wasn't strictly sensible of me to let my personal feelings get in the way of mine and my father's legacy, but if this wasn't personal, then what was it? I was planning to kill people and no one was paying me to do it. Of course it was fucking personal.

As much as I wanted to, I couldn't kill them both—that was a little *too* personal and would raise a few too many eyebrows. The Butcher hadn't killed in pairs. The police would suspect a copycat on a mission of pure vendetta; it wouldn't take them long to concentrate their suspicions on me.

On my first day back after spring break, I followed Darren around like a hawk. His dimwitted friend didn't leave his side. It was noteworthy but irrelevant, as I wasn't going to kill him in school. At the end of the day, I jumped the bell and hid in a small group of trees on the boundaries of the playground. The school board had jumped on the green wagon and instructed all the first-graders to plant trees, hedges, and flowers around the school, saving the world one pointless piece at a time. The high schoolers used it for clandestine illegalities as they smoked, drank, and fucked their way through recess.

There was no one there when I ducked inside and took up a position behind a low-hanging bush, where a used condom hung from a wilted leaf like snot from an infected nose.

Darren and Barry also finished early, trundling out onto the grounds like giddy hyenas on the prowl for their prey. They glanced around, scanning the throng that inevitably followed the chime of the school bells. They spoke briefly, voicing their frustrations, and then they left.

I waited for them to drift out of sight and then I set out after them, brushing painfully against a malignant thorny bush on the way. A few of the students gave me some perplexed glances as I emerged from the bushes. Their eyes darted past me to see if a female had also emerged, wondering who was desperate or dull enough to venture inside with me.

I kept my distance from the pair, sidestepping behind bus shelters, walls, and gardens whenever possible, peering at them surreptitiously from around my makeshift blockades. They turned around once—Barry's head inevitably following Darren's—to scan the backside of a middle-aged woman who strutted past them with the firm, comfortable gait of a teenager and the attire of a cougar desperately clinging to a lost and promiscuous youth. They didn't see me. Others did, giving me numerous inquisitive stares, but no one paid much attention. I was a nobody. To them I was weird and unimportant, even more so now that I was an orphan, and therefore I was probably always doing something suspicious and creepy.

A mile or so down the road, they turned into a large subdivision—a succession of streets and houses that branched out from a central block of apartments like the diseased arms of a dying octopus. They walked down to the head of the octopus, bypassing a succession of pebble-dashed houses, and caught up with another pair of degenerates that had stopped to trade cigarettes, sweets, or something less innocuous opposite a garden that had been used as a Dumpster.

I ducked into one of the gardens, through a gate that had had been ripped off its hinges and left on a small strip of yellowed grass. I hid up against a wall, pressing my face against the cold grainy musk of concrete and peeking around the corner. Darren and his friends were huddled in a conspicuous cluster, watching each others' backs with the privacy and agitation of drug dealers.

A loud, gruff shout dragged my attention away from the gaggle of cretins.

"What the fuck do you think you're doing!?"

It came from the house to my left, belonging to the garden and boundary that I had casually crossed. A heavyset man, his beer belly jammed inside an undersized tank top, was glaring at me like I had stolen his dinner.

My heart sank. He was only a few feet away, his body odor—an olfactory insult of cheap beer sweated through pores that hadn't touched water for weeks—invading my nostrils. I recoiled and moved away from the wall, in plain sight of the idiots further along the road.

I held up my hands defensively but they instinctively moved to my nose; his odor was too strong. "Jesus!" I spat as the smell hit me like a sweaty punch.

"What the fuck is wrong with you?" he roared.

"I'm sorry," I mumbled through a pinched nose. "It's just, well, you fucking stink."

"What!?" I had been a few steps away, almost at the curb, but he waddled forward like a dropped Weeble. At any moment, I swore he would kick out a leg, lower his head, and charge.

I stepped back, lost my balance over the curb, and stumbled into the road. I hit a parked car, righted myself after a collision with the hood, and then propelled myself off it with my forearms.

There was a small dent where my forearms had collided with the hood, a concave puncture in the cheap metal. I neatly pressed the edge of the bubbled wound, hoping my magic fingers would right the wrongs that my arms had caused, but instead I caused more damage.

The waddling behemoth stopped at the curb, his chubby face now red with unadulterated anger. He looked from me to the car and then back again, seemingly ready to explode.

"That's my fucking car!" he bellowed.

His forehead glistened with perspiration that appeared at an increasing rate, dribbling down his bulbous head like a freshly sprayed apple in a grocer's window. A vein at the right of his temple throbbed aggressively, on the verge of hemorrhaging and getting me out of a tricky situation.

"Oh, erm . . . sorry about that," I said calmly. I pushed my palms against it absentmindedly, forcing some pressure into it to try again to right the wrong. Somehow I managed to squeeze another indent into the surprisingly malleable hood.

He threw his palms to his forehead and screamed several obscenities at me. He took a few steps toward me and I took a few back, the effort far greater on his part.

In my defense, it was a shit fucking car. He did well to afford it, assuming he had actually paid for it, but it was a heap of mangled rust, and a few dents weren't going to make a difference. I could have told him that. I certainly felt like doing so, but before I could utter a word, I was halted by a familiar sound and an encroaching sense of dread. In the calamity, I had forgotten about the half-witted Darren and his no-witted friends. They had broken free from their cluster, split into a line of four, and were now rushing down the road, heading straight for me.

The big man was also preparing himself for an attack, his arms held out like an obese and hungry zombie, his chubby fingers grasping the air as if it were made of cake. I sprinted away as fast as I could. A roar followed me, a bellow concocted of adolescent excitement and middle-aged rage.

"Get the fucker!"

"Break his fucking legs!"

"*I can't . . . continue . . . running out of . . .*"

I sped away in no particular direction. There was no safety for me at home, only the comfort of having the shit kicked out of me in the privacy of my own house if they caught me there.

Out of the tentacled subdivision, across a graveled patch that kicked up flurries of stones behind my heels, the entrance to a park opened up invitingly in front of me and I headed straight for the woodland at its center. I was already breathless, ill prepared for the physical exertion. I didn't exercise and I rarely ventured outside the house. During gym classes, I found solace in the fact that no one wanted to pick me for any teams and even the teacher was content if I didn't take part.

They were gaining on me, clearly faster and fitter than I was. Darren headed the group; his two friends, two people I recognized from the year below, bounded just a few yards behind him. Barry was struggling at the back of the group, probably more upset by his distance from Darren than by his failure to catch me.

A wall of vegetation blocked my way, but I burst through like a runner scything through the tape at the finishing line. A few thorns sliced and picked at my skin, opening up wounds on my bare arms and piercing through my shirt and into my abdomen.

I slalomed through a succession of trees, listening with a heavy heart as the riotous group matched and bettered my every stride. The sound of their approach, their catcalls, and their heavy breathing broke through the sound of my own beating heart.

I hopped over a thicket, but my tired legs struggled and my right foot tangled among a twining of branches. I stumbled and nearly fell, but righted myself and plodded on.

I tried to detour, to cut right at an angle and throw them off my scent, but they were close enough to see me and follow. I struggled through the greenery, my legs growing tired with each stretch, my breath like razor blades in my chest. I made it to the edge, the light of the boundary and the street beyond—where a dozen alcoves, shops, and alleyways would have aided my plight— before I was crushed under the weight of an athletic dive from Darren Henderson.

I hit a number of bushes on my descent. The twigs picked and sliced at my knees and thighs; my stomach landed on something thick and heavy that refused to relent as bully after bully piled on top of me and pushed my torso down.

They kicked, stamped, and punched their way through my body like a baker preparing a lump of dough. They laughed through every moment of it, giving each other cheers when they decided to start jumping onto the bottom of my spine, laughing heartily when Darren pretended to take a shit on my head and rounded off his joke by farting.

They left me broken, bruised, and struggling to walk. When they had gone, I managed, with great difficulty, to stagger to my feet. It took me a few moments, but I ignored the agony in every muscle, forgot about the pain that coursed through my blood and bones like a visceral cancer.

I used the trees for support as I worked my way into daylight. I took a breath—an icy jolt of air into uncommitted lungs—sighed deeply, and staggered toward the boundary wall. I moved slowly and prepared to climb over the three feet of brick, an easy task made near impossible thanks to a torso that refused to lean and legs that wouldn't lift higher than a few inches.

I leaned forward against the wall and rested my palms on its cold and bracing surface, where the broken brains of generations past had scrawled their names and epitaphs with blunted knives and permanent markers. I tried to lean onto it, to shimmy my way on or over its surface and onto the path beyond, but I stopped halfway, my stomach bracing the edge, my right toe resting on its surface.

Barry Barlow had popped his head up from the other side. In my struggle, I hadn't been able to lean over. I hadn't been able to see him crouched there. He stood directly opposite me, a beaming grin on his dumb face.

He hopped acrobatically onto the wall and looked down at me as I struggled to release my foot and pull myself away. Darren Henderson stood by his side, his arms folded over his chest, a knowing expression pinned on his smug, narcissistic face.

Barry swung his right leg like he was kicking a football. The laces of his boot first made contact with my chin, and then, as my head recoiled from the impact, they lashed upward against my face, breaking my nose, busting my lip.

I lost consciousness. The last thing I heard, mingled with the sound of my own teeth cracking inside my skull, was Darren Henderson's sickeningly joyful laughter.

———

I returned home beaten, broken, and unsure how to progress. Darren was fitter and stronger than me. I couldn't take him in a fight or risk being seen in his proximity. If I was going to go through with killing him—which I was more inclined to do after the beating—then I had to have the advantage of surprise. I also had to make sure he was alone. I couldn't watch his back and anticipate his every move if Barry, the lumbering lummox, was doing the same.

Many weeks had passed since my father's death. Sympathy had been rife in the early stages. Bereavement cards filled the letterbox, pointless pleasantries succinctly etched on mass-marketed crap. A few of his friends had called, doing what they thought was the right thing, the final thing they would ever have to do before erasing our family from their mind.

My grandmother, his mother-in-law, also called. She was one of the few living relatives in our minimal family. She was half deaf and fully decrepit. She lived alone with only an apathetic caregiver to look after her disease-riddled body, yet, unfortunately for her, all of her mental faculties still remained.

The cards and the sympathy had quickly dried up after those first few days. The pitiful looks I received in the street and the whispered conversations, supposedly out of earshot, were replaced by the contempt and suspicion I had grown accustomed to.

My uncle came to live with me. He was a drunk, an idiot, and a failure. I got the feeling that his brother's death was a godsend to him. It dragged him out of the gutter and into a house, where the benefits of an overly generous government and a substantial life insurance policy would allow him to stock his liver with all the cheap beer he could drink.

He greeted me as I stepped into the living room. "Where have you been?" He sucked his head back, puffed out his chest, and unleashed a noxious burp.

I scowled at him, waiting for him to notice and comment on my face and my hunched posture.

"Well?" he said impatiently.

In that moment, I contemplated making him my first victim, but I felt I would be doing him a favor by ridding him of his pathetic existence and I didn't want to waste my effort with something that the bloated, diseased imbecile would construe as beneficial. Maybe his euthanasia would come in the form of methanol poisoning from the cheap booze he acquired from the back of suspect vans, or from blood poisoning the moment his liver spat back all the venom he had fed it over the years.

"School," I answered softly.

He burped again, glowered at me through lowered eyebrows. He checked his watch, tied to his hairy wrist with a plastic strap that threatened to cut off his blood supply.

"School finished an hour ago."

Bravo, you fucking tit. Apparently not everything goes over that head of yours.

"Detention."

He nodded knowingly, giving a cheeky smile that looked partly perverted and partly grotesque. "Naughty boy."

Drunks are incapable of subtle gestures, and I didn't know if he was about to rape me or if he was having a stroke. I ignored him, praying for the latter, before taking my beaten body upstairs.

I had adopted my father's office as my own. There was no way I could keep it locked, though; my uncle had become surprisingly materialistic about a house he now considered his own. But he wasn't a very bright man, and that, combined with his seemingly constant state of inebriation, allowed me to secrete my father's files around the room. I had started keeping files of my own as well. A small collection of what I knew about Darren Henderson and his brainless friend Barry.

I made sure the door was shut and secure behind me before adding the day's discoveries to the file.

———

My wounds healed slowly, but my determination grew instantly. The few days of school that followed the beating were tedious, painfully slow, and almost suffocating.

Before I had even arrived on the first day after the beating, I learned that Darren and Barry had spread around a story that I had followed them and then tried to fondle them. They said I had a crush on Barry and had tried to fulfill some kind of sexual perversion by following him home with the intent of watching him undress through his bedroom window. It took a great deal of energy to avoid another beating, and even the teachers were giving me quizzical and disgusted looks. In small-town life, and in small-town teenage minds, homosexuality is a joke, a sickening and alien orientation that is ridiculed, when the truth is that homosexuality is no different from heterosexuality. They're both disgusting, they're both unnecessary, and they both involve doing disgusting things with other members of the human race. Unlike my peers, I have nothing against homosexuality, just like I have nothing against people from other cultures and other backgrounds. I hate everyone equally. I was the most tolerant person in town.

During lunchtime, I had walked the halls of the school in an effort to avoid the playground and the inevitable physical and verbal abuse. On my idle journey, I turned a corner near the math block and then ducked behind a wall when I saw two teachers approaching.

"He was always a weird kid," one of them said. He was a gym teacher and was speaking with a relaxed tone, happy that he could forget his pointless existence—teaching hopscotch to fat losers—for an hour as he bit into his sandwich and flushed his body with a fresh dose of coffee and cancer. "But since his dad died, *Jesus*."

"You think the stories are true then?" a slightly timid French teacher inquired.

"That he's a little gay boy? Definitely." I heard him chuckle, a derisive sound that accompanied the pitter patter of his sneakers on the floor. "I've always said there was something odd about him, just have to keep an eye on him. Never turn your back."

That sort of attitude almost made me wish that I was stricken with sexual desires, just so I could have a little fun with him before I slit his throat. I contemplated waiting for him to turn the corner, jumping out at him, and ripping his throat open with my teeth. I was capable, and I would have been justified, but instead I turned and set off down the corridor at a brisk pace, disappearing around another corner before they saw me.

The news had even spread to the lower grades, where I was treated with equal disdain by petulant pipsqueaks half my size. A group of them shouted obscenities at me during recess; another feigned an invisible blowjob as I walked by, receiving applause from his friends for doing so. I ignored these idiotic actions and homophobic slurs with the knowledge that I was going to give the one who had started them the ultimate punishment.

A week later, I resumed my intentions to do just that. It had become even harder for me to blend in at school. The target on my back was visible for all to see. Instead I decided to go to Darren's home at night, to use darkness as my cover, something that my father, according to his notes, had done on many occasions.

I crept out of the house just after ten. It was pitch black outside and had been for a couple hours. A thin slice of moonlight and the heavy fluorescence of a dozen streetlights lit my way as I strode through the paved streets with my lowered head draped under the cover of a hood, my monastic silhouette cutting a sullen figure as I traced through the shadows.

It was a school night, but there was still an assortment of kids around: the young—a pool of pissants spread around the streets like a marmalade of unbroken voices, bicycles, and sportswear—and the adolescent converged near the shops in the center of town. I bypassed them all without raising my head, not wanting to kick-start a swarm of abuse or questions. They paid me little heed. Out of the corner of my eye, I saw a few familiar faces lift curious eyes my way, but nothing was said.

Darren lived on the edge of town, through the route I had walked the other day, on the outer tentacle of the public housing subdivision. There were back routes to his house from mine, ones much less traveled and much more conducive to a clandestine stroll, but they were used by nefarious youths who wished to keep their illegalities away from the main streets, youths that were sure to pay more attention to the rare passing of a hooded figure than their counterparts on the main street.

An unused field, bordered by a thick line of poorly maintained trees and shrubbery, lay at the back of the row of duplexes. The field was accessed by a short wall that traced around the border. I chose a neighboring house with the least activity—the windows black but for a small flicker of light in a second-floor window—and ducked inside, taking a route down the side of their house, through their back garden, and over the boundary wall at the back.

With my feet treading through moist mud, I scuttled forward, peering over the wall on my left, scanning the visible second-story windows in all of the houses.

I saw myriad blue flashing lights along the line—televisions and computers all buzzing with activity. In one window, a small boy sat smoking a sly cigarette, blowing the smoke into the night. In another, an elderly man stood gazing serenely at the nothingness beyond. I kept low and remained hidden, my pace steady as I made my way to the end house. I stopped in the trees and crouched further, taking in my surroundings. All the houses had small gardens at the back, between the house and the wall in front of me. Children's toys littered the weed-bitten grass. A stroller sat sullenly in the corner, its wheels nearly rusted off, its seat torn to shreds and faded under the constant gaze of sunlight and rain. A small trampoline took center stage in the middle of the garden, on top of an unmown patch of grass that looked thick enough to house a hidden tribe of pygmies. A hoodie lay strewn and torn to its left; a deflated football to its right.

The windows looking out onto this assault course were all alight. In one of them, next to the back door, a blonde woman stood washing dishes, moving gently from side to side to the rhythm of unheard music. A pleasant smile adorned her attractive face. She wore a long white T-shirt that at some point had belonged to a man. It hung heavily and loosely from her slim figure. The torso had been soaked with water, exposing a black bra underneath.

Through the window to the right of the door, a heavyset man sat watching television, the screen unseen but for a blue flicker that reflected against the glass. He was slouched so far he seemed to be sitting in on himself, his double chin pressing against his thick neck, his man-breasts caressing his pot belly. He was topless and seemed to be dressed only in his boxer shorts, the seam of which was just visible above the base of the window. On the second floor, in the room directly above the serene, swaying woman, the lights were on but the curtains were drawn.

I waited in the silence, studying the man and the woman. He picked his nose, inspected the contents, and then wiped it on the arm of the chair; he changed channels, seemed unsatisfied with all he encountered, and settled upon one that left him with a reluctant frown. She stopped at one point, bent down to satisfy someone or something small, and then rose with a wide grin, peeking down intermittently. At one point he turned his attention to the other side of the living room, away from the window. He was talking to someone; his head moving agreeably.

I scaled the small wall. The woman was facing me and occasionally glancing out the window, but with the light of the kitchen and the contrasting darkness outside, she would only see her reflection. I felt my feet crunch wilted flowers and compress damp grass as I carefully moved across the lawn and pressed myself up against the wall to the left of the living room window.

I dropped to my knees and hurried along underneath it. I could hear the television inside, the boisterous calls of a studio audience and the clichéd catchphrases from sitcom characters. I tuned into the conversation that mingled with the sounds of the television. I heard Darren's voice and that of the rough-spoken man whom I assumed was his father.

"Not my problem, old man," Darren said casually.

"Should I make it your fucking problem, kid?" his dad yelled back.

"You can't talk to me like that!"

"Do as you're fucking told!"

It felt exciting under that window, spying on their lives. I made myself more comfortable, shifting my knees out from under my body and relaxing onto my backside with the cold strip of paving that split the house and garden pressed into the seat of my pants.

"You can't tell me what to do. You're not my dad!"

As I should have suspected, the perils of a broken home. *You're not my dad. I hate you. You were nothing like my father. My mother's too good for you.* Freud would have been delighted with little Darren, if only his situation weren't a tired cliché.

At that point, the shrill calls of a youngster cut through the room. An incoherent and loud addition to the conversation. Daren shouted something at the youngster, which prompted an even shriller response as the child began to cry. The man then moaned and muted or switched off the television.

The woman entered from the kitchen and I listened to her as she consoled the child and then directed her aggression at Darren.

"What's going on?" she asked.

"He's trying to get me to do his fucking dirty work," Darren spat, aghast. "He thinks I'm his fucking lackey."

How dare he? Darren Henderson is no one's lackey. He may have the malleable mind of a modern-day moron, and he would probably do your bidding for a packet of cigarettes, a blowjob, or a pat on the back from his docile friends, but he is no one's lackey.

The man objected, "I just want him to—" but the sound of his voice was cut short as the baby started crying again, even louder this time. I heard their voices trying to shout over the top of his. I heard something about a hoodie. I heard Darren swear. I heard his mother swear back and then a silence descended. Even the baby toned it down.

I shifted uneasily. Then I heard a clicking sound, a bolt sliding open. My heart skipped a beat, thudding violently in my chest as if it wanted to leave. I turned sharply to my right and saw the back door swing open. I felt and saw an illuminating presence above me as an outside light illuminated the garden and bathed me in its bright glow.

Darren stepped out, mumbling disconsolately to himself. I watched him plod onto the lawn, feeling a lump stick in my throat as he did so. I felt rooted to the spot, unsure what to do or where to go, but knowing I would be seen as soon as he turned back around.

He shuffled around the garden, searching for something in the gloom. His hands stuffed into his pockets, his head hung low, his feet kicking angrily at any clumps of grass that dared get in his way.

On my right was a small fence that separated his house from a short stretch of land, beyond which lay the next tentacle of the architectural octopus. It was short enough for me to clamber over but not with great ease. He would surely hear the struggle and recognize my frantically stumbling stature as one that he had so often beaten to a pulp.

There was also an exit down a thin path at the side of the house, but that was on the other side, beyond the open door that was still shaking under Darren's angry exit and the kitchen window.

I swallowed thickly, trying to force the lump out of my throat. My head turned this way and that as I weighed my limited options.

Darren moved around the trampoline, kicking away the deflated football before inspecting the hoodie on the grass. He looked at it distastefully and then turned toward the window, toward me.

My heart sank. I felt it hit my stomach, a hollow depth charge in my chest. I waited underneath the ledge, expecting his eyes to light up and his fists to clench.

"I've got your fucking hoodie!" he shouted to the window. He dropped his pants, exposed his backside, and then began rubbing the sleeve inside the exposed cleft, mumbling obscenities as he did so.

I looked anxiously toward the open door and contemplated running right through it, hiding in the house and biding my time until an option for escape arose. But I would be running into an unfamiliar house, possibly right into a surprised mother, a crying baby, or an angry stepfather.

Darren pulled his pants up, gave a quick look to the far side of the garden, and then hurried over to the fence that separated his house from his neighbor's. I heard him mumbling incoherently as he scoured the far reaches of his neighbor's garden, hoping to foul the hoodie further with canine excrement, I'm sure.

I seized my opportunity and ran. I was over the fence in a desperate second, beyond the adjacent field as fast as my heavy heart and jittering legs would take me. I didn't stop or look back until I was on the outskirts of town, safe in the knowledge that Darren, and his house, were a good half mile behind me.

Despite my desperate escape I hadn't been followed, and it was too dark for Darren to have seen more than a suspicious blur. In my breathless exertions, my heart retaining normalcy, my mind pondered on what might have been if I *had* ducked inside the house. I envisioned myself hiding in Darren's room, surprising him on his return and butchering him with his parents, helpless and ignorant, sitting just feet away.

The prospect of spilling his blood made me just as excited as it always had, but after being so close to him and his home, after I had been given an opportunity and an opening, my need had turned into a deep desperation.

5

I wasn't sure what I had expected to learn from my first nightly escapade to Darren's house, but I walked away with more than I had known before. I didn't know what he did with his days or how he spent his nights, but I knew he had an overweight stepfather and a mother who was torn between the arguments of her son and her husband. There also seemed to be another child on the scene, suggesting that with a missing father, a nuisance adolescent son, and a needy baby, Darren's mother had a tendency to be preoccupied when it came to her eldest son.

The family also lacked a pet dog, a big plus if I decided to kill Darren in his home. I hate dogs. Their loyalty sickens me. Their dependency is deplorable, and their usefulness is limited. The lack of a dog is a plus in any home.

I went on more nightly excursions to spy on Darren. More than once, I discovered he had stayed out late or had slept at a friend's house, but I remained near the house, keeping a close watch on his mother and his stepfather. She fascinated me; there was something so sweet and soft in her eyes and so serene in her movements. But as soon as she opened her mouth, she changed into exactly the sort of woman I would expect her to be. She was the mother of a complete fucking idiot, after all.

I thought more about how I was going to kill him. The modus operandi of The Butcher was simple: the deaths were savage, clinical, and personal. He typically killed from behind, unseen, strangling his victim or slitting their throat with a quick and decisive slash of a sharp razor. On two occasions, he had killed with a single strike driven through the heart, the first through his chest wall, crushing his ribs on the way; the second with a similarly precise strike through the back.

I liked the idea of strangling Darren. I wanted to feel the life fade from his body, to drain every inch of oxygen from his veins and bathe in the warmth of his final breath, but he was stronger than me. He could easily overpower any attempts at asphyxiation.

To make sure I could hit the heart with a clinical strike, should it come to that, I practiced on a dummy I found in a Dumpster outside the school, discarded during a training session held during evening hours. I tied it to the light-fixture in the office and practiced sneaking up behind and driving a kitchen knife through its heart.

My uncle slept or drank his way through most of my studies, but not everything went over his balding head.

"There's a dummy in the office," he said to me one morning.

I had returned home from school to find him standing in the doorway to the living room with his hands on his hips. There was, as usual, a slight sway to his stance.

I nodded in reply. The dummy had been there for two weeks and he had failed to notice it. He had been home when I brought it back. I even carried it past him, dragging it up the stairs while he sat just a few feet away, wallowing in low-budget beer and television.

I thought about giving him a congratulatory clap or an exaggerated pat on the back, but nothing he was and nothing he did deserved a clap, facetiously or not. I also didn't want to touch him. He had a leprous quality, a contagious disgust that infects those on the fringes of society and forces them to remain there.

"What the fuck do you want with that?" he quizzed, lowering one eyebrow.

I replied with an apathetic shrug.

"You've been *playing* with it." He squeezed his eyes together and emphasized the word like it was dirty, which indeed was how every word sounded in that cavernous vestibule of pestilence he called a mouth. "I saw the holes."

"In the chest," I said with a bemused nod.

He frowned, both his eyebrows lowered now. "Is *that* what you're into?

I stared at him for a moment, checking to see if he was being serious. "Yes," I said, when I learned that he was. "I like to fuck dummies in the chest."

He raised an eyebrow, kept it raised during a silent stare that lasted for an interminable time. Then he shrugged casually, remembered he hadn't had a drink for nearly ten minutes, and then wandered into the living room to find his bottle.

The dummy wasn't mentioned again and the following week I got rid of it. I knew where to strike, I knew the rough layout of the human body; the rest was down to experience.

———

I kept close tabs on Darren and Barry at school and followed them home whenever I could. They caught me hanging around them more than once. They didn't suspect anything, but they beat me up regardless.

I discovered most of what I set out to discover. I knew when and where they usually hung out, and until what time. I knew who Darren's girlfriend was: a blonde-haired, skinny eighteen-year-old degenerate from the local college. And I knew whom he slept with on the side. He may have only been sixteen, but he was popular with the girls, or whatever the correct term was for these over-fucked, under-educated masses of hormones and venereal diseases.

A few months before the end of the year, the end of school for me and my classmates, I learned that Darren's parents would be on holiday during the summer and he would have the house to himself for a couple weeks. He boasted about the parties he had planned, the booze he would drink, and the orgies he would host. It was the perfect time for me to strike. The Butcher mutilated his victims, methodically tearing them apart and then leaving them in sickening death throes to horrify those who bore witness. The process was something that needed time and seclusion to complete. My house was out of the question, as were the streets, but his house, with his parents away, was perfect.

I prepared myself for that date. I even began working out, trying to increase my strength in preparation for any resistance and to retain the hope that I could, after all, strangle him. I also followed him on a daily basis, keeping track of every aspect of his life and that of his mother and stepfather.

During the final week of school, I was given a chance to get closer to him. A pretty girl with a porcelain face approached me after class. She tilted her head slightly to one side, a suggestion of innocence and curiosity.

Her name was Elizabeth Handle. She was intelligent and popular with both the delinquent students and the undereducated teachers. She had a glare of innocence to her radiant features, an almost angelic virginal aura, but there was nothing virginal about her. I was the only male in the class she hadn't slept with—even a few of the teachers had traded STDs with her.

It was only midweek. The final day of school was a couple days away, but already the excitement that school was nearing its completion and education was over created a palpable tension in the air. This was a big step in their lives; for many, the end of school signals a huge step on the road to a university education or a successful career. In the case of my fellow pupils, however, it merely meant that the Whitegate unemployment queue would get bigger and the local prostitutes would have more competition.

Excited pupils buzzed around the room like hyperactive flies, their varied conversations criss-crossing to weave a web of obscenity and incoherence.

"Herman, right?" Elizabeth spoke softly, her voice barely audible over the teenage static that swamped around us.

She had heard my name read out in registration every day for almost a decade and yet she was unsure when recalling it. I had been her science partner a number of times throughout the years, had spent the day in her proximity when teamed together to dress the school hall in preparation for a musical performance, and had, fairly recently, helped her with a math assignment under the instruction of a teacher who seemingly wanted me to do his job for him. She was playing the ignorant fool and at this rate she was on course for an Oscar.

"Yeah." I nodded with as much enthusiasm as I good manage.

She produced some small slips of cardboard, stacked and tied together with a purple rubber band. "I'm having a party," she explained, pulling out one of the slips and handing it to me. "You wanna come?"

I paused, wondering if she was joking. She had never invited me to anything before. Despite being classmates since the birth of our educational lives, I had never been invited to any of her birthday parties and didn't even know where she lived.

I checked the invitation. It looked genuine enough. Her name was embossed in italic golden letters at the top with a line of glitter running through. The words *booze* and *no parents* appeared below, suffixed with as many exclamation marks as the small slip would allow.

She was waiting with a patient smile. It was a look that I couldn't see through. She may have had ulterior motives, but despite her ignorance and naïveté, she was intelligent and experienced enough to hide it. Attractive teenage girls didn't get what they wanted from the male role models in their lives without being able to hide disdain or trickery behind benevolent smiles.

"Sure," I said.

She grinned and turned away, handing out more invitations as the crowd of vociferous pupils dispersed into the hallways. I caught a few looking at me perplexedly, no doubt wondering why I had been invited and possibly retracting their intentions because of my invite, but I didn't care. I wasn't one for parties or social gatherings, but there was a good chance that Darren would be attending and I doubted that even he would bully me at someone else's house during someone else's party.

I bought new clothes for the occasion. The invite declared *smart-casual*, so I picked out a new pair of jeans and a striped shirt. I intended to look my best and to do what my dad had done so well, to fit in with the masses, to become one of them. I used my father's aftershave, shaved what little bum-fluff had been clinging to my chin, and set out for the walk to Elizabeth's house with a leather jacket draped over my shoulders.

I arrived on time, to the minute. The house sat in a new-build subdivision on the edge of town. Rows and rows of four-bedroom houses, all with their own sizable lawns, garages, and driveways. A few of them, including Elizabeth's, also had conservatories at the back. The shimmering panes of glass glimmered with the reflected incandescence of the street lights.

I followed a train of guests into the house, slotting into the rear behind a pair of giggling blondes who reeked of perfume and hairspray. Music beat a pulsating rhythm from the house, the open door allowing the repetitive echoes of drum beats and bass throbs into the night air. A dam of bodies had wedged itself in the doorway as newcomers met with early arrivals and created a melee of conversation and activity. When this wedge departed into the house and the train shifted forward, the girls increased their volume, compensating for the encroaching music.

They talked incessantly about boys—who was going to be there, who they were going to kiss, who they were going to fuck. A high-pitched, excited giggle accompanied every mention of something sexual, but despite their wanton promiscuity, they changed their tones with immediate effect when entering the house and encountering a small Labrador puppy sitting with an expectant grin in the hallway.

The puppy already had a few admirers gathering around it, crouching down and mumbling cutesy noises. The addition of the two girls created a crowd. I slipped by them all unseen, glad for the distraction, and headed into the kitchen.

A few guys were already in there, one gave me a friendly nod as I entered, the others paid me no heed. I swung the jacket from my shoulder and carefully hung it over the back of a chair.

The kitchen was immaculate and looked new. The surfaces still shone with an untouched gleam. The knobs and handles on the many drawers and cupboards were unburdened by a single chip or piece of ingrained dirt or grime, as was the oven door, which offered a reflection of perfect clarity. No pictures on the walls, nothing but sheer and blinding whiteness. No chintzy magnets or Post-it notes attached to the large fridge.

In the center of a small oak breakfast table, a large punch bowl glimmered with a red liquid, on which bobbed a few slices of orange. A boy who I had seen around school took a ladle from the table and spooned some of the sugary booze into a cup before heading back out of the kitchen, through an open door, into a short hallway, and into the noisy living room beyond.

The counters were painted black with lines and lines of beer bottles. Beer, to me, is comparable to a product of the human digestive system because it tastes like piss and smells like a fart. But drinking beer is an acceptable norm for a teenage boy, and I wanted to come across as being as normal and inconspicuous as possible.

I took one of the bottles and popped the cap with a multi-tool contraption I found beside the alcoholic stack. The crimped metallic cap bounced off the edge of the marbled kitchen surface and scuttled to the floor.

The kitchen had cleared. The music from the living room had switched to another track, something equally repetitive and annoying, and someone had turned up the volume. I hastily drank the beer—my face scrunching in disgust when the sulfured taste of a defecating hop lingered on my tongue—before grabbing another and walking toward the wall of noise.

The giddy girls I had followed into the house had progressed toward the kitchen, the sounds of their excitement drowning out the music. I sighed inwardly, looked and failed to find an escape route—my only options being to advance toward them or to leave via a back door—and chose to remain standing, praying they wouldn't come my way.

They stopped in the hallway, thrusting their irritating tedium on whichever unfortunate person they encountered there.

"You've invited *everyone* to this!" one of the giddy duo declared excitedly.

I heard Elizabeth's voice in reply, partially drowned out by the music. There was an element of pride and feigned modesty to her tone. I edged forward, closer to the door and closer to them.

"This is so amazing," the second sycophant chimed.

I watched them through a reflection in a large mirror in the hallway, their jingling, twitching forms fully exposed before my voyeuristic eyes as I stood, out of sight, drinking my fart-scented beer.

"Everyone's here!" the first exclaimed, peering into the living room, unseen in the mirrored reflection.

The second giddy girl, hugging Elizabeth like she was a long lost sister, added, "She even invited Herman."

I stopped in my tracks, the bottle pressed to my lips.

After some awkward laughter, Elizabeth purred like a proud cat and made a show of looking around. "Have you seen him?" she wondered.

They shook their heads, following Elizabeth's darting eyes.

"Ah, I hope he comes," she exclaimed. "I have a few surprises set up for him."

More laughter, a friendly shove.

A previously unseen frumpy blonde appeared like a tubby pantomime villain, drifting out of an alcove and into the expansive hallway. "Ah Lizzie, tell 'em, you should totally tell 'em," she declared with a giddy sense of glee.

A small chorus of pleas erupted before Elizabeth hushed them with a wave of her hand. "Well," she said, her tone rife with the pride of attention. "I'm going to come on to him, pretend I'm drunk and desperate for a fuck. I might even tell him I've always fancied him." She laughed at this; her friends echoed her sentiments. "I'll take him upstairs, to my parents' room. I'll tell him to *get comfortable* and then slip into the ensuite while he does." More laughter, which cut through my boiling veins like a knife through hot butter. "You all wait inside there for me." She lowered her voice as she reached the climax of the story and her friends dipped their heads to listen above the sound of the music. I found myself inching closer to the door, my ears strained.

". . . wait in there with the camera and a few of the guys," she said. "He'll get naked, his puny little cock desperate for its first fuck. Then we burst in on him and get him on camera. The guys can hold him down if need be, then . . ." A nonchalant break in her story—I imagined her shrugging with a carefree attitude as she left the rest of my fate unplanned. "I don't know. We'll probably drag him outside, write *pervert*, or some shit like that, on his chest, and leave him butt naked in the middle of the street."

The laughter that followed was hysterical. I ducked out of the doorway, stood by the counter drinking what was left of my beer. The sour taste no longer bothered me as it rolled over my tongue and rushed down my throat.

"Come on," I heard Elizabeth say, her words shaking with excitement. "Let's find him."

I put the empty beer bottle down on the counter and quickly scanned the hallway mirror to see that Elizabeth and her friends had gone into the living room.

Even before I knew of her plan, she'd had very little chance of coaxing me into her parents' bedroom, and an even smaller chance of convincing me to strip naked and wait for her while she wandered into the bathroom. She was pretty, but I didn't want to sleep with her. The act of creating such an intimate connection with anyone, let alone a tramp who had traded saliva and other bodily fluids with Darren Henderson, was anathema to me. Once she, and more specifically, her drunken male friends, discovered I wasn't as pliable and desperate as they suspected, there was a good chance the night would turn violent.

I remained in the kitchen in silent contemplation. I entertained the notion of feigning to fall for Elizabeth's ploy, slipping upstairs with her and then giving her a few surprises of my own, but I quickly dismissed it. Instead I decided to slip out before they found me.

On my way to the front door, beyond the entrance to the living room, I brushed past a boy from my class. He was attached to the chubby girl who had chimed in during Elizabeth's plotting and was trying to slide a sly hand into her pants while she attached her mouth to his and they traded slurping sounds. It sounded like a cheap horror film. It looked like it, as well.

I stopped behind him, watching her face as it squirmed against his. Her closed eyes were facing me and I scowled into the sealed orbs. She didn't even know me and I couldn't recall ever meeting her or seeing her. She had no right to revel in my misfortune. I turned away, disgusted. Darren, my reason for going to the party, was nowhere to be seen. Therefore Elizabeth's words had not harmed me, as my attendance had been rendered redundant anyway.

The little Labrador puppy was still in the hallway, curled up into a small ball at the foot of the stairs. The initial interest from the teenage girls had waned once the drink had flowed and they had spotted the teenage boys. Now the puppy was on its own, murmuring to itself in its sleep.

They say dogs dream about chasing rabbits. Bull shit. Dreams are segments of life played on repeat, therefore only greyhounds should dream about chasing rabbits—everything else should dream about chasing anuses and licking their own shit. I bent down, planted a soothing finger on the little puppy. He looked up at me quizzically, his eyes snapping open as they left the dream world of jogging anuses. I picked him up, cradled him in my arms. He was warm, cozy. I could feel his beating heart against my own. He looked up at me with black and sorrowful eyes and then settled into the crook of my arm, content with the efforts of sleep.

I gave him a sorrowful smile of my own and carried him past the kissing couple and into the kitchen. I flicked a switch on the wall and then sat down with him at the dining table. In the living room, the sound of playful screams and shouts intersected the numbing beats.

After a few minutes, the dog was comfortable and had fallen asleep, a further ten minutes and he was fast asleep, twitching slightly under the influence of his dreams. Two people came into the kitchen in that time, but neither of them acknowledged me. I took the dog to the other side of the kitchen where the dwindling supply of bottles sat in haphazard formation, a scattering of bottle caps strewn around them. With the beer dwindling fast, attentions would no doubt turn to the punch bowl, the ratio of alcohol to fruit juice gradually increasing as the night wore on and taste buds were forgotten.

The puppy was asleep, stirring in my arms. I held him tightly and caressed him with one hand while I took the bleach out of the sink with the other. It occurred to me how easy it would be to poison the dog, to make all those girls cry and to create pure chaos, but I had no intention of doing that. I may hate dogs, but I still prefer animals to humans. Dogs, and other animals for that matter, act on primal instincts, devoid of all the emotions and characteristics that make humans human, and make them so deplorable at the same time. They are not as evil, simply because nothing they do can be construed as being evil. I'm not an animal lover, but when it comes to hurting an animal or a human, the human always gets my vote.

I left the puppy on the kitchen counter, curled up out of sight and out of reach of drunken idiots and giddy teenage girls. I then poured some of the bleach into the punch bowl before topping it up with vodka. It wasn't going to kill anyone, but it would make them sick, which would make me happy.

I left the party with a smile on my face. I wasn't humiliated like Elizabeth and her friends had hoped, and although I was sure they would still be looking for me, I knew that in an hour or so, when the contents of their stomachs were leaving via every available orifice, and her plush new house was covered with the biological detritus of a dozen teenagers, I would be the last thing on their minds.

6

I bent an ear toward associated cliques during the final few days of school and discovered that no one suspected me of poisoning the punch bowl, because no one knew I was there. A few people had seen me, but it seemed none of them had been paying attention. I noted a few embarrassed faces, a few friends that could seemingly not look each other in the eye, which suggested that the night had gone as I hoped it would and that those friends saw a lot more of each other than they ever wanted to.

When the school year and my educational life ended, I was delighted. My classmates were hiding their fears for ambiguous futures behind smiles of bravado and plans for a life spent drinking, smoking, and fucking, but the smile on my face was genuine. I had no aspirations of further education, no college, nothing that would prolong my harrowing stay in a flawed system.

My father had left me some money in his will, a will that had named my degenerate uncle as my sole guardian. It wasn't a spectacular amount. He was a man of great secrets, but none of those secrets involved a wealth of ill-gotten gains. With the mortgage and the bills burning a small but expanding hole in those savings, and the house not officially mine until I turned eighteen, I would need to find a job eventually, but until then, I was free to devote my time to my new vocation.

In the subsequent summer months, I spent more time than I would have liked at home. My uncle, whether suffering from a brain tumor or the mental ejaculations of an alcohol-based epiphany, had changed his tune.

"I'm going to be the man your dad would have wanted me to be," he told me one afternoon. I had stumbled in from a spying excursion, expecting to find him typically comatose on the bathroom floor, drenched in vomit and despair with a stench of inevitable death emanating from his soured body. Instead he was waiting for me in the kitchen, a cup of coffee in his hand, a look of sobriety on his haggard face.

"I'm sorry if I haven't been much like an uncle to you," he continued, straining his wretched face into a smile. "But things will change, I swear."

He hugged me and I stood rigid and uncomfortable in his musky embrace.

When he pulled away, he was grinning. I felt violated.

"What's gotten into you?" I asked him suspiciously.

"Nothing. I'm just—"

"No, seriously," I interjected. "What is it? Are you high? Is that it?"

He looked offended, but I hadn't finished. "Did you finally drink away all of your pathetic misery?"

His face twitched. "I'm just trying to be nice. I'm cleaning up my act."

"You still stink, though," I told him. "Clean up yourself first. Take a fucking shower."

My baiting didn't work. He sneered at me, did a double-take as if to say something, and then decided against it.

I found the source of his newfound sobriety the following day. A woman, short, skinny. Her eyes were sunken like the hollow crevices of death. Her clothes, although trimmed to supermodel proportions, hung loosely from her skeletal body. She was constantly grasping the edge of her sleeve with her palm and pulling it taut, hiding the needle marks that lingered on the pale flesh of her arms.

"I'm Joanne," she told me timidly, looking around me instead of at me. "Dave's friend."

"Dave?"

"Your uncle?"

"Oh." I gave her a succinct, uncommitted nod. "*Him.*"

She edged around the house with the timidity of an injured rodent. She refused to make eye contact, barely uttered more than a word, and seemed constantly ill at ease inside her own flesh, yet my uncle was infatuated by her. He never took his eyes off her, didn't seem to mind when his endless chatter constantly faced a weakened smile and a timid mumble.

Curiosity got the better of me and, for a few hours, I remained downstairs with the couple, watching television and trying not to sicken myself while studying my uncle's infatuation. After a while, I grew bored and decided to take my leave, but my uncle stopped me.

"It's late," he said, looking at his wrist, even though we both knew he was too cheap to own a watch. "Where do you think you're going?"

"I . . ." I paused and stammered, a little taken aback. "I don't know."

"Well, sit down then," he said with an assured nod, turning away from me.

"But I need . . ." I didn't finish that sentence. I wasn't sure how to. I didn't want to tell him my intentions, but for some reason I also didn't want to disobey him without knowing *his* intentions. I had images of him following me, or taking his newfound responsibilities to the extreme and reporting my disappearance to the police. The last thing I needed was the dense blue line following me around.

I returned to my seat with a scowl on my face. I saw my uncle exchange a dignified look of self-importance with his new mate and she grinned back, proud of his parenting efforts.

The malnourished girl stayed over that night. I retired to my room in the evening, stewing over my foiled plans, but I heard them—or rather *him*—talking downstairs throughout the night. They withdrew to bed early and he came to wish me goodnight, with her beaming a proud smile over his shoulder. I ignored him.

For an hour after that, I listened to their audible fucking. The bed squeaked angrily under their efforts, the mattress rebounding with a repetitive, springy rhythm. I prayed that his sweaty, desperate body would snap her fragile frame, forcing her out of my life before she became too comfortable and forcing him to hit the bottle again. Instead she seemed enlivened by the experience. The following day, skipping downstairs in one of his shirts—stained with years of sweat marks that no amount of washing could ever remove—she looked like a different girl. She was still the pale, pathetic female I had encountered the previous day, but she looked different. Lively. Fresh. She greeted me with a smile and a friendly "good morning."

I took my thoughts for a walk that evening, trying to collect myself with a brisk stride in the sunshine. When I returned I found my uncle, watched over by his ghostly mate, waiting impatiently for me.

"And what time do you call this?" Again he was looking at his wrist.

"Ten," I told him abruptly. "If you actually bought a fucking watch maybe you'd know that."

His eyes flared. He crossed his arms aggressively over his chest. "Get upstairs to your room!" He threw his hand toward the stairs in a wayward Nazi salute.

I smiled a stifled laugh. "You've gotta be fucking kidding me."

"Now!"

I met his annoyed stare. With the door behind me and his weakened frame just in front, it would have been easy to force his head in the jamb and use the door to split open his skull and end his—

57

"Now!" he ordered again, louder this time.

I looked from him to Joanne in the living room—she had been watching me but she turned away with shy uncertainty when our eyes met.

"For fuck's sake," I muttered softly.

He jolted his thrusting arm, as if to repeat the expression.

"Fine," I spat, mournfully slumping up the stairs and into my room. I heard him receiving praise and imagined the wide, simple grin on his moronic face as he soaked it up. I needed him out of the way, but as much as I wanted to, I couldn't attack or kill him. Not with a witness present. My career as a killer would be over before it started.

I decided that if I was to resume my plans of killing Darren Henderson that summer, I needed to make sure my uncle returned to being a terminal drunk.

————

Darren had started a summer romance, a new girl to force his unwanted sexual urges and sweaty desires onto. She hadn't gone to our school and looked a few years younger than him, maybe no more than fourteen. She was short and petite, with an Irish smile and bright red hair. She was fully developed for her age, but her soft features gave her away.

Wearing an inconspicuous disguise, I tracked him to the corner of a small, middle-class suburb. He waited there, checking his watch intermittently, while I pretended to examine the schedules at a nearby bus shelter. When he saw her—sauntering around the corner, her hair shining in the sunlight, her glittered face sparkling under its rays—his gaunt face lit up. He greeted her with a sloppy kiss and a casual grasp of her buttocks and then they set off together. When they brushed past me, my back to them, my eyes away, I heard him bragging to her about his exploits the night before, the bravado of stealing something inane and then running from the police. She didn't sound impressed, but she giggled along regardless.

They went to the park, sat briefly on a bench, and then took off sharply toward an enclosed, wooded area, the same section of park where Darren and his thuggish friends had jumped me months earlier. I had nothing to gain from following them and watching him awkwardly fondle her, but I had grown fond of the voyeuristic lifestyle. I felt a superior godlike rush when following him. It gave me a sense of power to know that I was watching and studying his movements without his knowledge.

I tracked them into the woods, keeping my distance and ducking behind trees for cover. I heard them ahead, their feet crunching twigs and kicking stones as they advanced deeper into the shrouded land. I heard their whispered conversation; him eager, her anxious. I stopped my tracking when I could no longer hear them. No crunching leaves, no conversation. I could hear only my own softened breathing as I waited for a sound to break through.

When I didn't hear anything, instinct got the better of me and I popped my head around the corner of the tree. Up ahead, the redhead was leaning casually against a tree, her eyes lazily wandering, a nonchalant patience on her face. Then I saw Darren, and he was looking right at me.

His face twisted into a darkened mix of anger and delight and he bolted straight for me. Shock and surprise held me momentarily rooted. I tried to turn and run when my body allowed but by then it was already too late. Darren pounced like a wild animal, grasping me tightly.

"Well, well, well!" he exclaimed, grabbing the back of my head with his thick, clubbish hands. "If it isn't my good friend Herman."

I mumbled something in reply, but even I wasn't sure what. I could feel the sweat of desire and anticipation soak from his palms onto my hair.

"You trying to catch a look at me and my girl?" he demanded to know.

At that point, the redheaded girl was moving cautiously toward us, her face twisting with a flinching moment of distaste at being called *his girl*. I watched her trepidatious steps with a hint of curiosity, but when Darren slammed my head into the trunk of the tree, I lost sight of her and pretty much everything else.

A sea of stars danced around my eyes like a glittering rave. A rush of pain shot from the front of my skull to the back before radiating an intense agony that covered every inch of my head. I dropped to my knees and threw my hands to my face, but Darren held me up.

"Sick little cunt!" I felt the cold sting of saliva on the back of my neck. "You make me sick!"

He threw me to my knees; I clattered to the ground with a joint-jarring thud. I felt the thud of a heavy-toed shoe as he swung his foot into the middle of my spine. I vaulted forward into the tree and felt my nose crunch painfully under the initial impact before my chin absorbed the rest of the grating grind of the caustic bark.

My ears were ringing with the sound of my own blood and through the noise I heard Darren laughing with glee. He yelled something at me, a giggling tirade of hilarity that I couldn't hear and only he could find amusing.

Wallow in your delight you pathetic little boy because soon I will tear every inch of existence from your unworthy soul.

I heard the girl shout something, a cross between a scream and a yell. It cut through to my ringing ears like a distant birdsong.

"Leave him!"

Darren grumbled something in reply, the bass of his discontented voice rumbling through without coherence.

I pushed my face away from the tree and flopped forward, flipping myself over so I was staring at a hazy, tree-blocked sky and the bemused expression of Darren Henderson standing underneath it. The girl came into view and put a restraining hand on his shoulder.

"Leave him!" she said. "What are you doing?"

"He fucking deserves it," he spat venomously. He threw her hand away and moved toward me, bending to pick me up by the collar. She stopped him again, more sternly this time. He snapped at her sudden touch, throwing her away a little more aggressively than he would have liked.

She toppled backward, losing her footing on the leafy ground and hitting the ground with a thud. He turned toward her, a look of regret and diminishing hope building on his face. She looked up at him with a sense of fear and newfound hatred.

"I didn't mean to—" he began, moving toward her, intending to help her up.

She kicked out at him, her heels digging in the dirt and flicking up specks of it. She shimmied backward, her eyes wide and alert. After staggering to her feet, she threw him an evil stare that said more than words ever could, then she turned and, with a final whimper, hurried away.

"No, please!" he shouted after her. "Sandy! *I love you!*"

He watched her go with solemn eyes, then he heard me laughing behind him, my laugher cutting through a bust lip and crackling through the viscous blood that spewed from my nose.

"What's so fucking funny!" he demanded to know.

I broke my laughter long enough to answer him. "*You*," I told him with a broken voice. "You're fucking pathetic."

A mixture of anger, self-loathing, and despair built a torrid and turbulent picture on his face. He moved with a frothing mouth to grab me, spraying spittle at my bloody face, then he decided against it, his despair taking over. He swung one last kick, heavy against my ribs, and then walked away, leaving me a bloody, agonized, and hysterical wreck on the forest floor.

———

I stumbled home, cutting a disturbed figure as I staggered along with my back hunched lamely, my face covered in dried blood, my arms holding my chest as if to prevent my lungs from falling out. A permanent smile on my face. Many people looked, but no one spoke and no one offered any help.

My uncle was asleep on the sofa when I staggered through the front door. I stood over him, breathing heavily. A drop of fresh coppery blood gathered in my mouth and popped out with my breath like crimson bubblegum.

He gently stirred to the sedate pulses of some unknown dream. A whimper on his lips, a twitch in his neck. The sight of him made me sick—so much waste of human life. He served no purpose to me or to anyone else, yet he still managed to get in my way.

An empty glass rested before him on the chair. Since he had taken to sobriety, he had been drinking a lot of water, whether in an attempt to flush out his system or to substitute his preferred tipple with something a little more innocuous. I hated him more for his sobriety, not just because he was a nuisance to me, but because he did it out of selfish greed, an act committed purely to get into the pants and the mind of a unwitting woman who didn't know any better than to inject her veins with filth and fuck the first dickhead who offered.

I flinched at the sound of the phone, a shrill siren that sparked the silence of my body into one terrified jolt. My uncle also flinched. He twitched violently, mumbled, moaned, and then turned over, his swollen body arching toward the other side of the chair.

I answered on the second ring.

"Is your uncle there?"

I recognized the timid tone of Joanne the addict.

"He's asleep," I told her with great difficulty, my voice grating in my throat.

She paused, hearing my voice and sensing the need to ask me if I was okay. "Oh," she said, deciding against it, her addiction and recovery having zapped any sense of social obligation out of her system. "I was supposed to come around later," she continued, half to herself. "It's just I'm back earlier than I thought and I was going to come around now."

I didn't reply. I enjoyed toying with her sense of uncertainty.

"Do you think I should?" She pushed through the silence.

Again I refused to comment.

"I'll come around soon," she said eventually.

"Okay."

"Okay, well, bye. I mean, I'll see you soon."

I hung up.

She was at the house within the hour. A timorous knock, a pitiful rat-a-tat of an approaching visitor almost apologetically alerting the occupants. My uncle didn't stir at the sound. Even I barely heard it.

When I opened the door and exposed my face, the blood now cleaned, the bruises and swelling more evident, she recoiled in surprise. She glared at me, a look of disgust on her face. No lack of social obligation would ease her away from the question now.

"What happened to you?" she asked.

I sighed heavily. "It's a long story."

I moved away from the door, standing sideways to allow her inside. She didn't move. She remained at the threshold, as though scared to bypass me and enter the house.

"Are you okay?" One of her initial recoiled steps had now been retaken, but she was still standing a few feet away from me.

I stared at her, absorbing the horror in her eyes, eyes that refused to leave my disfigured face. There was something behind her fear, a personal attachment to my wounds.

I replied slowly, following her face as I spoke. "I suppose I'll live."

She looked beyond me, her eyes apprehensive as they darted into the house, then to the street beyond, everywhere but at my face as her mind conjured up images that her eyes refused to acknowledge.

Then it occurred to me: she thought my uncle had beaten me. Her mind was weighing the possibilities of inquiring and finding out. Did she really want to have it confirmed that her new boyfriend was a thuggish brute? And if so, did that mean he had broken their pact and had started drinking again?

A smile tried to creep onto my face, but I managed to exchange it for a pained expression. "Wouldn't be the first time, after all," I said, throwing in a meek look and then staring off into the middle distance to establish a melancholic moment of reflection.

I heard her stutter. Her feet twitched uncertainly as they prepared a path of retreat; the primal fight-or-flight response in her body screamed for flight at every sense of discomfort.

"Di-di . . ."

I lifted my eyes to hers. She looked like she was ready to cry.

"Di-Did *Dave* do this?" she spoke in a whisper, almost silencing herself at the mention of his name.

I nodded solemnly and lowered my head to my chest. "He's drinking again," I said softly. "As soon as you leave." I tried my best to sniffle, emulating a suppression of tears when internally I felt like laughing. "He hides the bottles when you're here, he says that what you don't know won't hurt you."

I paused to let my words sink in. When I raised a surreptitious eye to gauge her reaction, I saw streams of tears rolling down her bony cheeks. She looked less agitated now; a feeling of desolation had taken over. She wiped the rivulets away with the back of a hand that seemed entirely composed of knuckle. She made a move to say something, one final word before running away in a fit of tears. I jumped in before she could.

"Please don't say anything," I told her. "He'll only beat me more."

I looked at her and she returned a look that shone with sympathy. Then she turned and left, walking to begin with, then running. I watched her all the way, grinning broadly as she departed from my and my uncle's life.

"Who was that?" my uncle asked as I entered the living room and discovered him rubbing his sleepy eyes with his palms.

"Nothing."

"I thought I heard a noise."

That noise was the sound of your last chance of sobriety and decency departing in a torrent of tears and regret. Now you have fuck all else to do but drink yourself into a putrid grave and give the earth back the carbon that you so recklessly borrowed.

"It was nothing."

That night, Joanne left a message on the answering machine. She told him it was over, that she didn't want to see him again, and that she would appreciate it if he never called or visited ever again. She sounded heartbroken, her voice cracking and breaking even more than usual. She sounded like she would burst into tears at any moment during the extended message of goodbye. She didn't leave him with a definite reason but did offer him plenty of excuses so he could pick his own.

"I don't think we fit together. . . . It's just not working out. . . . I have a few problems to work through . . ."

I was with him at the time. When the message started, he was smiling, happy to hear the voice of a newfound flame and pondering on what delights she would bestow upon him. As it wore on, his face grew gradually darker. By the end, when her weakened voice fuzzed its final excuse and faded into the electronic beep, he was distraught and looked like death incarnate. He left the house without saying a word, without even looking at me. He returned a few hours later, drunk, crying, and mumbling to himself. He had begun the day as a sober man on a gratifying journey to self-worth; he ended it as a drunk, passed out in a pool of his own piss and misery.

7

In the prevailing summer months, I was overcome with a fervent expectation and an almost quivering sense of excitement. I struggled to sleep, tossing and turning a number of empty hours away. When I did sleep, I dreamed about killing Darren in a multitude of ways. Sometimes I ripped open his throat; once with a sharp knife, another time with the clawed edge of a hammer. Sometimes I strangled or beat him. On all occasions I took great joy in his painful demise.

My chance to kill him came a few weeks after the incident in the park. His parents had gone on holiday, taking the younger child with them. Darren had either refused to go or hadn't been invited. He stayed at home, partying with his slow-witted friends and annoying the neighbors with loud music, drinking, drug taking, and general hoodlum activity. It would have been easy for me to slip into a few of those parties, so inebriated and diverse were the attendees, but I kept my distance and studied them patiently from behind the boundary in the back garden.

On four successive nights in his room, his friends stayed over and drank themselves into oblivion while Darren fucked any desperate and drunken teenage girls he could—the pretty redhead excluded. I made brief appearances just to check in on him and his erratic behavior, having no intention to stay out all night watching him and his cronies fuck and vomit their way into an abyss.

On the fifth night, he had plans elsewhere. It was a Saturday and he was going to the pub, an apparent lock-in—a much hyped episode broadcast to him by a semi-retarded blonde kid with aggressive acne. There was a promise of cheap drinks and a night of unadulterated drunkenness, after which everyone—except Darren, for reasons I didn't grasp—would be going back to the pizza-faced boy's house to spend the night. It was the perfect chance for me to strike. Darren would return drunk and alone. I would have all night to get my first kill.

I left my house at around eleven, at which time I was confident Darren would be at the pub, heavily intoxicated. It would give me enough time to sneak into his house and set up a plan of attack. My uncle was semiconscious. He had fallen asleep watching an old western, his beer-riddled half-corpse twitching to the sounds of simulated gunshots as I crept soundlessly into the night.

On the fourth night, Darren and his friends had spent some time in the back garden, sitting on the patio and staring at the stars while the remaining dregs of sunlight were drained from the glass of the day. This was why I hadn't spent much time behind the garden wall on that night, and it was also the reason I was able to sneak into the house the following night. There were no kids in the back garden on that night, but Darren was feckless and reckless enough to have still left the door unlocked, giving me the opportunity I needed.

The curtains were open and moonlight streamed in through the windows, offering me a partial path as I accustomed myself with the layout of the first floor. I skulked around, drinking in the details of the floor plan in case I needed to chase him around. I took a large kitchen knife from the drawer, the biggest and sharpest of a carving set that had seen better days. It made more sense than bringing my own weapon. I didn't want to carry a murder weapon home. I certainly didn't want to leave it at the scene of the crime.

I had bought a pair of gloves for the occasion. They were black, tight to my flesh, and allowed for easy manipulation of my fingers. The blade felt weighty and strong in my hands, as if brushing against my flesh and not a thin coating of synthetic material.

I found three bedrooms upstairs, two of which I dismissed quickly. One was clearly the master bedroom: a long-mirrored wardrobe rested along the front, a queen-sized bed pushed up against the opposing wall. The other was filled with an array of children's toys, while a single bed, adorned with a *Ninja Turtle* duvet set, stood against the far wall.

The final room was clearly Darren's. The musty smell, the rank, fetid air, and the detritus scattered around the floor like flecks on a Pollock painting all gave it away.

In his room, a sense of power and excitement overcame me. Stalking through the place where he rested his empty head and wanked his parental complexes away, with an instrument of murder clenched tightly in my fist, I felt a godlike power I had never experienced before. In a matter of hours, minutes, or moments, I would be taking a human life. I would have power over life and death. I would be the one to choose how much he suffered and for how long. It was exhilarating and overpowering, so much so that I remained standing there for many moments.

The sound of a key slipping into a lock finally snapped me out of my trance. In that time, the darkness had become my friend— my eyes adjusting to a light only they could see. Darren would turn the light on when entering, but not if I could get to him first. With a broad smile, I snuck in behind the bedroom door, the knife poised and prepared at shoulder height, waiting for the drunken idiot to stumble for the light switch before I pounced.

The smile dripped from my face like warm ice cream when I heard the sound of a female voice punctuating the silence. Darren wasn't alone.

I quickly scanned the room for a place to hide; a chest of drawers to duck behind, a wardrobe to dive inside. There was a small bedside cabinet, a set of drawers barely big enough to conceal a small animal, and a small wardrobe that sat on an unstable foundation. There wasn't even a bed to slide underneath, just a mattress slapped onto the floor like junkyard treasure in a homeless shelter.

I edged open the door, looked into the hallway. I could see the lights spilling from downstairs as Darren conversed loudly with his female guest, evidently breaking into his parents' liquor supply in an effort to appease or sedate her.

I slipped out, creeped across the hallway, and peeked over the banister, down the stairs. They were in the living room; on the opposing wall their illuminated shadows danced a tentative dance. They hadn't sat, hadn't rested. The front door was a tempting target at the foot of the stairs, but they were closer to it than I was.

I didn't want to kill them both. A double murder was too risky, too messy. Not now. Not at this point in my career. I wasn't that desperate.

I needed to be patient, to hold my nerve. I put my foot on the top step, prepared to move toward the door. The step creaked and groaned with a sound greater than I remembered on my ascent. It sounded deafening. I closed my eyes until that noise, and that of my own quickening heartbeat, faded. Then I took another step, my hand firmly gripping the banister to alleviate the pressure I was applying to the creaky floorboards.

"Come on," I heard Darren saying. The annoying laugh that had taunted me for many years was now present in its drunken form. "*Down it. Down it. Down it,*" he began to chant, almost grunting.

The female gagged a choking sound in reply, her voice strained through the efforts of forced alcohol consumption. She groaned, coughed. I moved onto the third step.

I heard the sound of a vigorous kiss, a sloppy, noisy caress. Then I heard glass on wood as a bottle was put down. I held my breath, praying they would do what they intended to do on the couch and leave me to an unheeded escape.

The kiss finished with a passionate breath. "Not here," the girl said. "Upstairs."

I gulped and instinctively moved my right heel backward, to the second step.

"What's wrong with here?"

That's right, you tell her. Couch, bed, floor, it doesn't make a difference; she can be equally disappointed on all three.

She sounded a negative groan. "Not here," she asserted. "Bed!"

I moved my left foot back to the second step.

"Fine!" Darren spat, annoyed. I heard movement, quick, eager footsteps.

I quickly turned, jumped the final stair, ran across the hallway, and ducked into the master bedroom on my left. The sound of my own heaving heart canceled out the noise of the creaky floorboards, but I was sure they would have heard me.

I listened, waiting for the inevitable questions, the paranoia and the panic. It didn't come.

In his parents' bedroom, with the sound of keen footsteps beginning their ascent, I headed straight for the walk-in wardrobe opposite the door and adjacent to the bed. It was large enough to accommodate me until I could make my escape.

I waited for them to go to Darren's room so I could slip out of the house during their thirty seconds of breathless passion, but instead they stumbled into the master bedroom.

Darren tugged the unfortunate female behind him with an eager and desperate lust. As he opened the door, the room bathed in light from the hallway and I twitched under its glow, fading further into the wardrobe and watching the action unfurl through a thin opening in the door.

I watched Darren pull his prey aggressively into the room, practically throwing her onto the bed before beaming down at her with a lustfulness that threatened to pop his eyes from his skull.

His eyes were wide, glassy and desperate. The crotch of his faded blue jeans bulged.

"You ready, baby?"

He whipped off his shirt. I threw up a little in my mouth.

I turned my attention to the girl. She was propping up her chubby physique with her elbows, watching the undressing simpleton with wanton eyes. She wore a short black skirt, tight around her ample backside and short enough to expose her thick thighs, the skin of which was bruised and red in places and heavily tanned everywhere else. She instinctively opened her legs, gesturing with her short dumpy body for Darren to enter her.

While Darren undressed, struggling to remove his pants, she stroked a finger between her legs, toying with a moistened pair of white knickers.

I found myself scowling at her face, at her dimpled, ruby cheeks, her glossy eyes and her protruding tongue. I didn't know who she was; she didn't go to my school and I had never made her acquaintance, but I had seen her before. She had been at Elizabeth's party. She was the little fat fuck who had been enthralled with the thought of tricking and humiliating me, even though she didn't know who I was. She was the one who had been swapping saliva with my classmate while trying to stop his hands from probing the depths of her infectious cunt.

Fucking trampy little waste of space.

Darren undressed and set to work on her, quickly tearing off her knickers and tossing them away. They flew toward the wardrobe, toward me. The moistened skid-marked material slapped at the wardrobe door and rebounded onto the floor with the faintest whisper.

In my head I urged him on, encouraging him to go where everyone had gone before and to contaminate her with whatever bulbous, warty disease he had festering and fermenting on his sweaty, unwashed, overused penis.

"Wait, wait!" she protested, trying to spit out his sloppy attempts at foreplay, blocking his pulsating cock with the palm of her hand. "*Condom.* We need a condom!"

Shame. I would have loved to see the mongrel offspring those two delinquents produced. The bastard, mutant child of two people who shouldn't be allowed to live, let alone reproduce.

"You're on the pill!" Darren objected.

"I have to be sure."

"But—but—" Darren was looking desperate. He swayed forward, hoping to slip in unseen. Perhaps thinking that he could get inside, do his thing, and then finish before she knew what was going on. She slapped him away again. "Come on," he urged. "I'm clean, I swear."

Quite frankly, I'm amazed they didn't hear my stifled laugh.

"I don't want to get pregnant!" the girl yelled. "Ya know what happened to my sister, *she* was on the pill and *she* got pregnant. Get a fucking condom!"

"Fuck," Darren spat desperately, looking like he was ready to explode. His eyes darted quickly around the room. "What if I pull out before I cum?"

I grinned at his desperation.

"Get a fucking condom!" she barked. "You're not putting that *thing* inside me without one. I don't want to get pregnant."

She didn't care about the wiggling, festering things that would climb into her vagina and prepare—with the benefit of reinforcements from the town's many diseased and desperate dicks—to fight an eternal battle against loosely prescribed antibiotics, but she did object to the idea of procreation. Thank God for small miracles and smaller minds.

Darren groaned noisily and I grinned widely at his audible discomfort. I heard him shift away from his inebriated mate and scurry out of the room. The noise of his desperate search filtered through to his parents' room like a lingering nighttime rodent scuttling through debris in an attic.

The girl called out to Darren, "I have some in my bag." But her words were heavily lubricated and soft, unable to seep through to her scrambling mate. She didn't seem to mind and clearly wasn't in a rush.

I saw her loll back onto the bed, groaning as she did so. Her skirt had been pushed up to her bulbous stomach, her exposed vagina glistened as she set to work on pleasing herself. I scrunched up my face and gagged a little, making a soft but audible noise. She didn't hear.

Considering what comes and goes through a woman's vagina, what plethora of typically disgusting fluids are ejected from its fleshy folds, it amazes me how men can find a moist one so alluring. When they're not cleaning out the ejections of other men's failed attempts at procreation, or wiping away the dribbles of their own spent urine, they're picking the crusts of dried menstrual blood from those apparently appealing folds. Clearly men will stick their penises anywhere.

Darren, who had yet to encounter a hole he didn't want to poke, seemed a little insulted when, after stumbling into the bedroom with a pack of condoms held proudly in his hand, he discovered the moaning mountain of flesh had started without him. He wasted no time in slipping on the latex and then jumping on top of her, where he quickly finished what had taken him many breathless moments to start.

He was practically wheezing when he finished. He rolled off of her and turned immediately away, his naked form curling into the fetal position. The girl looked perplexed. She hadn't seen him reenter the room and seemed surprised that not only had the sex started, but it had also finished.

"Is that it?" she asked.

He groaned in reply and held up his arm, exposing a filled condom that drooped toward the bed like a depressed, deflated balloon. He flung it across the room carelessly and the girl watched with absent eyes as it splattered against the far wall, hung there momentarily, and then began a slow decline, dripping down the magnolia like an anemic slug.

She groaned in annoyance, peeking over occasionally at his disinterested form before staring at the ceiling, her fingers tapping her stomach. She turned to his back, moistened with his succinct lascivious labors. "Will you be ready to—" She stopped speaking when she received a preemptive snore in reply. Darren was already asleep.

"Bastard," she muttered under her breath. She turned over, facing away from him. She tried to continue her solo efforts at stimulation, but she seemed unable to get in the right mood. A feeling of being duped got in the way of her desire and eventually she closed her eyes and forced herself to sleep.

I watched her attempts at slumber. She was distracted, uncomfortable, and annoyed; she wouldn't be sleeping too soon. I sighed inwardly and skulked to the back of the cupboard, resting my head against a soft and heavy piece of clothing and preparing myself for a long night.

———

I scrambled out of the wardrobe sometime later. Darren was still facing away, his naked and sweaty body rising and falling with the fluctuations of his rattling breath. The girl lay beside him, her body curved in a similar posture, the duvet half thrown over her body. Her suffering breath sang noisily as it strained through her dehydrated lungs.

I watched them momentarily as they breathed their rotten breaths into an air that already stank of their sweaty and brief exertions. Their naked forms looked so vulnerable and exposed. It would have been so easy to kill them both there and then, to slit her throat and end her miserable existence without Darren even stirring, giving me enough time to reset myself before suffocating the pointless life from his diseased body. But I was tired, stiff, and ill-prepared for a double murder. I retired from the room and descended the stairs.

The light from the hallway remained active; the house was bathed in a prominent glow. Despite the light and the sound of my footfalls on the stairs, still creasing and groaning an audible distraction, I was comfortable. There was little chance that either one of the comatose pair would awaken, and an even smaller chance that they would be capable of chasing me if they did.

A handbag lay at the foot of the stairs, next to two pairs of shoes that had been kicked off in a hurry. The handbag was of a tatty denim material, shaded and pale in parts, rather like the chubby legs of its owner. Also like her legs, the bag had been abused by a number of teenagers—the illiterate hands of a dozen feckless youths had scrawled a number of inane references onto the worn material.

There was very little inside. A purse, empty but for a fake I.D., a voucher for a fast food restaurant, and around $2 in change; a tube of red lipstick, glistening with the herpetic fluid of a hundred kisses; a makeup box, the colors and foundations of which were smudged into each other like a child's paint palette; a large pack of condoms, wholesale protection for a wholesale whore; and a small pill box.

The circular shaped pill box contained a number of contraceptive tablets. The pills themselves—small, white, innocuous—were embedded around the edges of the plastic device with the names of the days of the week above each one.

So desperate to avoid the sin of a mutant baby, borne to an incapable and promiscuous teenage mother and a septic, pointless father of any possible age and all possible retardations, she fought the threat with a double-edged contraceptive sword: condoms and birth-control pills. No doubt it decreased her chances of sexual success to a reckless race of boys who preferred their tiny organs to be unsheathed, but evidently she still found willing members of the masculine race, whether through sheer desperation or complete drunkenness.

There were two weeks' worth of pills left, yet I had no doubt that the condoms, a hefty pack of well over a dozen, would be used up before that in an orgy of debauchery, disappointment, and drunkenness. In two weeks, those condoms would stop a flood of potentially virile semen, with the pills acting as a safety net to catch any that managed to slip through the latex barrier. It would be a shame if anyone were to bring down those barriers and blunt that double-edged sword.

I took the pills to the kitchen and popped them out into the sink, using a flush of water from the faucet to send them down the plughole. The tiny tablets popped easily through the tiny grates in the drain. I found a small pack of pocket mints in one of the many drawers, spearmint flavored, white, roughly the same size as the pills. I put the mints inside the box, refilling it to within a pill of how I had left it. She might taste the mint as she washed them down, but I knew I wasn't dealing with the sharpest tool in the shed, so she wouldn't give it a second thought.

The box went back in the drawer after that, but before I closed it, a picture in the drawer caught my attention. I stopped in my tracks, entranced. The picture was of Darren's mother, sitting alone, sleepy, smiling warmly at the camera from underneath a cozy winter blanket. Her son, Darren's younger brother, was curled up at her feet like a dog.

I removed the photo, straightened it out on the counter. There was also a photo of her on the kitchen windowsill; she was grinning into the camera rather drunkenly. She wore a bikini and looked to be standing on some sunny beach. One of those lands of sun, sea, and sex, some distant cloudless paradise where no matter where you go, everyone you encounter is loud, horny, and British. That photo hadn't intrigued me, I didn't even give it a second glance, but this one was different.

I carefully folded the photo and stuffed it into my pocket. It wouldn't be missed, in a house full of junk, where the fridge was magnetized with a dozen trite slogans, postcards, pictures, and childish sketches, and where the floors were a battlefield of toys and the cabinets were mere storage rooms for the crap that couldn't be thrown away lest they serve a point in the future. One photograph wouldn't be missed.

In another drawer, one that rattled disconcertingly with the sound of a multitude of cutlery and gadgets, I found a small pin with a pea-sized green head. I used this to puncture individual holes in each of the condoms, passing the needle through the wrapper and out the other side. It left an unnoticeable—especially in times of need—hole that would further serve the purpose of impregnating the sleeping beast upstairs. Despite failing to kill Darren, I left with a smile on my face. His death could wait. His parents would be back soon and my window of opportunity would close for an indeterminable window, but I was happy to bide my time. They say good things come to those who wait and I was happy to do just that.

8

―

It was Christmas in our own little tinseltown, and the streets were coated with a tacky shade of festive folly. Lights, strung across the road from lamppost to lamppost, dipped in the center like the jagged-toothed smile of a psychotic clown. Tinsel hugged lampposts and signs like brightly colored bristly snakes. Dancing Santas, cirrhotic reindeer, and bulbous snowmen stood to attention in windows of shops and homes.

It was festive. It was joyful. It was merry.

It was fucking disgusting.

I hate Christmas and everything the season stands for.

I hate the sense of self-importance in the church workers or the heavily religious; they think it's their time to shine, their moment in the sun. Eleven months of regular church visits and senseless dogma all pays off when Christmas comes around and they can look down on the have-a-go Christians who go twice a year. *And where have you been, hmm? I haven't seen you since Easter.*

For the young, it's all about presents, about receiving an ocean of gifts that they barely wanted and will never play with. It is about pigging out on chocolate and flying through the day on a rush of dopamine-induced hysteria. For adults, it is a season of indulgence and a season of loss, where overeating, overdrinking, and maxed-out credit cards combine to make sure that, whatever they do over those few days, they will be paying for it for the rest of the year.

My dad was never big on Christmas, but he didn't want me to feel left out so he did his best for me. He would buy me something small and then spend all day cooking a meal for the both of us. He was a terrible cook and he had no taste when it came to presents, but it was the thought that counted, and he wasn't the source of my hatred for the season. I blamed everyone else. I blamed the smiley well-wishers on television, the presenters who always have a grin on camera, but are probably surviving on a diet of regret and cocaine off camera; the mail carriers, and paper boys and girls who are late and useless for fifty-one weeks of the year, but make sure they're bright and early during the week of Christmas. Christmas is the Las Vegas of holiday seasons, coated in lights and colors bright enough to distract your attention from the misery that lies underneath.

This Christmas was going to be different for me, though. This Christmas I was going to give myself the greatest present anyone had ever given me. It was going to be a momentous occasion. Christmas is a celebration of the birth of a powerful man, a God, a leader—a name that resonates throughout history. And this Christmas, a new God and a new legend would be born. This time nothing would stop me, because I knew that whatever happened, I was going to have my first kill. I was going to do what I was born to do.

"Where you going dressed like that?"

My uncle stood in the open doorway to my bedroom, looking me up and down with glazed-over eyes. Over the past few months, he had returned to being a miserable and worthless piece of shit. His girlfriend had left him, he had started drinking again, and I also suspected that he was using drugs. He had never looked worse, and I had never been happier. Some people don't belong in regular society; I should know because I am one of them. But while people like me will thrive in the shadows, feeding off the darkness, people like my uncle live on the borderline. They are on the edge of both worlds, close to both, loved by neither. There are two evils in the world. There are the people like me, the ones who nightmares are made of, and then there are people like my uncle, the ones who leech from society, taking everything, giving nothing back, and who have the tenacity to pretend they are normal.

Darren Henderson was also one of those people. He had nothing to offer the world and nothing to give anyone in it. He was a bully, a coward, a thug who would grow into a wife-beater, an addict, a waster. I didn't see myself as a vigilante, but I was certainly doing the right thing, whether or not people realized it.

I stared back at my uncle, gave him a little smile. I loved seeing him like this. It was early afternoon Christmas Eve and he was already dead to the world.

"I'm Santa Claus," I told him simply, gesturing toward my red outfit, my black boots, and the sack by my side.

He didn't reply and merely sneered at me.

"Can I help you?" I asked.

He shrugged. "You got anything in that sack for me?"

I nodded slowly. "As it happens, yes I do, but you'll get it later."

He perked up a bit, but as is so often the case with the terminally depressed, it didn't last very long. He had nothing to be happy about. "Should I get excited?"

"You can try."

I kicked out and caught the edge of the door, slamming it in his face. I heard him groan on the other side, heard the silence that followed as he waited and contemplated what to do with himself, and then I heard him slowly descend the stairs. He had a habit of taking them one step at a time, prolonging it as long as he could, as if hoping that by the time he reached the bottom, his life would be over or, at the very least, would be a little less shit than when he began.

I stayed in my room for another couple hours, keeping a close eye on the world outside my window as it turned from gray to black. It had been like that all day. No sunshine, no joy. The perfect day for what I had planned.

I spent a couple of hours downstairs, watching tedious television. All the programs that had done nothing of interest all year now had Christmas specials on and the nation was expected to tune in. There were also firework shows, talks with celebrities, and live music. I watched with disinterest, keeping one eye on the clock.

"Are you going to go anywhere in that?" my uncle asked, gesturing toward the Santa suit.

"Yes."

"Where?"

I paused and stared at him. I realized I could have told him every inch of my plan there and then, and he wouldn't have remembered any of it in an hour or two. He was already slipping into the abyss, his brain bathing in a cocktail of booze, heroin, and God knows what else since he first dragged his smelly, sweaty, and worthless ass out of bed.

"I'm doing some charitable work."

He raised his eyebrows. "Really?"

I nodded.

"What sort of charitable work?"

"You ask a lot of questions, don't you?"

"Do I?" He seemed amused at that one.

"If you must know," I told him, "I'm helping out some disadvantaged teenagers, kids who were never as lucky as I was, kids who, without my help and assistance, might end up as worthless drunks or drug addicts, leeching from their dead brothers and pissing off their nephews."

I wasn't entirely convinced he would put the pieces together, but he managed to do just that. The grin faded from his face and he no longer looked pleased with himself. "I try my best to look after you, you know that."

"No. You really don't."

"Your dad would have wanted me here."

"No. He really wouldn't have."

"It's not my fault things are like this."

I sat forward, leaning on the edge of the sofa. "Really? Then why don't you enlighten me? Whose fault is it? Is it the government? Is it your parents? Is it the little green men who sneak into your room at night and force the heroin into your veins?"

He stared at me for a moment and I sensed something happening behind his eyes. I didn't know whether he was about to cry or whether he was about to jump up and grab me by the throat. In the end, he did neither. His head lowered to his chest and he said, "I'm sorry. I really am. I tried my best and I was doing so well. But then she left and I couldn't face another day without a drink." He looked at me with sorrowful eyes. "I need help."

"Don't worry about it," I told him softly. "I'll help you."

"Really?"

I nodded. "Just give me some time and I promise, you'll be a different man when I'm finished with you."

He seemed content with that, and I was happy that *he* was happy, because it gave me something to look forward to.

We watched television in silence for another two hours, during which time he slipped into the abyss that had been calling his name all day. Realizing it was time to do what needed to be done, I turned off the television and walked over to him. I stood over him and watched him for a few moments, wondering just how bad one person's life had to be for them to turn into the polar opposite of what their brother had been. He had always insisted that life hadn't given him the breaks, but it couldn't have been just that. You make your own luck in life and you create your own breaks; there are options, get-out clauses if you will, that can take away your pain and make life more bearable, but these options come with side effects and invariably leave you a worthless, decaying pile of flesh by the time you reach middle age. My uncle had taken every available get-out clause and now his existence was an excuse, a lie. He lived to pretend that he *wasn't* living; he drowned out his mind, silenced his body, and dumbed down everything that made him human in an effort to ignore the pain, the regret, the fear, and the doubt, emotions that make us human to begin with.

I put my hand on his throat and wrapped my fingers around. I stared at his eyelids as I did so and he didn't stir. I tightened my grip, feeling his warm flesh yield against my palm. I felt a pulse; it was incredibly faint but it was still there. He would be lucky if he ever woke up again, but there was a good chance that he didn't want to anyway.

I backed away, picked up my Santa sack, and then left. I was heading out into the night, into the blackness and the chill of Christmas Eve, just a couple hours from Christmas morning. I was leaving my house a virgin and a child, but I would return as a man with experience. I was leaving as a nobody, but I would return as The Butcher.

PART 2

1

L ester Keats held his hands over his mouth as he watched the
video, and with each passing second, he felt like pushing
them up over his eyes. The onscreen image seemed fairly
innocuous, just one young man walking down the street, in tune
with his festive surroundings and as innocent as innocent could
be, but this wasn't the first time he had seen the video and Lester
knew what came next.

He still remembered the first time he had seen it. He had been
one of the lucky few who hadn't witnessed the crime scene in full,
the ones whose dreams wouldn't be haunted by everything they
had seen and the ones who wouldn't need to be medicated to keep
those dreams at bay. But he hadn't really been lucky; it had only
intensified the shock of what he had seen in the video.

The boy was wearing a Santa Claus outfit with a sack thrown
over his back and a big white beard covering much of his face. It
was Christmas Eve, just a few hours before the big clock in the town
square rang out the sound of midnight and the climax of the festive
season. The streets were empty and, although there was no sound
on the video, Lester had always been able to hear the dull, crunching
footsteps of the boy's big boots as they slapped on snow-encrusted
pavement. It wasn't quite a white Christmas, but it was close. He had
actually remembered the year and the excitement because his two

children had been watching out of their bedroom windows when the snow began to fall.

"Daddy, Daddy! It's snowing, it's going to be a white Christmas after all!"

They were half-right, but just twenty-four hours after their excited cheers, as Lester finished stuffing their presents into stockings and preparing for bed, someone was preparing a different-colored Christmas on the streets of a small town many miles away. He remembered the mince pie he had left out for Santa Claus and he remembered the bite he had taken out of it before leaving it on the table. But after that night, and across the entire country, Saint Nick had lost his saintly image.

This Santa left red footprints in the snow as he walked. The prints were too faint to be seen on the old CCTV recording, but they were still there in the morning when the press arrived. The image of those bloody boots backtracking to a slaughter in the town square was what many people saw on the morning news. Lester had lived a good hundred miles away from the town, but he still remembered the impact the prints had. He still remembered how that single image had come to personify evil, to strip a season of its joy.

The footage changed as the boy crossed the street and stepped out of one camera shot and into another. That followed a period where the boy disappeared down a side street and the camera seemed lost. It cut to another camera, this one located in the town square, which was surrounded on three sides by woodland, the fourth open to the main street. The camera pointed at four youngsters, roughly the same age as the kid in the Santa suit. There were two boys and two girls. They were nuisance kids who got into a lot of trouble, but were ultimately good at heart and certainly didn't deserve what they got.

Lester removed his hands from his mouth and sighed. He knew every detail of the video, but the next part was what haunted him the most. The young boys and girls were drinking and smoking, having their own little holiday fun. Their attentions were diverted when the kid in the Santa suit appeared, stepping out from the forest and stopping a short distance from them.

They were all sitting down, smiling and smirking at him as he stood there. Lester didn't know if the boy in the Santa suit spoke; he always imagined he remained silent, like some horror movie villain, waiting for the others to react. And react they did.

Barry Barlow, the bigger of the two boys, stepped forward first. He walked up to the boy in the costume and began talking down to him. He prodded him in the chest, laughing, joking, before turning around to face his friends and to get their support. He was facing his friends when the boy in the Santa suit pulled a machete from his sack.

They realized what was about to happen, but they were too shocked to react. Barlow, still playing the clown, never stood a chance.

The first blow was quick and deadly. Lester had always been shocked by how cold and simple it seemed. It was as if he expected some backing music, an excessive amount of blood squirting from the wound, or a kung-fu twirl from the attacker. But it was just a simple hack, the blade catching Barry on the forehead and penetrating his skull.

Barry slumped to the ground like a sack of potatoes. That was the first strike, the first casualty. It wouldn't be the last.

The boy moved quickly, taking his sack with him. One of the girls fought back, but he killed her just as quickly as he killed Barry. The blade severed several arteries in her neck and, just to make sure, he delivered another blow to her arm and then to her face as she fell, her body collapsing in stages.

The killer seemed to make a beeline for Darren Henderson, the second boy. In his desperation to escape, Henderson threw the other girl in his way, using her as a human shield before sprinting into the forest.

The killer was taken by surprise and nearly dropped his weapon. The girl could have stopped him there and then. If she had possessed the same spirit as her friend, the murder spree might have ended, but she was too feeble, too scared, and too submissive. He twisted her around, pressed her up against him, and then forced the blade through her back, into her heart, before throwing her limp body on top of her friends.

For a moment, he watched Darren trying to escape, beating a hasty and almost drunken retreat as adrenaline and fear took over. He looked over his shoulder several times, and with each glance he seemed to become a little slower, a little clumsier. The killer seemed to enjoy watching him run away. Eventually, he dug around in his sack and took out a crossbow. He stood on the nearby wall, took aim, and put an arrow through Darren's calf, just as he disappeared from view.

Acting as though he had all of the time in the world, the killer carefully reloaded and put an arrow through the head of each teenager. They were already dead, but he clearly wanted to make sure. He then took his sack over to Darren, out of view of the camera.

Lester had seen the pictures of the butchered boy. He had seen the agony and the humiliation that he had suffered. Lester had grown violently sick the first time and he hadn't been able to sleep properly for weeks. He was glad the rest hadn't been caught on video and that he didn't have to watch it happen in real-time. He had been on the force for two decades, he had seen children abused and raped, and he had also seen his fair share of graphic traffic accidents and murders, but none of that had prepared him to see what had been left of Darren Henderson, some fifteen years ago now.

"Right. Turn it off. That's enough," Lester said, slowly shaking his head. The tape continued for another hour and in the final moments of that hour, they would be able to see the killer walking back across the town center on his way home. But watching those dead bodies on the floor and knowing what was happening just a dozen feet away from them was still too much for Lester.

They didn't have much to go on, but they caught a few lucky breaks. The cameras themselves had been one of those breaks, and an ironic one at that. They had been installed a couple weeks prior to the event. The city's hand had been forced following a number of thefts from shops in the area, most of which had been committed by Darren Henderson, Barry Barlow, and their friends.

"This was the first time he struck, huh?" Matt Steinberg asked. He was one of the pencil pushers in the office. He hadn't set foot on the streets for years and had spent that time in the office, filing papers, scanning documents, and digging through the archives when requested.

"No. He was at the house first."

"Ah yes, that's right. I remembering hearing about this kid," Matt said. "Brutal stuff. He killed a young 'un as well, didn't he?"

Lester ran a hand through his hair and nodded. He hadn't slept much, the case playing heavy on his mind. He had been short with his kids and popping a few too many of the pain pills his "doctor" prescribed him. His mind was on the edge and the costumed killer he had just seen was the main reason.

"Just before he headed to the town square." Lester began, reciting a story about which he knew every detail, "he went to Henderson's home. He was expecting to find Darren there, but he wasn't. They had argued, changed their plans at the last minute. That was why Darren was out getting drunk and avoiding his family on the one night of the year he should have been with them." Lester sighed. He hadn't been there, but he had been fascinated with the case and the brutality of it. He had seen everything it had produced, including crime scene photographs and evidence.

"He killed Darren's brother and his father, but he left the mother. He tied her up, sat her down, and then spoke to her. She said he was bitter, that he had a lot of issues. She said he told her things about her son and his friends, how they were vermin and how they served no purpose. He told her that he wasn't a vigilante and he wasn't doing it to be a hero, but that Darren's death would be for the best."

"*Jesus.*"

"He let her go after that. There was something about her, something that he liked. He didn't try anything, no sexual contact or anything like that, but she sensed there was something there."

"Odd."

Lester nodded. "Hardly the oddest thing he did though, was it?" Lester allowed himself a cheeky smile. "She reckons that he had a thing for her. She said she could see it in his eyes, as if he was in a trance, 'like he was there but wasn't there,' was how she put it, if I remember." He knew that was exactly what she had said because he could remember every single word on her statement.

"Didn't he kill eight?"

Lester nodded. "He returned home to slit his uncle's throat, at least as far as we could tell from what was left of him. He burned the house down after that."

Matt shook his head in a moment of disbelief and reflection. "All that from a sixteen-year-old kid, amazing."

Lester nodded, although he didn't think that *amazing* was the right word to use.

"In hindsight, I suppose it's a shame he killed himself. It would have been great to know why he did it," Matt said.

"You think he killed all those people and then committed suicide?" Lester asked.

"Happens all the time, doesn't it?" Matt sat back, released a slow breath. "Wouldn't be the first bullied kid to go on a rampage and then kill himself."

It did happen all the time, but Lester had always suspected something was different about this time. The murders were swift and brutal, but he had known what he was doing. Not only did it take a lot of power to overcome four teenagers, and a lot of guts to butcher them, but to overpower three grown adults, tying one of them up and killing the other two, that required something else. There was a method to his madness. This was backed up by the fact that Herman's childhood home had been burned to the ground on the same night. It was an arson attack that cooked the remains of Herman's uncle and conveniently destroyed any evidence in the house.

"You realize they never found the body, right?" Lester reminded him. He'd heard the theory that Herman had died in the fire, as if his remains turned to dust. He hoped Steinberg wasn't dumb enough to believe that, but he wouldn't have been surprised.

Matt shrugged. "Doesn't mean anything."

It meant everything, actually. It also meant that Steinberg didn't know what he was talking about, which, Lester suspected, was why his role in the force now consisted of shuffling papers and making cups of tea.

Matt flopped forward on his chair. He shot a curious glance at Lester, as if he could hear his thoughts. "He was a loner. What was his name, Herman something, right?"

Lester cringed when he heard the name. Steinberg sensed his discomfort and mirrored it, shifting in his seat, looking around for a distraction and then settling for an exaggerated yawn.

"So how you doing?" Steinberg continued awkwardly. "Word around the station is that this Masquerade guy is sending you stuff, mementoes and what not, is that right?"

"That's confidential."

It was also bullshit. Lester's attitude had taken a nose dive over recent months and a rumor had spread that the reason he was so snappy, the reason he was constantly in a bad mood, and the reason he always looked tired was because The Masquerade had been toying with him. Lester was just fed up, sick of his life, his surroundings, and his job. It also didn't help that he had been working on this case for years and only seemed to be getting further and further away from discovering just who the killer was.

"I understand, I'm just saying, there's a serial killer out there that's targeting you. Mocking you. I can understand what you must be thinking and feeling. It's natural to jump to conclusions."

Lester glared at the man opposite and then picked up the remote for the television. "Stick to your computers and files, Matt," he said, handing it to him. "Leave the thinking for someone else." He left without saying another word.

2

The Masquerade had been active for eight years, killing a dozen people that they knew about. He wore a mask and he talked to his victims, unleashing a torrent of cynicism, telling them they were worthless or that he was doing them a favor by taking their life. There were few connections and he seemingly killed at random. At least, that's what the reports said and that's what the press said. Lester had his own suspicions. He considered The Masquerade to be some kind of fucked-up vigilante. Batman without a conscience or morals. Many of the people he killed had been on the police radar; some of them were just out-and-out cunts, by all accounts. Of course, there were also those who had done very little wrong, people who would be considered normal, even likable to the average person. The Masquerade was not the average person and he clearly didn't suffer fools.

None of them had survived to tell anyone about his proclivity towards soliloquies, his need to make them suffer, but there had been a couple of witnesses. The first was a homeless addict and not the best witness, but his story had been enough to give the press what they needed. The second witness had been there for the fourth murder, by which time the killer was already well known by his theatrical nom de plume. This witness had been an elderly man who lived in the apartment next to the victim, and although he hadn't seen anything, he had heard most of it.

"He told her how he thought what she did was pointless," Lester remembered the elderly man saying. "How being a nurse helped nobody and only served to prolong the lives of those already destined to die." The man also recounted a conversation about the army, most likely after he had seen pictures of her husband, who was serving in Iraq at the time. He belittled that just like he had belittled everything else, and he did it so he could be the center of attention and so he could have his moment while his victim breathed her last breath.

The old man hadn't known what was going on and didn't call the police until she screamed. By the time they arrived, the killer was long gone, leaving no sign of ever being there but for a bloodied and butchered young woman and an elderly neighbor whose life would soon be cut short by a massive heart attack, precipitated by chronic night terrors and unremitting paranoia.

Lester had another theory about the killer, something to do with the Whitegate massacre fifteen years earlier, but so far that was all it was, a theory. He hadn't told anyone about it yet, but Matt was a gossip, running his mouth to make himself feel important. It was just a matter of time before he put two and two together and Lester's theory became widespread knowledge throughout the office. Once that happened, Lester's life would be even less worth living than it already was.

"Keats, get in here!" He looked up to see Atwood standing in the doorway to his office. He was displaying a mean and self-important look, like he was ready to tear someone apart. This was normal. He scared the shit out of rookies because even when he was praising them, he looked like he was about to ram a fist up their ass and use them like a sycophantic puppet to sing his own praises.

Lester had turned fifty the previous year, five decades of underachievement and misery that had seemed like the good life until a few years ago. His boss, on the other hand, was forty-five and as accomplished as they came. He had worked on the beat and received commendations left, right, and center; as a detective he had been instrumental in bringing down some of the most high-profile criminals of the last generation. Now he was one of the big shots, getting paid a small fortune to sit on his ass and order everyone around.

He had become Lester's boss when Lester was a happy-go-lucky forty-five-year-old man with everything going for him, or so he thought. In truth, he was a lackey, a pushover, the one they all took advantage of because they knew he was too feeble and too mild-mannered to stir up the nest. Not long after that, Lester had lost his wife and drifted away from those he called friends. He had his kids, a beautiful girl and a talented boy, but without their mother, they became something that he hated. And in turn, they despised him.

"How are things going with the Morrison girl?" Atwood asked.

"She's still dead," Lester said blankly.

"Is that supposed to be funny?"

"No, sir."

"This girl was butchered by a fucking psychopath you're supposed to be tracking down."

"Yes, sir. I know, sir. I'm sorry."

He was actually a sociopath, or so Lester gathered, but he knew that correcting his boss at that moment could cost him his job. He had lost interest in everything else in his life, but his job still meant something to him. Even if it wasn't very much.

"How did the evidence pan out?" Atwood asked.

"It didn't, sir," Lester said, still standing. There was only one chair in the office and now Atwood was sitting on it. He preferred it that way, as he thought it gave him the power in any argument. Allowing them to sit down would only be offering them comfort, and comfortable was the last thing he wanted any of his officers to be.

"The partial print?"

"Old boyfriend."

"Possible suspect?"

Lester shook his head. "Addict and probable dealer. He's an idiot, not a seasoned killer.

"What about the blood stain? It didn't come from the victim, so who was it?"

"The boyfriend again, sir," Lester said. "He had a nosebleed, or so he said. The truth is that Morrison probably smacked him, but either way it wasn't our killer's blood."

Morrison, by all accounts, was a feisty young girl. She was a user, but there were no signs of addiction. She lived alone, having done so for much of her young life. It was clear that she was strong and independent, experienced beyond her twenty-five years. And judging by the contents of her bedroom closet, she was also very kinky. She didn't have anything heavy in there, but she liked to dress up and she liked her men to do the same. Her boyfriend seemed to be a complete contrast to her. Scum of the earth; a snotty-nosed, self-righteous prick who thought the world owed him a favor despite never contributing to society. He was an addict, a thug. He didn't deserve her.

Lester always found himself being drawn to the victims, putting them on pedestals. He never got to see them when they were alive, only as lifeless, helpless, soulless vessels when they were dead. They were like abused animals, their eyes wide and pleading, their minds unable to communicate, unable to speak of their suffering. Everything he knew about the deceased came from the people who knew them, and no one had any bad words to say about the dead. Lester knew deep down that the women probably weren't as saintly or as innocent as he imagined them to be, but lately his irrational thoughts had been outnumbering the rational ones. He also didn't want to think for a minute that The Masquerade had a valid reason, that he was justified in killing them. As far as Lester was concerned, everyone had their vices, everyone had something that made others resent them. But no one had the right to use that as an excuse to end another's life.

"Is the boyfriend in the cells?"

"Of course. We'll let him sit and sweat for a bit."

"Good." Atwood nodded to himself, his attention sweeping lazily across his desk. He was distracted. Lester could see that, but he didn't want to address it.

"Is there anything else, sir, because I have some work to get to."

Atwood seemed annoyed by the perceived tone of impatience. "What is wrong with you lately, Keats?"

"I'm not sure I know what you mean, sir. Everything is fine with me."

"Come on, Lester, don't piss in my pocket and tell me it's raining. I'm your boss, your friend, you can tell me what's going on."

Lester stared at him for a moment, trying to understand his angle. A perpetual wickedness was still plastered across Atwood's face. He was also trying to look sympathetic, but he was failing miserably. Atwood played the part of a human being well, but he wasn't human, certainly not in the typical sense.

He wasn't a murderer and he didn't have a lust for blood, but Atwood displayed all the symptoms common in psychopathy; he just didn't know it. His work led him to believe that all psychopaths were murderers or rapists, that people like him were just driven and determined to succeed, but the only thing that separated him from them was that he had chosen a different career path. He was nothing like The Masquerade, who was a whole different breed. The Masquerade was so devious, twisted, and intelligent that Lester often found himself admiring him in a way that poisoned his morality. He had never admired his boss.

"Everything is fine, sir."

"I don't believe you. If you ask me, you're one step away from fucking up big time. I've seen men in your position before and I've seen what happens when they finally snap." He paused to let his words sink in, seeing that they had almost no effect whatsoever. "How's your home life?"

"Wife's still dead, children still hate me."

"I'm sure they don't hate you."

"Only because you haven't met them."

Atwood shook his head and looked solemn for a moment, a major feat for a man who struggled to understand the basics of human emotion. "Just watch yourself, Lester."

"Yes, sir. Can I leave now?"

Atwood waved his hand at the door and Lester wasted no time walking out of it. He returned to his desk and turned on his computer. He was immediately greeted by a barrage of open documents and pictures that he kept either on display or minimized to remind him of his job and his purpose. He pulled up an image of Herman on his computer and studied it. He was a plain looking kid and he'd led a sorrowful life.

He had lost his mother when he was young and, not long before the murders, he had also lost his father. He had no friends that anyone knew of and no social interaction other than regular run-ins with the school bullies.

Lester almost felt sorry for him. Lester himself hadn't been very popular at school either, although he had always tried his best to fit in. He hadn't been bullied quite to the extent that Herman had, nor had he ever contemplated doing what Herman did, but there were dark times in his youth when he had wished the worst on the people who made him feel bad. He had always taken things with a grain of salt, part of the experience of growing up, but he was starting to wonder if the bullying in childhood wasn't just a preparation for something much worse in adulthood.

Lester spent the day learning more about Herman, digging through the few scraps of information he hadn't already read. He read and reread the reports given by Irene Henderson—the one survivor from that night—even though he knew them word for word. He watched the CCTV footage a few more times, trying to make sense of what he saw. What struck him as odd, and had always struck him as so, was how premeditated it had been. This was a boy who had clearly practiced and prepared for what he did, a boy who had probably suffered further bullying and tormenting as he prepared. To have the patience and the restraint to hold back, to not let his anger get the better of him and to wait for the right time to strike, was a virtue not many people possessed, let alone many teenage boys.

Lester had listened to the opinions of a number of colleagues and friends throughout the years, the case having acquired an almost cult status in police departments up and down the country. The ones who believed Herman was still out there were often treated with the same disbelief and contempt as conspiracy theorists, even though the evidence was on their side.

"He probably topped himself, he seems the sort." That was how many of them saw it, because that was how many murder sprees ended. They were moments of violence, premeditated to some extent, that were precipitated by anger, mental illness, or religious extremism. School shootings often ended that way, as did other acts of explosive violence in public places, but Lester had never believed Herman to be a spree killer. Yes, he killed eight people in one night, but what happened after he disappeared? What if he had been preparing for that moment all along? What if he continued to kill and to hone his craft before transforming into The Masquerade? It was all speculation and Lester had nothing to go on, but if it was true, then Herman would be one of the most prolific serial killers in the country's history.

Another possibility was that Herman had links to The Butcher, whose activity ceased around the time of those first murders. The way he treated Darren Henderson was somewhat reminiscent of The Butcher's murders, but was Herman a copycat and a crazed fanatic, as the media had believed, or did he actually know the killer? Something told Lester the story ran deep, that it had to be more than a coincidence that The Butcher, The Masquerade, and

Herman, one of the most notorious spree killers in recent history, all resided within a hundred miles of each other.

Lester had a headache just thinking about it, but what pained him even more was that there was very little he could do. He didn't want to tell his boss his theory for fear of being laughed at. "Good detectives don't work on gut feeling," Atwood had once told Lester and the others. "Gut feeling gets you fuck all in a court of law. Stick to the facts and if there are none there, then find them. That's your job."

Lester knew as well as anyone that he wasn't special. He didn't have any talents that half the world didn't possess; he didn't even have the ingenuity, the knowledge, or the gut instinct that half of the police officers in his division had. If there was a link and it could be found, Lester knew that the chances of him finding it were very slim. That didn't sway him, though, because while the destination was unlikely, he knew the journey itself was what his life needed right now.

———

Lester's mobile phone rang in his pocket and he jumped at the muffled sound. It was late, well into the night shift, and although the office wasn't empty, it was dead. The men and women on duty were slumped over their desks, tediously tapping away at computers, mumbling sedately into mobile phones.

"Where are you!?" a familiar voice bellowed at him as he pressed the phone to his ear.

"I'm in the—" he paused and opted for a lie. "I'm in bed."

"Bollocks!" his daughter spat. "I'm at your fucking front door!"

Lester sighed and moved the phone away from his ear as his daughter assaulted him with a barrage of obscenities. A few people in the office looked up at him, able to hear her screams on the other side of the phone. They tuned out when they realized that whatever it was, it wasn't interesting enough to keep them from pretending they had to work.

"—back here and open the door, now!"

He hung up without saying anything, knowing she wouldn't listen even if he had. She was an eighteen-year-old with a mind of her own and a mouth straight out of an eighties dockyard. He blamed her mother, a selfish cow who had gotten herself run over by a drugged-up driver. Lester had been on his own since then, and considering he hadn't been a very good father when she was alive, he didn't have much hope when she died. He had always cared for his kids, he bought them presents and he gave them love when he felt like it, but he was usually working too much to ever feel like it. They had always gotten their love from their mother, and even though he tried to be more like her when she passed on, they hadn't been interested.

His kids blamed him for her death, for the same reasons he blamed his wife. The person who was really to blame, a middle-aged man who saw speedballs as a way to get him through the tedium of a twenty-hour shift, had also died in the crash. The fact that there was no one to get angry at, no one to direct those feelings of loss and rage at, made things worse. If her killer were in prison, Lester would feel better, as he could at least visit him and let the kids write to him. If he were a free man, then they could vent their anger at the courts for being so inept and forgiving. But he was dead, and the dead didn't give a shit about your anger.

"Who's this?"

Lester arrived home to see his daughter, Annabelle, leaning against a motorcycle. The rusted machine was straddled by a pimple-faced kid with a mustache made entirely of wispy-ass hair.

"This is Sparky."

"Of course it is."

Annabelle rolled her eyes. "Are you going to open up and let us in?"

"Where's your brother?" Lester wanted to know.

"He's out."

"Where?"

She shrugged nonchalantly and turned away, indicating that she did know.

He took a lot of shit from his daughter, but there were a few things he couldn't stand for and this was one of them. She was the older child. He had tasked her with looking after her younger brother, Damian, but she was often too busy getting high to pay attention to him. She had gone off the rails when she was fourteen, the same age as Damian was now, and although he hadn't exactly stood by and let her, all of his attempts to stop her had failed. There was little hope left to save their relationship, and he didn't know if there was any hope left to save *her*, but what he did know was that he didn't want Damian to go down the same road.

"Tell me where he is or you're not getting in."

She released a long and exaggerated sigh. "Fine!" she snapped. "He's at Richard Mass's house. Are you happy now!?"

"Mass? The drug dealer?"

Annabelle waved her hand dismissively. "He ain't a drug dealer, stop being so dramatic. It's just pot."

"Ain't nothing wrong with pot, Mr. Keats," Sparky chimed in.

Lester looked at him like an unexplained smudge of blood in his stool before turning back to his daughter. She was pretty and smart. She could do better. But she either didn't know that or she simply wanted to date the lowest of the low, a man for whom evolution had been one step too far, to get at him. "It's—" he checked his watch. "One in the morning and you've left your brother with a known criminal?"

Annabelle just stared at him. "Are you going to let me in or not?"

"What about Fonzi here?" Lester nodded to Sparky.

"It's Sparky, Mr.—"

"I know what your fucking name is!" Lester spat.

102

"Dad!"

"Annabelle! Get in the house." He tossed her the keys and then turned to Sparky. He knew the neighbors would be watching; this was usually a quiet cul-de-sac and he would be waking a lot of them up, but they were used to it. His kids were always causing trouble and making noise. The only difference was that this time Lester was getting in on the act.

"You shouldn't shout at your daughter like that," Sparky butted in after Annabelle disappeared into the house. He had lost his confidence, his edge, but was trying his best to maintain an air of ego.

Lester stood over him, pushing his face close. "Do you know what I do for a living?" he asked.

"Of course I know," Sparky said, sensing what was coming but refusing to back down.

"Do you know what I can do to *you*?"

"You can't arrest me if I don't do anything wrong, *pig*."

Lester threw his hand around Sparky's throat. The reaction took the teenager by surprise and a yelp escaped his lips as Lester's grip tightened. He felt the youngster try and fail to swallow, saw his eyes bulge in terror as he feared for his life.

"I never said anything about arresting you," Lester said, pressing his forehead against the youngster's. "*Prick*."

"Get off me. This is police brutality."

Lester squeezed harder. "Actually, I'm off duty. This is nothing more than a pissed-off dad trying to stop some perverted little tit from fucking his daughter."

Sparky mumbled something, but his words struggled to leave his mouth, blocked by Lester's tightening grip. His face turned red, more through fear and disbelief than anything else. His air supply hadn't been cut off long enough to cause such a transformation.

"Now you listen to me," Lester ordered. "As soon as I let you go, you're going to drive this bike of yours away from my house and my daughter, and you're never going to come back, do you understand?"

Sparky did his best to nod, but Lester wasn't convinced.

"You may be younger and stronger than me, but I know what I'm doing. I have friends in high places and my job allows for a number of *perks*. I can do things to you that you didn't even think possible, and afterward, regardless of how much blood I spill, how much damage I do, I can walk away as a free man." Lester paused to let that sink in. It was nonsense, of course; he didn't have *any* friends and he certainly had none in high places. His job didn't allow for any leniency either. If anything, he would suffer more, with the press and the public keen to make an example out of every cop that stepped out of line.

"Do you understand?" he said once Sparky's face had turned a deeper shade of red, his minuscule brain deprived of the oxygen that it needed to shit, wank, and daydream about underage girls.

Sparky nodded and Lester let him go. There was a moment of utter relief in his young eyes, followed by an explosion of anger. Spit frothed on his lips when he was finally able to breathe again and his face turned to a brighter shade of scarlet. "You're out of your fucking mind," he said as he revved up his bike and Lester stepped back.

"Exactly. And don't you forget it."

He watched the nuisance teen depart. He had never threatened any of his daughter's boyfriends, and since the death of their mother and her rise into adolescence, there had been many. Since she was fourteen, she had been dating older boys, but any attempts he made to stop her, mostly by talking to her, only seemed to make things worse.

Annabelle had seen everything from the house. He knew she would have been watching and the only thing that surprised him was that she hadn't rushed out to face him. It was further proof, if he needed it, that this was all a game to her. She didn't care about any of her boyfriends and only cared about tormenting her father.

She was a sick little child plucking the legs off a spider one by one, before tossing it back into the wild.

"I hate you, you know that?" Annabelle stood in front of him, an expression of utter contempt on a face that Lester had once looked upon with pride. He tried not letting her see that her comment hurt him, but he was having a hard time hiding it. "How can you do that to me?" she begged to know. "I loved him."

That was just another part of her act, her manipulation. He decided to go along with it.

"You're a child," Lester said. "You don't know what love is."

"How dare you say that to me!" She looked like she was ready to slap him, and he would have welcomed that, but she didn't. Instead she stormed up the stairs, her heavy heels slamming into every stair as she went. He knew she wasn't finished, though, and when she reached the top, she glared down at him. "Our love was more than you could ever understand. You're just a bitter old man. Bitter because no one ever loved you!"

She stormed into her room, slamming the door behind her. Lester stayed where he was, staring up the stairs. That comment didn't hurt him; he had heard a lot worse from her. What did hurt him was that he felt like he had completely lost her, and that his son was going the same way. Without either of them to rely on and live for, he only had himself. And what was he these days? A failed policeman? A failed husband? A failed friend? A failed father?

"You know what," he said to no one in particular. "Fuck you."

There was only so much bullying, only so much torture, and only so much hatred that one man could take. He was going to do his best to save his son, and if he had already failed, then he was going to take revenge. He knew where Mass lived. He had been there before, fulfilling his duties as a police officer. Now he would go to fulfill his duties as a father.

He grabbed his coat and opened the door, just as a bombardment of loud music exploded out of his daughter's room and flooded down the stairs. He paused for a moment to listen to it, slowly shaking his head to himself. Her taste in music was even worse than her taste in men, which was saying something.

He took a pen and a piece of paper, scribbled out a note that said, "Gone to do the right thing. If you need me, tough—piss off somebody else for a change," and stuck it to the door on his way out. She would see it and it would annoy her. She hated it when he talked back, when he had the balls to say *anything* to her. The fact that he wouldn't be there for her to vent that annoyance and that hatred would send her around the bend.

3

—

Richard Mass was a thirty-year-old waste of space who had been a blight on the town since his early teens. Nearly two decades ago, when Mass was a preteen and Lester had only been on the job for a few months, they had run into each other at Mass's school. He had lashed out at another kid, breaking his glasses and giving him a lifelong scar above his cheek that would remain as a testament to Mass's anger. Lester remembered sitting in the headmaster's office with Mass's parents and listening to how their child was quiet, how he was the victim. They said that he was a tortured soul, an intelligent boy who wasn't emotionally or mentally challenged enough at school, so he got into trouble to stimulate his brain. The teachers, the parents, and even Lester had all believed it, but while such stories and such children did exist, Mass was just a fucking idiot. He couldn't read, couldn't write, couldn't multiply, and probably couldn't tie his own shoelaces. This was no tortured soul. This was a disturbed little nuisance who could only put two and two together when selling drugs, whose only knowledge of biology came from fondling teenage girls and masturbating to lingerie catalogues, and whose only understanding of the solar system was that the sun revolved around the earth, Pluto was Mickey's dog, and Venus had something to do with female hygiene products.

Mass had lived with his parents for much of his adult life, and throughout it all, they still believed he was a tortured genius. Some of the evidence they cited to maintain their denial was that their son often just sat doing nothing. To them, that proved that he was contemplating the universe and the human psyche. To everyone else, it was obvious Richard was just incredibly high and incredibly vacant.

He had moved out of his parents' house a couple years ago and now lived in an apartment on the edge of town, paid for by the government and frequented by the police. Atwood once joked that they should place police headquarters there to save on fuel costs.

The apartment building was stuck in the middle of a small strip of unwanted wasteland, once a thriving piece of real estate with the potential to be a park, a family home, or even a business, now a desolate swamp of potato-chip bags, beer cans, broken glass, and used needles. After a few drug dealers moved in and their friends followed, the entire block became a haven for depraved hedonism.

When Lester arrived, he noted an old three-seater parked just outside the building. Its doors and windows were open and a subwoofer blasted out something barely recognizable as music. Several youths gathered around the car, drinking and smoking. A number of adults were with them, wearing the same clothes and the same glum, disinterested expressions. Lester scanned their faces as he approached and they stared back at him. He couldn't see Mass or his son among them.

He parked away from the small gathering, locked his car, and then advanced toward the building. His car was just as shitty as theirs and all the others scattered around the block. That wouldn't set him apart, but his clothes and his mannerisms would. They all wore designer sports gear, Adidas tracksuits, Nike trainers. But none were clean, all were stolen, and Lester knew the closest these delinquents got to sports was when they were being chased by people like him. He'd seen them and people like them day in and day out for years, and while he began his career thinking that everyone had something good inside them, that everyone had hope and everyone deserved a chance, he now understood they were all worthless, hopeless, and rotten to the core.

As he moved closer to them, Lester knew trying to hide, to fit in, would be pointless. He had been in the police long enough to pick up a few habits those on the wrong side of the law would spot. He had also dealt with many of them before.

"You're in the wrong part of town, pig!"

Matty Ferguson, a kid playing tough at the front of the pack, hadn't always been as bad as the others, but he hadn't had a chance in life, and eventually he became just as hopeless, just as worthless, and just as despicable. He was from a family of no-hopers, a family where violence was as common, as natural, and as frequent as a morning bowel movement. He spent his childhood on the right side of the law, steering clear of a family that had more psychological issues than Charles Manson. The blood that had been passed to him from an insane mother, and to her from an insane grandmother, finally infected his mind when he was fourteen. A friend he had known for as little as three weeks forgot his birthday, and in response Matty forced his way into the friend's home, took him by surprise, and proceeded to assault him, barking incessantly like a rabid dog as he did so: "How dare you forget my birthday!"

Lester stared back at the sixteen-year-old cretin and wondered what it took for a mind to turn so bad so quickly. He'd always been a firm believer in nurture over nature, evident in his own children, who had rebelled when the warmth and love had been sucked out of their lives.

"Fuck off back to your sty!"

Matty's brother spoke up. He was older and had always been insane. Just like his mother, his grandmother. Just like his brother. Lester felt an unshakable pity, looking at the Ferguson pair. Maybe nurture had played a part. They had grown up without a father, after all. Lester himself had witnessed how an absent father, whether physically or emotionally, could turn good kids bad. And these kids barely qualified as good to begin with.

Lester lowered his head, tried to shake their shouts and his thoughts away. They continued though. Some of the shouts didn't make it above the rattle of the music, but Lester ignored them all regardless. He turned to face them as he opened the door to the apartment building and he saw they were all still staring at him. A couple even spat at their own feet, indicating their disgust either at him or at their own knock-off trainers.

Lester had seen it all before, but it resonated more now than it ever had. The pity he had felt for the Ferguson brothers had blossomed into anger. He was angry at himself, knowing that his son could turn out to be just as worthless, just as insane, and that it would be his fault if he did. He was also angry at them; he didn't deserve that sort of hate. He had arrested them before, but had been nothing but professional and, in Matty's case, he had even been sympathetic. But despite that, they didn't think twice about treating him like shit. They were just as bad as his daughter. The only difference was that he couldn't and wouldn't hit or hurt her. He couldn't and wouldn't show her just how much he hated what she said to him and just how much her actions hurt him. But there was nothing stopping him from expressing that anger toward the gang of delinquents.

He made a beeline for the oldest and biggest member of the gang. He looked a few years younger than Lester, built like a brick shithouse with tattooed arms exposed through a sleeveless vest. Lester had seen him around but had never arrested him. The older ones had the experience and the sense; they knew that if they needed anything doing—robberies, drug deals, someone to sit on their stash—there was always a line of kids waiting to do it for them. Kids like Matty Ferguson and his half-witted brother would take the risks and the flak so they didn't have to.

The big man puffed out his chest and took a step forward as Lester approached. It was all bravado, keeping up appearances.

Lester knew the big man wouldn't hit him and would be careful with every single word he said, but the same didn't apply to Lester. The big man was about to mock him, taunt him, but as soon as he approached, Lester swung. He felt one of his knuckles pop as he caught the big man square on the jaw. Even above the sound of the music—the bass pounding through the earth, through his feet, and through his soul like a second heartbeat—he could hear a crack as he broke the man's jaw.

The man stumbled backward, slipped. The back of his head rattled off the side of the car and he slipped into unconsciousness, his body slumped up against the vehicle. Lester paused, a little shocked at his own power, at what all of that anger, hatred, and venom had morphed into. He had been fit and strong in his younger days, but he didn't know he still had it in him. He turned to the others, who had already retreated several steps. They looked both angry and terrified, but their fear was the dominant emotion. They exchanged glances, wondering whether they should all attack, but no one was willing to make the first move. That was the problem with delinquent gangs. Take away their machismo and test them, and they lost their allegiances in a second. They talked a big game and stood proudly by their idiots-in-arms, but test them and they backed down like the cowards they were.

Lester grinned at them all, feeling a hell of a lot better about himself. He didn't say a word to them, but he didn't need to. He had told them everything they needed to know, and he had given himself all the satisfaction he needed with that one punch.

He turned his back on them and headed for the building, confident none of them would jump him. Once inside, he looked out through the glass to see several of the kids had retreated further, their glum and cocky faces filed with fear and uncertainty. Some of the others had gathered around their fallen friend, unsure if they really wanted to be there when he woke up and didn't find a dead cop next to him.

Lester focused on Matty Ferguson and found himself thinking about his son again. The anger had dispersed, but he was still determined not to let the child that he had hugged, loved, and kissed so many times fall into the traps laid by a broken home, a damaged psychology, and a ruthless peer group.

He studied the displaced knuckle on his right hand. It hurt like hell and would hurt even more when the adrenaline faded, but it had been worth it. A noise from above interrupted him and he looked up as a drunken teenage girl stumbled her way down the stairs. She was wearing high-heels and with every step, he waited for her to break an ankle. She looked like she had been dragged through a hedge—her hair was a mess, her makeup had run, and her clothes were twisted. She wore a skirt so short that Lester could see her knickers and, when she finally made it to the bottom of the stairs, she caught him looking.

"Are you staring at my pussy?" she asked.

"How old are you?" he asked.

She lowered her eyebrows and nearly lost her balance as she tried to stand up straight. "What's it to you?" she said, cockily slurring her words. "You're not a cop and you're not my father."

Lester clearly was a cop and the fact that she wasn't experienced enough to realize that indicated she was as young as she looked. That made her no older than fourteen, the same age as Damian, the same age Matty had been when his corrupt genes caused him to flip.

"Go home," he told her bluntly.

"You can't tell me what to do."

He sighed. "Just go home, kid. You're fooling no one."

He ascended the stairs she had stumbled down, stopping on the second floor, outside Mass's flat. The front door was wide open, looking straight into the hallway and one of the bedrooms. The door to the bedroom was missing completely, with a few remnants of broken wood lying on the floor and stuck on the hinge.

From where he stood, Lester could see a young boy and a young girl in their late teens, getting heated on a bare mattress inside the bedroom. The boy, who had long and messy hair that probably hadn't been washed in months, had his shirt off and was trying to remove the girl's top as she batted him away, seemingly aware of just how exposed they were.

A middle-aged man walked out of the living room next to them. He stopped and stared when he saw Lester standing there, a cigarette hanging loosely from his mouth, a smile stuck stupidly on his face. The blank stare remained for a few moments until he turned toward the bedroom, standing in the doorway and egging on the two lovers while grabbing his crotch and asking them to make room for him.

Lester felt sick to his stomach to know that not only was this the environment his son was currently exposed to, but it was one his daughter had been living in for the last couple of years. These were her people, her friends, her boyfriends. The thought that she could be just like the girl in the bedroom, batting away the advances of a horny teen as he prepared to fuck here in front of a block of imbeciles, made him sick to his stomach.

Receiving another blank stare from the drunken pervert, Lester entered the flat and prepared to barge into the living room. He waited to see if the man would react, if he would stop him or alarm his friends, but he seemed more interested in the unveiling pornography ahead of him than in anything Lester had planned.

Mass was seated in the middle of a tatty couch, his glazed eyes staring at the television, which played an old repeat of *The Simpsons*. The room was thick with smoke and people, at least half a dozen, many of whom sat on the floor. They weren't talking to each other but the occasional mumble and laugh indicated they knew of each other's presence. Lester stood in front of Mass and blocked his view of the television, his hands on his hips.

"Where's Damian?" he demanded.

It seemed to take Mass a few seconds before he realized someone had interrupted his time with his animated and less-than-animated friends.

"Who the fuck are you?"

"Where's Damian?" Lester repeated.

"*Who. The. Fuck. Are. You*?" Mass repeated.

Lester grabbed Mass by the collar and lifted him off the chair. He was thin and light. He felt like a mannequin in clothes as Lester dragged him across the room, kicked the television off its stand, and then pinned him against the wall behind it, making sure that everyone was now paying attention to him.

"I'll ask you again," Lester said slowly. "And if you don't answer me this time, then I'm going to hurt you. *Where. Is. Damian*?"

Mass sobered up a little, but his body was still limp and he seemed incapable of resisting, or even twitching. "Hey, aren't you that copper? I think I've seen you before."

With his hands busy, Lester used his knee to drive some sense into the drug dealer, delivering a precise shot to his groin. He felt genitals crush into bone as Mass's balls flattened against his own pelvis. Mass squealed and began to froth at the mouth. There was movement in his arms and his legs now, his body zapped into life by a jolt of electricity.

"This is police brutality!" he snapped.

Lester dropped him and watched as he struggled to retain his footing. He backed away and Mass turned to his friends, stuck motionless in their original positions. "You see," he said, "they ain't got the balls, these pigs, they're all the same."

At first Mass didn't see the chair coming, swinging at him like a bulky baseball bat, and by the time he did, it was already too late. He crumpled into a heap on the floor, writhing in agony and struggling to retain consciousness.

Lester grinned, wiped some spittle from his mouth, and then looked around, his eyes on fire as he met with the horrified stares of drug addicts and users, some of them Damian's age. "Where is my son?" he asked.

At once they all responded. Most of them pointed toward the door, but one of them shouted, "*Bedroom!*"

Lester checked the first bedroom. The kissing had stopped and the boy was now completely naked but for a pair of stained boxer shorts. She was trying to get away but he wasn't letting her.

Lester shook his head and moved onto the second bedroom. This bedroom had a door, but it wasn't locked. It was smoky and it stank of booze, must, and sweat. Damian was in there with a girl, sitting on the edge of the bed with a bong in his hand as she watched eagerly. He looked up when his dad entered—he was about to take a hit, his lips open and the bong poised.

Lester ripped the contraption from his son's hands and tossed it to the other side of the room.

"What you doing?" Damian screamed. "I paid for that."

Lester didn't answer, and when his son yelled and kicked with the energy that had eluded Richard Mass, Lester overpowered him and dragged him to the floor.

"You're embarrassing me!" he spat. "Get your fucking hands off me." Damian managed to release his arm and he swung for his father, catching him on the leg. Lester ignored him and dragged him a couple of feet as he continued to hurl abuse and kick out.

After the third or fourth kick, Lester let go and stood over him. Damian was silent and still in anticipation as Lester, frothing with anger, eyes burning with an intensity that Damian had never seen in him before, towered over him.

Lester stood on his son's arm and this time Damian didn't flinch. "You move an inch and I will break your fucking arm," Lester warned. "Do you understand?"

Damian nodded.

"I'll be right back, but if you run away from me, then you better make sure that I don't catch you. Do you understand me?"

Damian nodded again.

"You can't treat him like that!" The girl who had been on the bed with Damian was now standing in the doorway, defending her fling.

"It's okay, Shelly," Damian said, his attention still on his father.

"Get off of him before I call the police," she continued. "Or his father, he's a policeman. So you better watch out."

"This *is* my father," Damian said, swallowing thickly. "Please, just go back in the room. I'll be okay."

She gave Lester another fearful look and then disappeared.

Lester ducked into the other bedroom to see that the boy's stained boxer shorts had been removed and he was several minutes away from raping the girl. She wasn't going to scream, kick, or run, even though she had the chance, but she clearly didn't want to be with him and she looked disgusted as he approached her and tried, with increasing agitation, to get what he wanted.

The boy had his back to Lester as he entered the room, but Lester saw the fear and the disgust in the girl's eyes. She was his daughter's age and he saw some of Annabelle in her, which angered him even more. He thought of Sparky doing the same to her, forcing her, trying to get his own way. He saw red.

Lester grabbed the boy by the hair and yanked him off the bed. He heard the hair rip and the boy scream as he was pulled off the bed. He fought with him, his arms and legs kicking and swinging, but Lester silenced him by throwing him headfirst into the wall. The thud was loud and dull, strong enough to remove a chunk of plaster, which rained snowy debris onto the filthy carpet and onto the naked body of the boy beneath it. He groaned in agony and squinted away the pain as a large cut opened in the middle of his forehead and made a mess of his already messy face.

"*What have you done?*" the girl screamed.

"Excuse me?" Lester said, baffled. He took a step back as she raced around the bed to attend to the young man who had tried to sexually assault her.

"He tried to rape you," Lester reminded her.

"So?" she spat, her disgust now directed at Lester. "I can deal with my own problems. What gives you the right to come in here and beat up my boyfriend?"

"Your *boyfriend*?"

"Do you have a problem with that?"

"He tried to fucking assault you."

"*So?*"

"Are you fucking kidding me?"

"Ah, baby, I'm so sorry." She bent over her fallen beau and used his discarded boxer shorts to wipe away the blood.

Lester shook his head in disbelief, realizing that out of pity alone, he had probably helped the dirty little pervert get what he wanted from his psychotic girlfriend. He left them to it and returned to his son, who was still lying in the hallway.

"Now, are you going to play nice and come with me?" Lester asked. "Or do I have to drag you all the way home?"

Damian held up his hands and slowly rose to his feet. "You win, Dad," he said. "I'm all yours."

4

—

Are you fucking kidding me?" Atwood slammed his fist on the desk loud enough for everyone in the office to hear, heavy enough to topple a small glass of water. "What the fuck is wrong with you?" he barked.

Standing in front of his boss with a vacant expression, Lester merely shook his head. He was wondering the same thing. Maybe his kids, his job, and his life had finally gotten to him, maybe it was The Masquerade, maybe he had just ceased to give a fuck.

Atwood brushed the empty glass to the floor before wiping his hand on the seat of his pants and dropping a sheet of paper on the spillage. He stared at the paper as the water slowly seeped into it, turning it translucent. Lester watched his boss's face the whole time and noted, oddly, that he seemed to calm down. Eventually Atwood flopped back on his chair.

It was early morning and the room outside his office was buzzing with activity; tired, hung-over, and eager detectives sat at their desks or hot-footed it around the office, all pretending not to be staring, not to be trying their best to eavesdrop. Many of them couldn't believe what was happening. They had seen their boss angry before, but not at Lester. He was an exemplary worker, the one who did everything by the book and never stepped out of line.

"Who do you think you are?" Atwood asked. There was malice in his question, but he spoke calmly, almost through gritted teeth.

"Excuse me, sir?"

"You heard me," Atwood said. "And don't call me *sir*. I know you don't give a shit about me, about what I think and about the orders I give you. If you did, you wouldn't have taken the piss out of me last night."

Lester nodded politely and kept his attention fixed on the floor, where it had been for most of the morning. His boss had had an early start, and for most of that time, he had been trying to reach Lester, getting angrier and angrier. When Lester finally did show, ambling into work an hour late, Atwood was at his boiling point and had practically dragged Lester into his office.

Last night, when Lester was being shouted at and then ignored by his children, when his daughter was calling him worse than shit and his son was worrying he would die of embarrassment—if his friends didn't get to him first—the police were called to Richard Mass's house. When Annabelle and Damian were conspiring in Annabelle's room, concocting a plan to run away from home, and while Lester was downstairs drowning his sorrows with a large bottle of blended scotch, Mass was telling the police everything that had happened, along with several things that hadn't. When Annabelle and Damian were making plans to move out of town and stay with their grandmother, and when Lester was unconscious on the sofa, drooling like a sick dog, Atwood was waking to news that one of his detectives had gone rogue.

"You're lucky," Atwood told Lester, who didn't feel very lucky at all. "Mass is an addict, a waste of space, and a liar. He is also the biggest idiot we've ever come across, and that's what's saved you from being locked up instead of him."

Atwood couldn't have been more correct in his assumption of Mass, but it was one that Lester had also made. In his anger and his disbelief, Mass had immediately phoned the police, telling them it was an emergency. He had hoped they would catch Lester before he left, giving him the satisfaction of watching the police arrest one of their own, but his haste had been his downfall. He didn't have enough time to hide his drugs, nor did he have enough time to inform his friends he had invited the enemy to his door.

It began as a simple investigation, but it resulted in a raid involving several police vehicles and a forensics unit. They arrested Mass and a number of his friends, with many of them facing serious charges of possession and possession with intent to supply. Mass had also attempted to grow his own supply of cannabis, and while the product of that attempt was pathetic at best, it was still enough to add another tick to his rap sheet.

"What he says still has to be recorded," Atwood warned. "I can disregard most of it, and I don't think too many people will ask questions about that, but you're still in deep shit."

"I understand."

"Do you though?" Atwood wondered. "I mean, why? Why did you do this? This job has been like a second home to you for over twenty years, this is your life now, why would you risk that?"

"Maybe that *is* why," Lester said. "Maybe I'm tired. Maybe I'm sick of this."

"Maybe?"

Lester shrugged. "Maybe it's just because my kids hate me, my wife is dead, and I missed *Eastenders* last night. Maybe I don't really know why."

Atwood nodded slowly and then picked up a pen from his desk. He tapped it idly against his chin and then against his desk, watching it absently. "What do you want me to do?" he asked eventually, the pen now immobile.

"What do you mean?"

"With your job, Keats, with your fucking job."

Lester smiled. "You could give me a raise."

Atwood managed a half smile, his face twisted. It looked like he'd had a stroke during the point of orgasm. The expression was enough to wipe the smile from Lester's face.

"I can't keep you here," Atwood said. "I think you need a break."

"You're suspending me?"

Atwood nodded and for the first time that morning, Lester felt a stab of panic. Not because he was losing his job, or because he would be going back to an empty house filled with nothing but pictures of times gone and all but forgotten, but because he was finally getting close to The Masquerade and he didn't want to throw that away.

"Please, don't."

Atwood looked confused. "Pardon?"

"I know I fucked up, but I need this job."

"You're a strange one, Keats. First the blasé attitude, the 'I don't give a fuck' expression that you've worn for weeks, and now this? What gives?"

Lester sighed. He hadn't wanted to tell anyone about his theory until he had something more substantial than a feeling, but he sensed his chance would slip away if he didn't open his mouth.

"It's about The Masquerade, sir," he began, bringing a half-smile to Atwood's face as he grew more animated. "I have a theory that I want to test."

"Go on."

Lester sat on the end of Atwood's desk, turning his half-smile into a brief look of revulsion, but Atwood was too intrigued to stop him.

"Do you remember the spree killer a few years ago, the kid who dressed up as Santa and—"

"Murdered a bunch of kids, set his house on fire. Of course I remember," Atwood said slowly.

"Exactly," Lester said. "There was no trace of him after that. Some assumed he died in the fire or killed himself some other way, but there was never any proof. They had him pinned as a loner, a spree killer getting revenge on the kids that had bullied him, so it made sense."

"Okay." Atwood shrugged. "What's this got to do with The Masquerade?"

"Very little, truth be told." Lester hopped off the desk and paced up and down in front of his boss, firing an accusing stare out of the office window as he did so, making sure that none of his nosy colleagues were listening in. "But I remembered something that the mother of three of the victims said. She said that when he killed her son and her husband, he sat down next to her and talked to her."

"Where are you going with this?"

"She said he was bitter, cynical, that he hated the world and wanted the world to know it. She said he was also very intelligent for his age, but that she had never seen or heard anyone so twisted in her life."

Atwood nodded. "And you think that this guy is The Masquerade, right? Because he talks to his victims?"

"Exactly." Lester had stopped walking and was standing in front of his boss's desk, taller and prouder than he had stood for a long time.

Atwood wasn't convinced, but he didn't fail to notice the detective's manner or the look on his face. "You know that this doesn't mean shit, right? These are killers, psychopaths—"

"—Sociopaths."

"Whatever. They want to control their victims, they want that power, that dominance. They're like Bond villains, only they actually go through with the murder."

Lester nodded. "I understand that."

"And these killings happened, what, one hundred miles apart?"

"Yes, but we don't get that many sociopathic serial killers. It's not farfetched to assume that Herman left town, got as far away as he could, laid low for a bit, and then resumed his work."

Atwood paused for a moment and then asked, "And what if it *is* him? What does that mean, we still don't know where he is. If Herman's file is still open then we're still looking for him anyway, what difference does it make?

"If we expose him then we strip away his mask, we take away the thing that has defined him. Then—" Lester shrugged. "I guess we just wait for him to make the next move and hope he fucks up."

"He hasn't put a foot wrong yet, what makes you think exposing his identity will make him do so?"

"Just a feeling, sir."

Atwood nodded and then laughed a little. "This is fucking crazy," he said. "But I'm with you on this. If you're prepared to do the legwork, then you can investigate this. I'll give you time off, let the men above me think I'm punishing you, and in that time I want you to investigate this Herman kid, see what you can dig up. How does that sound?"

Lester grinned from ear to ear. "Perfect."

5

Whitegate was a metaphorical hole in the ground, and one that few residents ever escaped. It was a rural town, far from the hustle and bustle of the major cities, and a short drive to a bigger town where the shopping centers, cinemas, and other amenities of modernity made day-to-day life a little less shitty. Lester had never been to the town before, but he knew he hated it before he stepped foot in it. His mother actually lived not too far away from here, in a nearby town. That wasn't where she had always lived and, thankfully, it wasn't where Lester had been forced to grow up. But the place she now called home was a stone's throw from this madness, this depravity. He had never understood why she moved, and he had never really cared either. She probably did it just to piss him off. He wouldn't have been surprised.

After the incident at Mass's house, Damian and Annabelle had run away to spend some time with their grandmother. They had threatened all night and, while he didn't think they would follow through with their threats—because they rarely followed through with anything that required effort—they did just that. Their grandmother's house was far from a haven, but it was a long way from their friends, a long way from the drug dealers, the boyfriends and the bad influences, so Lester was happy. They'd actually done him a favor.

There were towns like this all over the country, towns that had once flourished, but were now home to the unemployed, the unambitious, and the uneducated. If Britain truly was broken, these were the towns on the fault lines.

This was where delinquency was applauded, ambition was questioned, and intelligence was viewed with suspicion. As Lester sat in his car outside the main shopping street—a collection of boarded-up and poorly maintained shops, vomited onto the landscape by an unenthusiastic deity—he watched the people traipse up and down and tried to imagine what Herman had thought when he witnessed these same sights.

A group of kids, no older than thirteen, were waiting outside a newsstand to harass anyone who entered into buying them booze. On the other side of the road, a heavyset man leaned against a lamppost with a dog on a tight lead. Whenever the dog moved, he yanked the lead, obviously enjoying the squeal that followed before berating the dog for making a sound. Several feet ahead of him, two women stood in the middle of the road chatting, oblivious to the old man in the car who had to slam on his brakes so as not to run them over. Both of the women were smoking despite the fact that one of them was heavily pregnant, the bulge clearly visible due to her insistence on wearing a tank top several sizes too small.

"Excuse me, mate, you got a light?"

Lester turned to see a kid looking up at him.

"You've got to be fucking kidding me," he said under his breath, half expecting the young one to hold up a bowl and ask for more food.

"What?"

"Should you be smoking at your age?" Lester asked.

"I'm fifteen," the kid—no older than ten—lied, somehow thinking that made everything okay.

"In that case, you should stop smoking, it's stunting your growth."

The kid glared at him before Lester walked off with a smile on his face. He had seen it all before. There were kids like that everywhere, but in towns like Whitegate they weren't the exception. Kids needed to look up to their parents, but when their parents were hanging around street corners getting drunk, committing petty crimes and generally being a drain on society, there was no hope for them.

Lester didn't care. He wasn't there for them and he certainly wasn't there to feel pity for Herman or to understand what he had done. He was there for Irene, for her children, for her husband, and for the others who had perished. He was there to learn everything he could about Herman.

Irene Henderson was a difficult woman to track down. She had lost everything important to her. Her husband and her youngest child had been brutally murdered in front of her; her eldest child had been butchered like an animal near the dead bodies of his friends. He knew she wasn't a particularly smart or ambitious woman and had been content with what little she had—her biennial holidays in Spain, her nights out with the girls. Her family was her life, so when that was taken away, she didn't have much left to live for.

To Lester, Irene was a vital piece of the puzzle. She was one of the few to have seen Herman's darker side and survived, one of the few who had seen him at his worst and didn't view him as some pathetic, weak loner. He had tried his best to find her in the police records, but there was no information about her whereabouts. There was, however, an intriguing mugshot, taken just a year before the murder. She had been arrested for being drunk and disorderly, stripping off in a public place. The report said she flirted with a female officer and then tried to hump a male officer's leg. She spent the night in jail and was given a slap on the wrists and a mugshot that portrayed a happy, red-cheeked mother with a lifetime of regrets ahead of her.

The next mentions of her were from the night she lost everything. She had given a number of statements to the police that Lester had already read, but she was grief-stricken and in a state of shock at the time. As far as the police were concerned, she had said enough. She had confirmed their suspicions that the murderer was Herman and that was all they had needed to know, but the information Lester sought went much deeper than that. He wanted to get into the killer's psyche, and he also wanted Irene to confirm a suspicion that he had, a suspicion that linked the Herman to The Masquerade.

After some online searches, and a check on her car and house records, he discovered Irene had stayed in that house for just three months before she sold it and disappeared. She hadn't claimed benefits, and she hadn't bought a new house or a new car. She just disappeared.

He visited her old house but a new family had already moved in. He watched from a distance as two young children, probably brother and sister, played in the small front garden while an overprotective mother watched from the front window. The kids were barely older than ten or eleven and as Lester watched them, he forced himself to remember that despite their youth, despite their size, and despite the fact that they were still wrapped up in a world of make-believe, so far removed from reality and its horrors, these kids were probably older than the youngest child to have lost his life that night. The mother who was watching from the window was probably just as loving and protective as Irene had been, and yet Irene had been forced to watch as the one she tried to protect the most was murdered while she was incapable of helping.

Lester dissociated from the most horrible crimes; it was the only way he could pull through. He saw the crime scene with a detective's eye, looking at the details and the facts and not the emotion or the loss, but he had struggled with that of late. Seeing such a peaceful scene before him and realizing how this had played out years ago, and what it had led to, made him despise himself, the world, and the human race in one bitter moment.

When the mother noticed Lester, she called out to her husband and they both watched. They probably knew what had happened in their house, and although that didn't put them at any greater risk than their neighbors next door or their friends across town, it would have been enough to give them sleepless nights and to turn them into paranoid, neurotic parents. Lester moved on when he realized the mother was most likely a few minutes away from phoning the police and the father a few seconds away from confronting him. He caught a glance and a smile from the young boy in the garden as he walked by, and as Lester winked at him, the little boy waved, much to the annoyance of his parents.

Lester walked to the town square, knowing the route he was taking had probably been the same one Darren Henderson took nearly fifteen years ago. He hadn't been the innocent kid his little brother had been. Lester had met plenty of teenagers like him and he had despised nearly all of them, but that wasn't to say he wasn't going to better himself, that he wasn't going to turn things around. After all, there wasn't too much difference between Damian and Darren: both were mischievous, both were mixing with the wrong crowds—Damian had even been sent home from school before for bullying. The only thing that set the two apart was the fact that the kid Damian bullied might grow stronger because of what happened to him—his pain and his isolation might turn him into a successful and wealthy adult. Whereas the child Darren had bullied had gone down a different path. There were many bullied kids in the world and a lot of them had the resolve to put those experiences behind them; some fought back and ended it there and then, a select few ended their own lives, but then there were the Hermans of the world. Herman had taken a lot of grief from a lot of people, and he had given it back with interest. These kids deserved to be fed their own medicine, and Lester had always been a proponent of revenge, of "an eye for an eye and a tooth for a tooth."

But Herman didn't think that way. If you took Herman's tooth, he took your head; if you took his eye, he took your life.

Whitegate was one of the few small towns that had CCTV cameras, due to the increased levels of antisocial behavior and a government scheme to clamp down on it. After the murders, there had been a panic, as expected, and that resulted in more cameras being fitted. It was all pointless, but it was what the people wanted, and if it was what the people wanted, regardless of how pointless it was, then it was what the local government was willing to give them. It was amazing how much could get done when elections were just around the corner and the world's media was watching. Whitegate was now one of the most well-guarded and heavily watched areas in the country, although as the paranoia faded and people realized how stupid they had been, those cameras fell into disrepair and the rest of the town soon followed.

The killings had created a tourist boom at first and local businesses had thrived. Fast food restaurants opened and shops sold macabre mementoes. Lester remembered a story about a local shopkeeper-cum-conman who sold Herman's school uniform to a rich businessman in France, with suspicions only being raised when he made the same sale to three dozen other customers around the world. Most of Herman's actual belongings had been destroyed in the fire, but for a short time there was a black market trade in them as he achieved cult status. It wasn't just because of what he had done, or because of his age—it was the fact that he hadn't been found that piqued interests more than anything else. He was a modern Jack the Ripper, and just like Jack the Ripper, everyone had their own theories, each as insane as the last. Some said he had been abducted, some said he had never existed, that Herman's uncle was the real killer and that the CCTV images were a disguise of some kind. And of course, there were those who were quick to point to a government conspiracy, with talk of mind control and assignation. As if Darren Henderson and his friends were Russian spies or powerful diplomats, and not delinquent losers.

That sort of interest eventually faded, though, becoming nothing but a faint recollection for most and an obsession for few. Herman's crimes made great material for the press and documentary makers, but the articles published about him and the films made about his life only proved that very little was actually known about him. He lost his mother when he was young, probably running away following a breakdown in her marriage; his father died not long before the murders, and his uncle then moved in with him. Between that, the bullying, and a fairly standard academic record, there was little else to learn. He had no friends and his neighbors and classmates knew little about him.

Once the hype faded, the town returned to normal. People stopped caring, stopped showing up to take pictures and buy mass-produced crap; the businesses fell into disrepair, the gift shops that had opened in the hope that Whitegate was the next hot tourist destination closed down before fulfilling their first year's rent. The world moved on to new stories, new psychopaths. The house prices dropped, the unemployment rate increased, and Whitegate found itself in a worse position than when Herman had called it home. He was still their claim to fame, though. Herman was still a legend. And the irony of this was that the school kids were the ones who adored him the most. The delinquent teens, the disillusioned youth—the very people who had bullied and tortured Herman and the very people who had kickstarted the massacre and sated his bloodlust.

———

Lester went to Irene's parents' house, just out of town. He had phoned in advance and, although they were very friendly and welcoming, he sensed something else as well. A wariness, a fatigue, a fear.

"You must be Barbara." Lester smiled a pleasant greeting when a well turned-out octogenarian answered the door. Her creased face broke as she returned the smile.

She gave a dismissive wave of her hand. "Please, call me Barb. This is my husband, Reg." She pointed to the living room where a less well turned-out and less smiley man sat slouched in an armchair. Lester waved and the man nodded in reply. "And you must be Detective Keats."

"You can call me Lester."

"Oh, thank you, Lester. Is that what you tell all the old ladies, or just the pretty ones?"

"Actually, it's just the ones I don't arrest," he said, sharing a smile. "You know what the older generation are like."

She laughed softly, but there was still a stiffness to her, hidden behind a friendly facade. It would have remained hidden if Lester hadn't seen it before. This was what happened to families that had been through hell, families that had stared into the devil's eyes. They say time heals all wounds, but it didn't. Time just made it easier to get on with your life. The pain never goes away, the changes never revert. The fear, the tension, the depression, it all remained, as did the reluctance to think about the thing that caused that chaos in the first place.

They made him a cup of tea and then sat in silence. There was a somber air in the house, and one that the arrival of a police officer did little to ease. He saw pictures of Irene on the fireplace and on the walls—she was pretty, bubbly—but Lester couldn't fathom a reason why Herman hadn't killed her. She wasn't particularly stunning and he doubted she would be very friendly either, especially to a boy who had just butchered her family. Herman had seen something in her he had obviously not seen in the younger girls he had killed. And if he was The Masquerade, it was the same something he had not seen in the women he had murdered in their homes and on the streets.

"She was a lively woman," Barbara explained when she caught Lester looking at the pictures.

Lester didn't like that Barbara used past tense to talk about her daughter, but he had searched the obituaries. As far as he knew, Irene wasn't dead.

"She's not lively anymore?"

Barbara shook her head solemnly. "But she was a family woman." She smiled meekly.

The house was immaculate. The carpet, the sofas, and the television all looked new. Lester took their wealth as a sign that Irene hadn't remarried and didn't have any more kids, otherwise they would be more inclined to save their money and prepare a nest egg for their grandchildren. Parents and grandparents who had lost children were always more protective of any more that came their way, always willing to give up their own happiness and their own fortune to ensure a long and prosperous life for what they saw as a second chance legacy. Those who experienced loss suffered an increased paranoia, a worry that lightning would strike twice.

"And you don't know where she is?" Lester asked.

Barbara shook her head. "As I told you on the phone, we haven't heard from her in years."

She smiled softly and she looked genuine. She had sounded genuine on the phone, as well, and Lester almost hadn't gone because of that, but when he caught a glimpse of the father, of the nervous twitch in his upper lip and the way he feigned a smile and then looked away when his wife spoke, he was glad he had made the trip. They were lying and he just needed to prove it.

"I can understand how she must be scared," Lester said. "Wherever she is. For all she knows, Herman is out there somewhere. He took a liking to her and she's probably worried that he'll find her again." He looked into Barbara's eyes. There was a flare of recognition there. She was listening more intently than before, the knuckles on her bony hand turning white as she tightened her grip on the cup.

"But her silence could be costing lives. You see, I have a theory that your daughter is right to be scared, because I believe that Herman is still out there and he's still killing."

Barbara gasped and nearly dropped her cup.

"But he has no interest in Irene anymore," Lester said quickly, keen for her not to have a heart attack. "Whatever that was about, it's over now. She has hidden away from him for long enough and he's no longer interested. But there are other women out there who *can't* hide, women who *can't* run away. They need your daughter's help."

Barbara lowered her head and stared into her tea, as though the scalding liquid held the answer to all of her problems. Her husband watched on, and in his eyes Lester sensed desperation. Reg wanted to tell Lester where his daughter was. He was the voice of reason, but he had been forced into silence by his paranoid wife. Lester saw it all in the look they exchanged when Barbara finally raised her head.

"I understand," she said. Lester felt his hopes diminish when he saw she was smiling again, back to her world of fake-grins and denial. "But I can't help you. We don't know where she is. Isn't that right, honey?"

Both Lester and Barbara turned to Reg and he looked at them each in turn, spending a little longer on his wife, before confirming, "Yes, that's right."

Lester stared at Barbara in disbelief. He had liked her at first, but now he despised her—that bright and toothy smile hid so many lies. She was putting lives in danger and she didn't care. It was an attitude he had seen time and time again, one that penetrated deep into the fiber of his being. It was all about families and friends to these people; they didn't care how many people died and in what ways they died, provided that their own were okay. They would happily sacrifice the lives of dozens to avoid their own child even getting the sniffles. And why would they care? It was number to them—they didn't see the faces of the dead, they didn't have to look into their eyes and wonder what those lifeless orbs had seen last. They didn't have to ring their families and let them know his wife had been butchered or her daughter had been raped and murdered. Some would have allowed for ignorance with Barbara, considering the loss she had suffered, but as far as Lester was concerned, that should have given her more reason to help him. Yes she had lost, yes she had suffered, but that didn't mean that other parents, grandparents, and siblings needed to suffer as well.

He picked up a picture of Irene and smiled. "I see the resemblance in her," he said.

"I'm sorry?" Barbara asked pleasantly.

He held up the picture to show her. "Darren," he said.

Barbara's face changed in an instant, the smile fading. "Oh."

Lester nodded. "You know, I've seen the CCTV footage of that night so many times. I've seen the crime scene photos more times than I can count." He shook his head. "What happened to him was horrible, and yet, in a way, he was lucky."

Barbara gave him exactly the reaction he was hoping for. She shot to her feet, her teeth bared and her hand thrusting outward. The smiling old woman had gone, replaced with the face of a vicious matriarch, and it was all Lester could do to keep from smiling. As much as he despised those who blinded themselves to the world, those who didn't give a fuck what happened outside of their home or their family circle, they were easy to manipulate.

"How dare you say that!" she blasted vehemently. "Darren was tortured, he was butchered out on the street, next to his friends, next—"

Lester shrugged. "I've seen worse."

"My grandson was—"

"That's the problem," Lester said, keeping his calm. "He was your grandson, and that's something that's going to haunt you for the rest of your life. I appreciate that and I truly apologize for it, but the girls I pick up off the street, the ones who are raped, tortured, and killed by this man, each one is also someone's grandchild, someone's daughter, someone's fiancé, and someone's wife."

Barbara seemed to calm down as Lester's words drilled into her. The Masquerade had never raped anyone; sexual assault seemed to be beneath him. He didn't spend a lot of time torturing them either, at least not physically, but a few embellishments wouldn't hurt if they got his point across.

"Darren suffered, but believe me when I tell you that *they* suffered more. The killer was young then, he was learning his craft; he's experienced now. He's much sicker, much stronger, and he has an appetite for murder that cannot be sated."

Barbara sat back down, flopping into her seat and immediately lowering her head to her chest.

"I need your help," Lester said. "I think that your daughter can help me, but I need you to tell me where she is."

Barbara was silent, but Reg finally decided that enough was enough. "She lives just a few miles from here," he said. Barbara glared at him in protest, almost instinctively, but she immediately retracted that look. "I can tell you her address, but I would prefer it if you let me ring her first and explain who you are. She is very temperamental these days."

Lester nodded, doing his best to hide his smile. "Thank you."

6

Lester had seen the beauty in the pictures, he had caught a glimpse of what Herman might have fallen for, but none of that was left. These days Irene Henderson looked haggard, and even though only fifteen years had passed, she looked a good three decades older. She was thinner, gaunter, and if she wasn't hooked on drugs, she looked like she could use some.

The short drive to her house was a trip into the bowels of hell. From the quiet and affluent cul-de-sac where her parents lived, into the desolate and empty town whose dreams had been realized and then destroyed thanks to Herman's massacre, and then on further into the smaller, uglier stepsister of that small and ugly town. Irene lived in what could be best described as a village, but not the picturesque English village that graces so many magazines and stereotypical images. It was something much worse, something much *less*. It was served by a small shop sitting wearily in the middle of the village, surrounded by kids in hoodies and tracksuits. The rest of the village was an expanse of old houses, most of which were boarded-up and half destroyed, despite the fact that people still clearly lived in them. This was a rural version of an inner-city jungle; the same people, the same deprivation, the same absence of hope.

Irene lived in a semi-detached house at the end of a long street. The house was big and at one point had probably cost quite a lot of money, but these days—judging by what surrounded it—anyone brave and stupid enough to live there was welcome to it for the price of a padlock and a baseball bat.

When Irene answered the door, Lester thought he had the wrong house. She was nothing like her former self, and drawing a resemblance between the two would be like searching for recognition in the before and after photos of a meth addict. She looked very tired. She had probably spent nearly a decade sleeping with one eye open, alert and awake to the sound of any movement.

The house was horrible, the street was worse, and the village was the modern-day extension of hell, but Lester doubted she cared or even acknowledged any of that. This woman had been through much worse, so much more than a gang of delinquent teenagers or drug dealing neighbors could ever throw at her.

"I don't sleep these days," she said when she caught him looking at her.

That much was obvious, and he understood that "these days" probably stretched back a good fifteen years. The irony was that while those years had no doubt dragged on slowly, feeling like centuries, the night she lost her family and her hope probably felt like yesterday.

He gave her a sympathetic and pitiful smile and she did her best to reciprocate, but smiling was alien to her. In her pictures, she had one of those lively faces that seemed almost constantly prepped for a smile, as if she spent her life in a perpetual state of joy, but that smile and that face were now a distant memory.

She showed him into the living room, a small and musty room that light was barely allowed to enter. Not only had the curtains been drawn, but there was a set of blinds underneath them that had also been closed. The kitchen door was open and, from where he stood, Lester could see that the windows above the kitchen sink had also been covered, while a square of glass in the top half of the back door had been taped up.

"The light does me no favors," she said, following his eyes. "Please, sit down." She gestured to the sofa, which had seen better days and probably had several generations of creatures living inside it, but he didn't want to be rude and so he perched himself on the edge and watched her as she sat next to him, curling her legs underneath her.

"I still see him when I close my eyes," she said. "It's like I'm stuck on repeat, always going back to that day, telling myself that I should have done more, that I was to blame and that it was all my fault."

"That's not true, you know that."

"I know, or at least I *should* know, but it's not always easy convincing myself. I mean, he didn't kill me, he kept me alive for a reason, so maybe it *was* all about me."

Lester shook his head but he didn't elaborate; to do so would mean dragging her dead son through the mud. Her sane mind knew that it had always been about her eldest son, that his bullying had driven Herman to do what he did, but she struggled to grasp that sane part of herself.

"Darren was alive at that point," Irene said, a tear rolling down her cheek as her already bloodshot eyes reddened even more. "I didn't know what he was going to do, but when he tied me up and left me there, Darren was still alive."

Lester nodded. "You couldn't have known. You had more important things to worry about."

He didn't want to drag her back to reality, to remind her that she couldn't have possibly contemplated what Herman would have done when she was surrounded by the blood and flesh of her husband and her youngest child, but it was the only way to stop the guilt. Guilt had obviously eaten her over the years and that, combined with a constant state of paranoia, had turned her into the pathetic excuse for a woman that she had become. Some people sought justice and revenge, some people turned to drugs or drink to block out the memories, some people killed themselves, some people just sucked it up and managed to get on with their lives. Then there were people like Irene. They were the ones who had been to the brink of suicide and drug addiction, but had refused both. They were the ones for whom death or inebriation were the only options, but couldn't bring themselves to do either and therefore just remained in a constant state of purgatory.

"So . . ." She lifted her eyes and looked directly into his. He didn't see pain there, he didn't see anger. He saw emptiness. "What do you want from me?"

He told her about his theory, watching as her entire body seemed to twitch when he mentioned Herman's name. "Not a lot has been written about that night from your perspective," he added. "You confirmed their suspicions, but after that . . ." he shrugged and allowed himself to trail off.

"After that I disappeared."

Lester nodded.

"The police stopped caring," she explained. "Like you said, they got their man—*boy*," she corrected, expressing great distaste as her tongue curled around that word. "That was all they wanted. It was the press who tried to track me down. The people who wanted to write articles, film documentaries. My parents even got a request for someone looking to sell off items in my home."

She gave him a look of disbelief at that point, as though she had never heard of or imagined anything more disgusting than that. He gave her an understanding smile in reply, but he had heard a lot worse.

"I guess there is no end to the sickness of the human race."

Lester nodded again—she was onto something there. "So, you never did any interviews, any documentaries?"

She shook her head. "They found me in the beginning, when I was still living in *that* house, but when I moved I didn't tell anyone. Except my parents, of course. This house is rented in a false name and paid for with cash. The landlord doesn't have an issue with that, and I don't think that he would find a tenant otherwise. It's not like I'm going to wreck the place." They both looked around, but she clearly wasn't embarrassed by the state of the house. It wasn't a home. It was a hideout, a refuge.

"Why didn't you just stay with your parents?"

"I couldn't do that to them, and they—they just handle things differently."

"How do you mean?"

"You've met them, right? There's no grief there, not on the surface anyway. They hide everything. They go around smiling, laughing and joking as if nothing ever happened. I can't do that."

"I understand."

Irene sighed and slipped her legs out from underneath her. She took a cigarette pack from the armchair and clawed one out with her trembling fingers before offering the pack to Lester. When he refused, she put it to one side, lit the stick in her mouth, and then watched him as she sucked and inhaled. "So," she said, breathing a cloud of smoke into the fetid air. "You're the first person I've spoken to about this in years. What is it you want to know?"

"I want to know everything," he explained. "We know he did it, we know who he is, that's all irrelevant now. I want to know *why* he did it and *what* he is."

"I don't like the way you say *is*," she said.

"I think he's still out there," Lester said, seeing her shudder. "But don't worry, he won't harm you."

"How can you be so sure?"

"He's moved on."

She nodded, but she didn't look convinced. "There's not much I can tell you," she began, her eyes on the tip of her cigarette, which she held loosely between two fingers on her right hand. "He took us by surprise and before we knew what was happening, he had beaten my husband and my little boy—"

"I know all of that," Lester cut in, keeping the painful memories to a minimum. "I want to know how he was with you, what did he want from you? I mean, what I don't understand is that there was something there, something that drew you to him. He was fascinated with you, but there was no sexual assault, right? Did he even touch you?"

She shook her head softly, a half-smile on her face. "You know the weird thing? I've seen the documentary and I've read the stories. Sometimes I think that if it's in my head all the time anyway, why not try to embrace it, right?"

Lester shrugged.

"Well, they all say that he had something for me. That I was his crush. There are even some who say I was the reason he went to my house that night."

"But you don't think that?" Lester asked, intrigued.

"Of course not. Some of them also say that he touched me, some even go further than that. I suppose it makes sense for them to say that—hell, it would make sense to me if that had happened, but he didn't so much as hold my hand." She paused to take a long draw of her cigarette, the misery at the memory now turning into a bitterness as she spoke about the boy who had ruined her life.

"It wasn't sexual. It was weird. I mean, he just sat there and talked to me, ranting and raving like some cynical old man."

Lester nodded; it had been Irene's statements about that cynicism that led him to link Herman to The Masquerade in the first place.

"But there was something else, something in his eyes when he looked at me. It was like. . ." she shrugged. "I'm not sure. Pity maybe. Regret. Loss." She took another draw, another inhalation, another billow of smoke into the fetid swamp. She raised her eyes to look at Lester as something seemed to dawn on her. "It was like I was his mother, or like he *wanted* me to be his mother."

That surprised Lester. "His mother?"

She nodded slowly and watched as her cigarette burned to the end, and as a cloying stench filled the musty air when the flame began to eat into the filter. "I think he wanted my company, my approval." They locked eyes at that point; pity on her face, realization on his. "I think he wanted my love."

———

Lester had never looked into Herman's mother. It had never been an angle he had even considered. She was gone, out of the picture, probably living it up in a disturbingly British part of Spain with a disturbingly hairy Spanish man, or shacking up with her second husband, who proved to be just as much of a disappointment as the first. There was also a chance that she was dead, just like Herman's father, but there was nothing on record and if that was the case then Herman certainly hadn't known. She had simply disappeared out of his life, and that, Lester realized as he left the stagnating town Irene called home, was probably a sizable part of the big picture he had overlooked.

Sociopaths weren't created because their mothers left them. If that were the case, then the world would be an even more horrible place to live than it already was, but if it didn't explain the cause, it certainly went some way to finding a solution. Lester had known nothing about Herman other than his name, which was now irrelevant; his father, who was now dead; and his house, which was now ash. But with this new link, it opened up a whole new world.

He discovered that the mother's name was Gertrude, or Trudy for short. The name made him wince and he wondered if it was she who had chosen Herman's name, perhaps as a way of projecting her own misery onto her newborn child. There were records of where she was born and where she gave birth to Herman, all of which were angles previously explored. But what he couldn't find was any information on what had happened to Gertrude around the time she had disappeared.

The police reports said she had been reported missing by Herman's father. She had gone to the shop in the morning and had failed to return. Lester saw cases like that all the time. They were much more common than they should have been, but this one was different. He remembered looking into a similar case a few years back. The father had gone to buy some cigarettes in the morning and hadn't returned. The mother phoned the police just five hours later, as worried as you would expect her to be. But this, this was different. According to the report, the shops were a ten-minute walk away from Herman's home, but at no point did Herman's father attempt to find her himself, and he didn't phone the police until forty-eight hours later.

Why had it taken him so long?

Trudy worked at a local factory, peeling potatoes and stacking boxes for much of the day. Herman's father also worked, so it would have been difficult for them to juggle their child and their careers. Their jobs didn't pay well enough for them to hire a nanny, and as far as Lester knew, there were no relatives nearby other than the uncle, someone who Herman had clearly despised. None of it stacked up, and as with Herman before her, there was little information to help him. It was as though the entire family worked on the fringes of society, trying their best to stay out of the records and away from the public eye.

"Anything interesting?"

Lester looked up from the computer screen, tucked away on a partitioned desk at Whitegate Police Station. A local officer named Matthews was standing above him with a cup of coffee in one hand, a biscuit in the other, and a look of intrigue on his face. As much as Lester hated this little town, he hated the police station and its officers even more. They were cleaners more than anything else—people whose job it was to skim the scum off the surface of the fetid swamp and then stand back as others delved deeper. They dealt with delinquents, addicts, and domestic abusers, and when anything interesting happened, the detectives were called in and they were shoved to one side. This turned them into nosy, annoying little twerps who insisted on offering their worthless two cents in the hope of getting a buck in return.

"Anything I can help you with?" Matthews pushed.

Lester thought he would humor him. "You knew that Herman had a mother who ran out on him, right?"

"Of course," Matthews said confidently, looking like he was about to step above his station and claim some underserved respect. "She went out one day to get some milk or something. Never came back."

"Did you know how long it took his dad to phone the police?"

He shrugged. "In these cases? I don't know, usually a few hours. I mean, the shops are only—"

"Forty-eight hours," Lester cut in.

Matthews seemed surprised. "You're shitting me?"

Lester shook his head. "She also worked for most of the day, and so did he, yet I can't find any information on who looked after Herman during that time."

"Well then." Matthews straightened up and looked like he was going to say something profound, which Lester knew was unlikely. "That is a toughy, isn't it?"

Matthews breathed out deeply and then took a long sip of his coffee. He made several lip-smacking noises, followed by a long sigh, and when his eyes finally returned to Lester, and when his mouth finally opened to do something other than ask questions and feed his face, he simply said, "A toughy indeed."

"Well, thanks for all your help," Lester said, doing as little as possible to hide the sarcasm. "I'll let you know if I need anything else."

Matthews paused and looked Lester over, seemingly trying to work out if he had been insulted or not and what his next move should be. Lester hadn't forgotten this wasn't his territory, and he knew he was stepping on other people's shoes, but as distrusting of them as he was, and as much as he walked around thinking he owned the place, none of them stood in his way. That was another issue with small-town cops—they had been stuck in a rut for so long they no longer cared. It was just a job to them, and Lester couldn't blame them for that. They didn't deal with murderers, rapists, or even armed robbers; they dealt with the bottom rung of society's worst, and no matter what they did, the ones who were destined to climb that ladder and commit bigger crimes would still go on to do so.

Eventually Matthews walked away and Lester watched him sit behind his desk, put his feet up, and then pick up his tablet and begin to browse his Facebook profile, playing the latest mind-numbing game and generally doing whatever he could to avoid doing any actual work. Lester watched him for a few moments and then decided he needed to get some air—just being in the same room as Officer Gump and his numb-nutted friends was sapping the life out of him.

He took a stroll down to the local park, a hotbed of dog-walkers through the day, a place for the local yokels during the night. The poorly manicured lawns, overgrown hedges, and graf-fitied trees were a testament to a town that had stopped caring. At one time, maybe even during Herman's time, this had probably been a decent area, with lush green lawns that stretched on as far as the sun shone, but those green lawns were now dry, patchy, and covered in dog shit and broken beer bottles.

He sat on a park bench, which, according a number of mis-spelled, poorly penned graffiti etchings, had at one time been party to three different varieties of the name Maddison (or one girl who hadn't decided how to spell her name), a promiscuous boy with a small penis whose sexual failings had been scrawled for all to see, and an unfortunate girl whose name looked like a brand of cheap wine.

Lester had only been in the town for a couple days and already he could understand why Herman had done what he did. He was clearly a bright kid, and for someone like that to be stuck in a place like this, surrounded by these people, was enough to send anyone over the edge.

Lester was interrupted from his thoughts when his phone rang. First he ignored it, realizing that no news was ever good news and he'd had enough bad news to last him a lifetime. Then curiosity got the better of him so he decided the least he could do was take a look at who was calling. As soon as he reached that point, he knew there was no turning back.

It was his mother, who, as pleasant as she was, never had any good news for him. She was listed on his phone as Banshee due to her high-pitched voice—brought on by a throat condition—and the fact that she only rang him when someone was dead or dying. Four years ago, she called to tell him the family dog had died; then, almost in yearly intervals, she informed him about his father's passing, his uncle's demise, and the time that his cousin was diagnosed with a terminal condition. He dreaded to think what news she had for him this time, but he took solace in the fact that very few members of his family were still alive.

"Hello, Mother."

"Son, I have some bad news."

Lester rolled his eyes. She always started the conversation like that; it was her way of saying hello.

"Of course you do."

"It's your kids," she said, before immediately pausing.

Lester felt his heart stop. The kids had cited the fact that he was an asshole and they never wanted to see him again as their reason for leaving, but he was happy to watch them go. If nothing else, it would keep them away from their poisonous friends.

"What is it?" he asked, his voice turning dry.

"They're with me now."

"I know that, but—"

"I didn't know if you knew, so I just thought I would tell you."

"I did know. I—"

"I mean, they don't seem very happy with you. In fact, they have quite a lot of bad things to say—"

Lester moved the phone away from his ear and let her talk to herself. She wasn't deaf, but anyone would be forgiven for thinking otherwise. She rarely listened to anything that anyone had to say and always liked to make drama out of everything. It was a diet of daytime crime dramas that did it, coupled with the fact that she had fuck all else to do but scare the living shit out of people.

"Mum!" he said, cutting her short. She had broken into a conversation about something else entirely, a neighbor who was either terminally ill or dead. That was her favorite topic and, considering she lived on such a small street and had such a fascination with the macabre, Lester had always wondered if he should be investigating her as a potential serial killer. "You said you have some bad news about my kids, what is it?"

"The kids? The kids are fine. I wasn't talking about the kids, I was talking about Mrs.—"

Lester hung up. He had no interest in her neighbors. If he had known them when they were alive then he would have maybe cared, but he had no idea who these people were. His mother knew that, and she just wanted to vent. Now she would take it out on his kids, telling them all that she couldn't tell Lester. The thought actually pleased him a little; it would teach them for running away and thinking they could hole up with their grandmother for a few weeks. When he was struggling to explain to their teachers why they weren't at school, and when he was being threatened with fines because of their truancy, he would take solace in the knowledge that they had suffered.

He smiled at his thoughts and their misery, but that smile quickly turned into something else.

The grandparents. That was the answer he had missed. That's where kids go when the parents are at work. That's who brings them up, providing all the services of a nanny for none of the cost. Herman's father's parents were out of the picture before Herman was born, but his mother's parents had never been mentioned, and it was the mother's side that usually took the responsibility. It had been the same when he was a child and it had been the same for his kids, as well.

If they lived nearby, then that's where they would have taken Herman while they were at work. From the stories he had read and the documentaries he had seen, the grandparents were never featured. He could recall mentions of Herman's father's parents, but never of the other side of the family.

"So what the fuck happened to grandparents?" he asked himself out loud.

He went straight back to the station. Officer Matthews was still at his desk, talking to one of the other slouches who had spent the morning pretending to work and trying to hide the fact that he had actually been playing online poker. The officer shared a joke with Matthews, no doubt at Lester's expense, before walking away.

"Herman's grandparents," Lester said, getting straight to the point as he stood over the officer's desk. "What happened to them? Were they alive at the time?"

Matthews inhaled deeply, the breath whistled through his teeth. He leaned forward and rested his elbows on his desk. "Well, the dad's side died before he was born, but on the mother's side he had a grandmother who lived through it."

Lester was shocked to hear such a nonchalant answer. "You're kidding me?"

Matthews beamed like a chubby kid who had finally broken into the cookie jar. His pathetic job was finally being validated.

Lester ran a hand through his hair. "I don't understand, why am I only hearing about this now?"

Matthews shrugged.

"You didn't say anything before."

"You didn't ask."

"So, did she look after him when he was a kid?" Lester demanded, irritated to be in the company of the incompetent officer.

"Possibly," he said with a shrug. "We never asked. It wasn't really our case."

It wasn't his case because they left it to the ones who actually knew what they were doing.

"So why was there nothing in the news, why does no one mention her?"

"She is frail and very old, plus she rarely saw him after his parents split. I guess she never got on with his father. We decided—well, in truth we didn't have much say in the matter, but we helped—that it would be best if we kept her out of the picture. She lives in a quiet neighborhood, a retirement community really. If we mentioned her link to him then they'd be queuing up halfway down the street, bugging her day and night. Poor old cow is too old for that shit."

"You said *is*. She *is* far too old. You mean to say she's still alive?"

Matthews sat back in his chair, his chubby ankles on top of the desk again, his hands folded over his bulbous stomach. The smile on his face indicated that job satisfaction was a rare occurrence for him, and he was going to milk this for all it was worth. "Of course she is."

"Well?" Lester said, his eyebrows raised, his tone already annoyed. "Where the fuck is she?"

7

River Acres was a peaceful and picturesque part of suburbia. Here there were no hooligans roaming the streets; no domestic violence waiting behind closed doors and occasionally spilling out of open windows; no children playing in the street, kicking balls against cars and windows and into gardens. There was no loud music either, but if you walked down the empty pathways, passing the rows of bungalows set back from small and flowery gardens, you would be greeted with the noise from dozens of television sets.

This was where the old and infirm came to die. The people who lived here weren't capable of much activity and they certainly weren't capable of causing a nuisance. Police cars did come here, but only because of burglars, door-to-door cons and, on one occasion two weeks ago, to arrest a ninety-year-old woman who decided that stripping naked and going for a powerwalk around the block would work better than her medication ever could.

Lester had been briefed on the area by a local cop, a man who laughed at the suggestion that a place as dull as River Acres could be holding something so vital to Lester's case.

"You came all the way to our quiet little town to find the quietest little spot, what gives?"

Lester didn't need to tell a local gossipy officer what his motives were, not when the people who needed to know already knew. He was a long way from home, but this wasn't a fleeting visit.

Lester hated River Acres as soon as he drove down the empty road that cut a line through the middle of rows of identically drab houses. He hated it even more when he stepped out of the relative quiet of the car—with the engine roaring and the radio turned down—into the complete silence of the street. It was too quiet, too creepy. Death walked these streets, and in a single year you'd see more ambulances and hearses parked outside these doors than you would cars, indicating that the grim reaper was closer to the residents of River Acres than any of their family members.

He stopped outside one of the houses and listened. He could hear the television blaring through the front door and although the curtains were tightly shut—despite it being early afternoon—he could see the lights from the set flickering through a small gap. He checked a slip of paper in his hand, double checked the number by the door, and then buzzed the intercom.

When he didn't receive an answer, he held his finger down on the buzzer until he did. An old voice trickled down the line, sounding half-asleep, half-dead, or both.

"Who is it?"

"Is that Mrs. Johnson?"

"It's *Ms.*," she said bitterly. "And I'm not buying anything."

He heard her click off. She sounded old and frail, and although he had expected as much because of her age and the area in which she lived, a part of him, knowing who she was related to, had anticipated something a little more lively and a lot more feisty.

He sighed to himself and held the buzzer again until she answered.

"I told you," she snapped. "I don't want any of your shit. Now fuck off and piss on someone else's doorstep."

He grinned to himself. That was more like it.

"I promise, I'm not here to sell anything. I'm with the police." He looked over his shoulder as he spoke, knowing that if they were capable of hearing him then several dozen old men and women would be turning off their TV sets and dragging their chairs in front of the window.

"Oh, well, why didn't you say so?"

She clicked off and he waited. He heard her turn off the television. The noise of a daytime mystery was replaced by the grumblings of a woman who was talking to herself, but was probably too deaf to realize it.

He heard several bolts yank open, followed by at least two locks. It took her a good five minutes before she opened the door and when she did she was already on her way to the kitchen. "I'll make you a cup of tea, sweetie," she said with her back to him.

He had his badge ready to show her, but she didn't ask. She didn't even look at him.

"Thanks," he said meekly, stepping inside the house. He closed the door behind him, seeing several curtains twitch in the houses across the street.

————

The elderly woman beamed at him as he sat sipping his cold cup of tea. There was a good chance that it had been hot when she poured it, but by the time she made it across to him, stuttering and struggling with every step, it was tepid and half empty. There was an equally good chance she was senile and had made it with water from the tap, or that she had simply given him a cup that had been left by a recent visitor, but he didn't want to seem impolite so he drank it and pretended to like it.

"Do you want a biscuit?" she asked, holding out a biscuit tin with shaking hands. The tin looked at least fifty years old and was as dusty and frail as she was.

"Oh," he said in feigned delight. "I don't mind if I—" he recoiled when she opened the tin and exposed contents that looked as old as the tin. "I'll pass, thank you."

"There's some chocolate ones in there," she said.

"Oh God, I sincerely hope not," he whispered under his breath. On closer inspection, he saw a thick brown, clay-like substance stuck to the bottom of the tin that had at one point probably been chocolate.

"I'm not much of a biscuit lover," she said as she pulled the tin away. "I just keep these for the guests."

"You don't get many guests these days?" he asked.

"Sorry?" she said, turning to him and pointing her ear at him.

He sighed. "Nothing, it's nothing important."

She smiled and settled back in her chair before saying, "Although I don't get very many guests these days."

Lester rolled his eyes and took another sip of tepid tea before putting it to one side and vowing to leave it alone.

"I've come to talk to you about your grandson," he explained.

"My son-in-law? Ah, I thought so, he's a sly one. Good man, though."

Lester paused, but decided against pursuing that. He knew nothing about Herman's father. "No, your grandson," he reiterated. "Herman."

"Who?"

"*Herman!*"

"Ah, of course. Lovely kid. Are you a friend of his?"

"No. I'm a policeman."

"So you said, dear, but are you a friend of his?"

"No. We're not friends," Lester told her, struggling to imagine a boy like Herman ever having friends. There were people who believed his lonely upbringing was what caused him to do what he did, that he had taken all he could take until he decided enough was enough, but Lester believed otherwise. Lonely children were not murderers. You needed to have something in you, something dark, sinister, and yet at the same time empty, to do what Herman had done.

"That's a shame. That boy needs a good friend."

Lester decided that she didn't need to hear his theory. "Maybe."

"He's a mischievous little fucker, isn't he?"

Lester raised his eyebrows. He didn't know what was more surprising, that she had sworn out of the blue, or that she had just referred to one of the nation's most notorious spree killers as mischievous.

"So," she continued. "How can I help you?"

———

Lester got all that he needed from Mrs. Johnson. By the time he left her house, the skies were turning an eerie shade of gray. It was only afternoon but without the streetlights above him—pinning an orange halo around him as he stood, documents in hand—he wouldn't have been able to see his own hand in front of his face. This was the sort of weather The Masquerade would thrive on. Lester felt a stab of regret at that thought. He had left his home, his territory, one that had been torn apart by this killer, to come to this piece of purgatory. The people he was paid to protect and serve were now in the hands of a sadistic killer, but Lester knew there was no risk of The Masquerade doing anything while he was away, because he knew that the masked killer would soon follow him.

Lester was now more convinced of his theory than he had ever been. He had little doubt that The Masquerade and Herman were the same, and the evidence that he now had would convince others, as well. This was a crucial time, a time when revealing such information could be very costly and could anger one very disturbed individual, but he had to tell several people, and eventually one of them would leak that information anyway.

Lester had been quick to dismiss false rumors that The Masquerade had targeted him in the past, but as he stood under the eerie glow of the streetlight, watched by countless senile eyes, and with his own eyes perusing the documents from the old lady, he had a feeling that the rumor would become much more widespread and much more real very soon.

PART 3

1

"A re you going to buy that?"

Above the creased rim of the paper, I studied the questioning glare of the shop assistant, his arms folded smugly over his chest, his eyes glaring at me over spectacles that had slipped down his colossal nose. A laminated tag on his shirt declared his name was Scott, but by his body language and facial expressions, he clearly thought he was God.

I furrowed my brow, wondered where his motives lay. "Maybe."

"You have to buy it then."

I stared at him for a moment longer. His dark eyes bore the shadows of a superiority complex borne out of a lonely, friendless childhood, his only acquaintances probably an older, promiscuous sister or a workaholic mother.

I dipped my eyes back to the pages, paying him no heed. I didn't have time for a stuck-up narcissistic cunt with an Oedipus complex and no grasp of social etiquette. I had gone in to check the local papers, to skim through the personal ads and pick up one that had what I was looking for. But he was making that task very difficult.

I heard Scott *harrumph*, the sigh of the well-to-do and the pretentious social elite. Of which he was neither.

"Are you going to buy it *then?*" he pushed in a childish, contemptuous tone.

I peered above the paper again. His arms were still folded, his eyes still bearing down on me, asking what right I had to be in his world—how dare I think I was as good as he was?

I wanted to jump over the counter and split his arrogant head open on the till, to squeeze the life out of the little pompous prick. But I didn't. I remained calm.

I began to explain myself. "I just want to see—"

"—You *have* to buy it," he ordered.

When he interjected, I found myself shooting him an instinctive and fleeting stare. A look of utter contempt, a look that fully expressed my desire to rip open his throat and paint the shop with his blood. He didn't appear to catch it.

"But first—"

"—You have to buy it."

I closed the paper and folded it up. I hadn't seen the personals section. I wasn't even sure it had one.

I pulled some coins out of my pocket, counted up the required amount, and placed them on the counter. Scott the Snobbish Assistant didn't even glance at the money; his eyes were fixed on me.

"There's a good boy," he said when I finished, a mocking smile on his thin lips. "That wasn't so hard now, was it?"

I absorbed his comment without even flinching. It didn't matter, I'd have my revenge. I'd follow him home to his one-bedroom dilapidated flat; to the single pet—the derisive, callous feline or the tuneless, institutionalized bird. To his meals for one, his energy drinks, and his expired milk. To his spacious collection of fantasy books and dusty academia. To his bedroom, devoid of the brain-numbing atrocities of television, and stale with the spent force of a million angry matriarchal masturbations. And there, among the collections of comic books and manga pornography, I would open his larynx with a Stanley knife and watch his pointless existence soak into his Spiderman bedsheets.

"What're you fucking staring at?"

The bespectacled narcissist was glaring at me, his arms unfolded and ready to fight, his glasses pushed back to the bridge of his nose.

I picked up my paper, slipped it under my arm, and turned to leave. "You'll see."

I took the paper to a nearby bench, carefully positioned myself in the center so no one would feel the desire to sit next to me, and continued to flick through the pages. I found what I sought in the back: three whole pages of personal advertisements—a plethora of singles, swingers, and sex nuts spouting their personal wares in small, neatly laid-out columns.

The ads were an assault course of abbreviations, juvenility, and cringe-inducing desperation. One middle-aged man wanted his perfect girl, holding hopes to the highest that he would find someone who was *attractive, athletic,* and *professional,* as well as three different synonyms (and one abbreviation) for *good-humored,* and two for *intelligent.* He was clearly none of those things himself. His ad was akin to a lottery ticket.

God loves a trier but the world hates a dickhead.

Another man didn't seem as picky, stating that he liked his women *fat or thin* and didn't have a preference for features, hair color, or creed. I skimmed the first two pages, bypassing more desperation and impossible hopes. I found the gay section on the final half of the final page and slowed down, reading intently.

Among a plethora of poor spelling and egregious grammar, one of the ads stood out. It was longer than the others, the writer presumably having bought two squares. And there were no abbreviations, spelling mistakes, or grammatical errors. It stank of desperation and lies, of someone who was possibly just as confused sexually as I was and had been living a lie for at least some of his life. This was the twenty-first century, after all, with speed dating, online dating, and mobile dating. There was very little need for classified dating ads and the only people who used them—those who could actually spell their names—were hiding something.

He posted his email address, so when I returned home, I sent him a brief email. I told him I was a professional looking for some fun. I told him I was "new to the scene" and "needed someone to show me around." I felt goose pimples crawling on my skin as I wrote it. It was terrible. Cringeworthy. But it was better than the truth, and it seemed like the sort of tripe that would wash with someone who signed his safety away to a personal ad.

The dating scene wasn't for me, and even if it was, I struggled to imagine what scenario I would be comfortable with. There were very few men or women who interested me in this world, and none of them did so for sexual reasons. A blind date would be tedious and would result in me trying to kill them before dessert just so I could have an excuse to leave. Dating sites were the worst, a place for big egos and bigger idiots where so many beautiful people were available that everyone felt entitled and capable of shooting above their station. I would have tolerated meeting people at clubs—that way I could only talk to those who intrigued me and only if there was anyone intriguing to begin with—but the atmosphere of such places was anathema to me. With so many sweaty, drunk idiots, it would be difficult to stop myself from killing every last one of them in order to assist with the advancement of the human species.

I expected a reply to the email but I sent my phone number out of courtesy. He phoned me the following afternoon.

"Is that Mr. Anon?"

He sounded posh, which took me by surprise.

"It is."

"Rather cliché, don't you think?"

He also sounded like a dick, but that came as less of a surprise. I told him I was nervous and wanted some assistance. I noted an edge to his voice, an irritation, an urgency. It didn't take me long to ascertain he was probably in a heterosexual marriage. After all, other than serial killers, adulterers, and plain weirdos, who uses the classified ads?

I told him to meet me several miles away from my house on a street corner. Anyone else would have been worried at that point—few people will meet strangers on street corners for anonymous sex—but that was the beauty of the classified ads and of a married man who wanted to get his end away with a homosexual virgin. I had used the classifieds before. They were a good way to satisfy some urges and kill some time. But I didn't meet all my victims on there, at least not the special ones.

A job had never suited me, but I still needed to earn some money. In the beginning, I tried to get work in factories and as a laborer, but the hours were tedious and the people were worse. My lack of official documents also made it nearly impossible to get anything worthwhile. I had been offered cash-in-hand jobs, possibly on the assumption that I was an immigrant without any legal papers and not a serial killer on the run. But the cash was meager and would barely cover the cost of a lunchtime sandwich.

I earned my way by killing. When it eventually occurred to me, it seemed obvious, but it took some time to do so. Killing was so natural to me and getting away with it was easy. When there is no motive and no link to the victim, few killers are caught, and that's why serial killers become serial killers and not just murderers. I wasn't a hit man, and would have never associated with any gangs, certainly not those who considered me as anything other than their superior. I was only doing what my father had done, satisfying my urges by killing anyone who I found interesting, anyone I deemed worthy of death. I wasn't continuing his legacy anymore, but my methods and my motive was the same. In the beginning, I killed for pleasure and for experience. I was honing my craft. But I also killed to get the money I needed to survive.

My first murder for cash was a woman I met through the classifieds. She was wealthy and looking for a young and kinky man. A bit rough. I gave her more rough than she could have ever hoped for and I took her for every penny. I cleaned out her purse and her bank accounts, and I also took all of her jewelry before dumping her body. I had also used the Internet a number of times. My favorite pastime was to pose as a young girl, getting horny old perverts to meet me in secluded areas, bringing enough cash for us to run away together. It was a win-win for me. They brought a lot of money with them and they were unlikely to tell anyone where they were going. Few of them had anyone to tell.

————

I picked him up an hour later. He was well-dressed, in his mid-forties, but his suit was well worn and creased, as was his face. He was a businessman, his attire and his stance gave that away, and he also had a fair bit of money.

He flashed me a smile when he entered the car, but it wasn't a contented smile. He was on edge, still without his fix. I would have preferred him relaxed—that would have made my job easier—but if the fix he needed required me to suck on whatever horrid member he kept hidden in his polyester pants, it wasn't going to happen.

"You okay?" I asked.

He was tanned and it wasn't fake. It didn't have that chemical taint so common with self-tan products, and he didn't have the raccoon eye indicative of spray-on tan or sun-beds. If he was married then the tan line of his wedding ring would have been obvious, but in an effort to hide that, he was wearing a bandage that covered two fingers on his left hand.

"Broken finger," he said when he caught me looking.

I gave him a smile and then drove on. When we arrived at my flat, he nearly bolted out of the car. I let him into the house and offered him a drink, at which point he excused himself and went to the bathroom. I could have poisoned his drink at that point, but that would have been too easy and poison wasn't my style. Instead I waited for him to come back and then realized that he had been ingesting a poison of his own.

The edginess had gone. He was smiling and he looked content. Whatever he had snorted or shot up hadn't fixed the tiredness or the red streaks in his eyes, but it put a smile on his face and had calmed him down.

"So . . ." I asked, playing the part of the anxious fool. "Where do we begin?"

He took the glass of whiskey from my hand, sat down on the couch, and then patted the seat next to him. "Let's relax first," he said. "We can see where we go from there."

I wasn't great at relaxing in strange company. I had developed enough social skills to fake it, but I wasn't sincere. I didn't have a pocket full of chemical glee to make the anxiety go away.

As the night wore on, I realized that I was correct in my initial assumptions: he was a prick of the highest order. He was a narcissist, an ignorant fool, and he was also a terrible liar. Not only did he drop several names and contradict himself on stories of meeting celebrities—most of whom I had never heard of—but he also told me that he had been single for ten years, even though he accidentally dropped the name of his wife, and what I assumed were his kids, into the conversation. He was apparently an "openly gay" man who was actually so far in the closet he was one step away from Narnia. He also told me that he was a self-help guru, a yoga master, and a student of insight meditation, when it was obvious that the only insight he got came in crystallized form and could be traded for a blow job.

I have nothing against the homosexual lifestyle. All forms of human sexuality confuse and disgust me equally. If anything, I am more understanding of the homosexual side of it. To me, it seems that a relationship with two men or two women will have fewer disagreements and fewer arguments than a heterosexual relationship. In terms of procreation, it has its disadvantages, but who needs more humans?

Once he finished talking about himself, he told me more about himself. We had moved into the kitchen by then. I had gone in to get away from him and to pour myself a large drink, but he followed me like some energetic kid with abandonment issues and an inability to shut the fuck up.

". . . I hate people like that," he was saying. "So stuck up their own ass. They need a good slap, or a good fuck, if you know what I mean." He laughed and shoved me on the arm. I wondered how long it would take to squeeze the life out of him if I started now. "I also hate the ones who think they know it all, like they have life sorted out. I mean, I've come close, but those guys? They haven't got a clue. That's why they're stuck in their nine-to-five with their obnoxious kids and their ugly wives. That's why they have a shit job, a shit car, and a home that's falling to bits—"

He either didn't understand irony or he didn't realize that he was talking about himself in third person.

"You're smiling," he noted with a lethargic and somewhat drunken nod. "You agree with me, don't you?"

"You could say—"

"Of course you do." He paused to take a sip of whiskey, making the pause as short as possible in case anyone else tried to steal his limelight. "You know . . ." He pointed the glass at me as he prepared another rant. "I think it's people in general. I'm not a people fan. They do so much that pisses me off, so much that I can't stand."

I could agree with that, but there wasn't a hope in hell that he would let me.

"I hate people who love themselves. I hate people who project their own failings onto others. I hate the old. I hate the young. I hate the weak. I hate people who state 'there is nothing worse than' and then follow it up with something trivial, because believe me, there are many things worse than overcooked steaks, running out of eggs when you're baking a cake, or whatever other shit they come up with. I hate people who pronounce *cashew* like a sneeze. I hate the news: why do we only hear about the deaths, the wars, the rapes and the football results?"

He was on a roll. I allowed him to continue and he allowed me to move behind him, almost forgetting there was something else in the room other than his own ego.

"—I hate religion, all of them, take your pick. I hate the fact that we're all dominated by television, that there are no new ideas, no more great minds, and that everything we do and everything we are is dictated by some stupid fucking TV show penned by some coked-up fucking idiot in Hollywood. I hate the modern world, the computers, the super-quick, super-sleek shit that serves to turn us all into zombies and—"

At that point, I opened up his throat with a kitchen knife. His skin split like a ripe tomato and ran a torrent of crimson down his suit.

I wasn't offended by what he said. I agreed with most of it. I just didn't like his extroverted way of expressing, or anything else he had done or said. If anything, the diatribe of personal dislikes had been the highlight of our date, and it was the memory I retained of him as I dragged him into the bedroom, carved the smug expression out of his face, and carefully flayed his skin. The bedroom was set up for such an event, covered from floor to ceiling with sheets of plastic that would be disposed of later. I had actually gotten the idea from a television show—ironic, as I doubted my date would approve.

The killing happened far too quickly for my liking and I took very little satisfaction from it. It felt like routine, as if my hands were moving on a predesigned course. It wasn't that it was too easy—although it was—or that killing for me had been rendered monotonous on the whole, because it hadn't. I just didn't enjoy killing "innocent" men as much as innocent women, not anymore anyway. Darren had been fun, but he was far from innocent and deserved everything he got. His brother and his father, although accidental, had also been somewhat fun, but more because of the anger I had felt toward Darren.

I had enjoyed killing the perverts and the pedophiles I met online. I didn't particularly like kids and wouldn't think twice about killing them, but there was still something so innately sickening about those people. The children are the ones I hate the least, the ones who have yet to adapt to the world and have yet to turn into the horrible, despicable adults who they are destined to become.

I had hoped this murder would provide a nice change, that it would take me back to those early days. But it didn't. I couldn't put a finger on why I got more satisfaction from women. It wasn't sexual, I had no interest in that—it just felt right. It had always bothered me, and this egotistical prick had been an experiment more than anything, part of a desire I had to feel as much when murdering men as I did when murdering women. But that experiment didn't have the desired outcome.

I enjoyed killing for vengeance, there was no doubt about that, and when it came to the female population, I felt that vengeance and I got the same satisfaction, even if they had done nothing to me personally.

"Odd, isn't it?" I asked the skinless corpse of the talkative idiot on my bedroom floor. Humans pride themselves on being different, on their individuality, but deep down they all look alike and in death they all act alike. This man seemed to pride himself on his uniqueness more than others, but underneath his skin, he was exactly the same as the next man.

It had occurred to me that I could have been homosexual. The truth was that I could see the beauty in people, I could see the things that made both men and women attractive, but still neither of them appealed to me. If anything, something in me leaned more toward women, and to a certain kind of woman. Irene Henderson, the first woman I had ever spared and one who I had dreamed of killing many times since, had been one of those women, but there was nothing sexual about it.

I cut off his penis and popped it in a pickle jar after removing the pickle. It wasn't very big, which might have gone some way to explaining why he was such a pompous, overcompensating prick. I had been a little grossed out by the penis when he was alive, as I was with female parts, but once they were dead, I didn't mind. After that, it was merely a hunk of meat deprived of the filthy connotations it'd had when it was attached to the human.

There was a cupboard underneath the stairs where I kept all of my souvenirs, safely tucked away behind a false wall. I moved around a lot, but wherever I went, I took those mementoes with me. I rarely ever took things that people would notice missing. That would only create problems for me down the line, and I got the same amount of satisfaction from collecting something small and insignificant. It all depended on how satisfying the murder had been, on how long it would linger in my memory. This one would struggle to remain in my memory for long, but the penis would be an apt reminder. The victim was a cock.

I smiled to myself as I put the jar next to a small box. It was the same box my father had used to store his memories, the same box that had led me on this path. It was a good reminder of that part of my life and of my father's legend, but it was also a disappointing one, as I had let my father down.

I never quite assumed the role of my father's legacy. I did try, but things didn't go as planned. Darren was supposed to be home alone that night, with his parents and his brother spending the night at a relative's house up north and him insisting, as usual, that he would rather spend the holidays with his friends. But something changed, something went wrong. I had already anticipated and planned for a party or a gathering of his friends at the house, but I never expected his family to be there. I never expected his mother to be there. There was no turning back, though. I wanted to do it. I wanted to kill. I was ready. It was a trial by fire, but it was a rushed, messy trial and one that plastered my face all over the front pages.

Still, I went there to lose my virginity, and I did just that. I went there to see if killing was as exciting and satisfying as I thought it would be, and I discovered that it was even better than I had ever imagined. The Butcher died that night. I was too young and too sloppy to have been connected with him. A night of violence brought on by years of bullying had nothing to do with the clinical, vicious acts of a calculated killer. In the eyes of the press, he had gone into retirement. No one had found any evidence to the contrary.

I wanted a large kill count because I wanted people to fear me and to respect me. I wanted the legend that my father came so close to being, but there were kills that I was not proud of, kills that I did not enjoy and made me feel dirty, and now this was one of them. It had nothing to do with his sexual orientation, or the fact that he was an obnoxious prick, but more to do with the fact that my previous victims had been young, beautiful women, the sort of women who made an impact wherever they went. Their deaths would terrify women all over the country, a tightening fist around the hearts of everyone who had known them. That was the sort of fear that created legends, the sort of fear I lived to create. But no one would miss this guy. No one would fear me because of his death.

There had been others, many others in fact, even ones that I hadn't met online or in the classifieds, and there were many reasons why I had not been linked with their deaths. I once killed a neighbor who had persisted to annoy me with loud music night and day. I crept in through a window the morning after a party and beat him to death with a baseball bat while his girlfriend was passed out on the sofa. I left no evidence and no fingers were pointed my way. In my earlier days, when my confusion regarding my sexuality was a little more problematic, I paid to have sex with a prostitute. She saw my youth and my naïveté and she made an incorrect assumption that she could manipulate me and rob me. She told me that if I didn't pay her double, then her pimp would beat me up. She was dirty. A skinny addict with rotting teeth and a rotten soul. And although I enjoyed killing her, I didn't want the credit.

The talkative, egotistical prick whose penis I now had in a jar had less than a hundred quid in his wallet, inside which was a picture of his wife and two kids. They looked happy, but death had a way of bringing the skeletons out of the closet, and although he would have preferred it a different way, he would get his chance to be the openly gay man that he professed to be. There were a number of credit cards in there that I would find a use for, and in his other pocket was a vial of morphine and a capped syringe. It wasn't what I had been expecting, but perhaps it fit the bill. He probably thought it was cooler and more upmarket than heroin or cocaine.

The parts that identified him would be eradicated and the rest, whatever was left, would be tossed into a bath of highly corrosive acid. His existence had been extinguished in a heartbeat, and his memory would be wiped off the face of the earth in a similarly short time. Everything that he had done, everything that he had tried to be and everything that he ever would be, was now pointless, cast into the dust of life along with the physical remains that tied him there. The idea of life being so fickle scared a lot of people, but it fascinated me. Life is something that we hold so dear, something that literally means everything to us, yet it is so fragile, so fleeting, so utterly pointless. My existence will be a little less pointless, of course, and when I do slip off this mortal coil, my memory will remain.

———

"That's some pretty potent stuff you're buying."

A fellow customer was looking at me. A peppy prick with a 1950s quiff and clothes better suited to an aging hillbilly with a passion for chewing tobacco and fucking with the English language was looking at me. He was judging my purchases as though I weren't carrying a knife and a severe distaste for the human race.

"Excuse me?" I said.

"The acid." He nodded toward the vat I had just removed from the shelf. "Are you trying to hide a corpse or something?"

Why, do you want to volunteer?

I returned his smile and gave him the cheery small talk he sought. "Yeah, my wife. I've finally had it with her cooking and figure I'd make a fresh start."

He chuckled. "Going for a newer model, eh?"

"Of course."

"Can't blame you, I need one of those myself. Well, good luck to you."

I smiled as he walked away. "You too," I said, wondering if I should follow him, kill him, and give his wife the opportunity to get herself a new husband. Small talk is the bane of my existence, giving people the assumed right to butt into other people's lives. Altruism and politeness is dead, and once everyone realizes that and gets on the same page, then the world will be a better place.

I dropped the vat on the counter and dug out some cash, stolen from the wallet of the guy who talked me to death and then provided me with a little memento for my collection. There was something so wonderfully ironic about using his money to pay for his eradication.

"Lovely day out there, isn't it?"

For fuck's sake. Not another one.

"Yeah," I said vaguely. "Sun and everything. All good."

Now fuck off before I kill you and burn your store to the ground.

He gave me a serious look, wondering for a moment if I was playing around, if there was something wrong with me, or if that was just how I talked. It was probably a mixture of all three.

"You hear about the news?"

Nothing like a vague question to force me into a conversation I don't want to be in.

"No, what news?"

"The Masquerade," he said, immediately grabbing my attention. "They reckon they know who it is."

"Bollocks."

He gave me another look and I tried to smile away my snappy response. It seemed to work.

"It's true. A detective reckons he has the case all figured out, some Keats bloke or something. He says he knows who it is."

That amused me. I liked Keats, but he didn't have a clue. He was one of the detectives assigned to my case. One of many, but the one I liked the most. I made it my business to learn about my adversaries and I knew all there was to know about him. I knew that his wife had died many years ago. I knew he had a daughter named Annabelle and a son named Damian. I knew he had a mother who lived not too far from the dive I once called home and, thanks to his daughter's willingness to open up to strangers online, her desire to post everything she ate, thought, and did on social media pages, I knew that his kids hated him and had pissed off to the grandmother's house, or whoever else would have them, at every opportunity. I also knew he wasn't capable of finding me. If he were, then I wouldn't be buying a vat of acid to wipe another corpse from the face of the earth.

The shop owner hadn't finished talking. "You remember that spree killing in that little town a few years go? Whitegate, I think it was called."

My face dropped at that point. I was sure it was noticeable, but I couldn't help it. "Vaguely," I said slowly, fearing the worst.

"Well, he reckons The Masquerade and that lad are two and the same."

"Fuck off."

"It's true."

Fuck. Off.

I paid for the acid and left the shop as quickly as I could. I dumped my purchase into the backseat of my car and headed for the newsstand across the street.

"Oh, you again."

It was the prick who had served me the previous day. I had kept my cool then, but as I picked up a newspaper and he waited to berate me, I knew I wouldn't be able to do it again. Lester Keats was plastered all over the front page and my heart sank into the pit of my stomach when I saw the headline: WHITEGATE SPREE-KILLER IS BACK.

How the fuck did he figure it out?

I ripped open the first page, quickly scanning the story. The news report hadn't come from Lester. It had been leaked by an inside source. There were no official lines on it yet, but there didn't need to be. They were right—they had their man and it would take a miracle to divert their attention from the truth. It didn't mean much for me—the memory of the boy I had been was just as elusive as the man I became—but it was the first sign of weakness, the first indication that the people in charge of finding me weren't as incompetent as I thought they were.

I jumped when I felt a hand on my shoulder. I dropped the newspaper and turned to see Scott, the shop assistant, standing next to me, his eyes flaring with determination. This was his moment to shine, his moment to do right and put the wrongdoers in their place. After all, I read a newspaper without paying. That was probably worthy of capital punishment in his eyes. This was his chance to become a vigilante like the heroes in the comic books he so fervently masturbated to every night.

"I told you not to—"

I hit him. It was an instinctive response, and one borne of surprise and anger. I had let the moment get to me, taking it out on him in one swift and powerful blow. He fell backward and only just managed to maintain verticality before stumbling into a magazine rack. He held a hand to his face as a look of astonishment spread over his gaunt features.

It wasn't enough to put him down and he came at me, his eyes alight with vengeance and justice. I stopped him quickly by thrusting my hand into his throat. He dropped to the floor, choking and gagging, struggling to suck air into his lungs.

I bent down beside him, the adrenaline pumping, the anger still coursing through me. "I want to do so much more to you right now," I told him. "So count yourself lucky that I'm going to turn around and walk out of this shop."

"*You. Have. To. Pay. For. That,*" he spat in broken breaths, throwing a hand toward the paper in my hand.

I could feel the knife in my pocket, almost begging me to use it. Not since Darren Henderson had I wanted to kill someone so badly. I slid my hand into my pocket and felt the handle against my palm, but I was interrupted by the jingle-jangle of the bell above the door as someone entered the shop.

It was the man I had spoken to in the hardware store. He smiled when he saw me and then that smile vanished when he saw the shop assistant on his knees in front of me.

"Is everything okay here?" he asked.

I grinned and took my hand out of my pocket. "Asthma attack," I told him, standing up and brushing myself down. "He'll be fine."

I was furious and I wasn't used to sitting and stewing on my anger, I wasn't used to not being able to vent. I left the shop in a hurry, brushing past the baffled man in the doorway and listening to the choked gags of the flunky on the floor. I tossed the newspaper into the car, clambered behind the wheel, and then hit the road. The have-a-go-hero in the newsstand wouldn't feel my vengeance, certainly not in the way I wanted, but someone would.

2

I drove for hours, my destination first unknown, but later very clear. I cruised through what passed for red light districts and what passed for prostitutes. These women didn't charge much, and you definitely got what you paid for.

"Twenty bucks for the lot," one of them barked into the car as I approached and rolled down the window.

"The lot?"

She gestured to herself, the yellowed fingers on her emaciated hands seemingly pointing out her worth.

"Twenty bucks can buy me a lot in this day and age. What makes you think I should spend it on you?"

"Excuse me?" She was even uglier when she looked confused. She could have made a decent living as an extra in a horror movie, or scaring teenagers away from shopfronts.

"Why should I purchase your services over all of these fine ladies?" I asked, nodding through the front window to the small cluster of half-naked woman gathered around a lamppost and looking like they were one degree away from losing a limb.

"Are you right in the head?"

I couldn't help but laugh at that one. I rolled up the window and intended to ignore her, but she banged on it. She had an impatient look on her face that made her look even uglier than when she was confused. She really didn't have much going for her.

"Are you just gonna drive away?" she asked when I rolled the window down again. "Are you just here to fuck with me? I'm a professional woman, you know. I deserve respect."

I *was* just fucking with her. I felt better about myself when I talked to people like her. Society was pretty uninspiring to begin with, but people like her were the worst. They were the leeches, the pests. They were not parasites, as many would suggest—parasites are admirable creatures. They take control of the living and they live through them, essentially hiding in the shadows, stealing their nutrients, drinking their life-force. I was a parasite, and I was proud to call myself that, but these, these *people* would need to go through several stages of evolution to be deemed worthy of kissing the ground that I pissed on.

"You're a professional, are you? Well, why don't you give me your business card and I'll get back to you if—"

I paused when she reached into her bosom and produced a card. At that moment, she had more of my respect than I had ever given to anyone like her. I took the card and gave her a nod of approval.

Touché, you dirty little pest.

She stood back and waited for me to drive away, a proud expression on her gaunt face. That was one of the few expressions that didn't make her look ugly, but it was also likely to be the one she used the least. I actually felt some sort of inclination to do something with her, even something sexual, but I reminded myself how unpleasant that would be and moved on.

I had a destination by then, but I took things at a leisurely pace, using the time to calm myself and stop myself from doing anything stupid. As superior as I was to many other people in this world, I was still human and therefore susceptible to human emotions. I got angry, I made mistakes. The only difference was that

I could often anticipate that anger and act accordingly. I was in tune with my body and could see moments of rage coming. In the newsstand, the anger had been a surprise and I had acted out of line, but those moments were rare.

Even as a child, I had been able to control my emotions more than most, making me infinitely more intelligent and worthy than any of my peers. Of course, I was never deemed to be a particularly intelligent child. The intelligence was there; they just didn't see it. It was that cognitive superiority that had helped me restrain my anger when Darren and his half-witted friends had beaten me day after day. Instead of acting out, getting involved, and putting my plans into jeopardy, I had let them do as they wanted while I waited and plotted.

I had never excelled in my classes and although it wasn't intentional, I like to think that my subconscious mind stopped me from doing so, understanding the problems that would arise with being seen as an extraordinary child possessed of the greatly developed brain that I had.

I parked the car in a densely populated car park and made my way into the center of the town. This was a night-life hotspot, where several residents from nearby towns and villages spent the night on the dance floor. They saw it as the ultimate destination, the entertainment capital of their little world, but only because it had more than one nightclub and most of the bars served neon-colored, gasoline-strength booze for the price of a bottle of pop.

It was late evening and other than the bars and nightclubs nothing was open, indicating the cars in the parking lot belonged to the drinkers and that even without my assistance a few of the dim-witted locals were going to die tonight. I encountered some of them on the street—young males wearing matching short-sleeved shirts, despite the arctic conditions, and stinking to high heaven of knock-off deodorant. They had clearly been bathing in the stuff, but it was probably cheaper than bath foam.

The women were just as bad. Dressed like the prostitute I had run into earlier, only with higher heels and more perfume—a little more upmarket, but probably a lot cheaper. By the end of the night, they would be opening their legs for some deodorant-drenched bro because he bought them a bottle of Barcadi Breezer.

"Take a picture, it lasts longer," one of the bitches barked when she saw me looking at her legs, visible underneath a ridiculously short skirt and reddened from the intense cold. They looked like a pair of chorizo sausages and probably tasted just as funky.

"You got a problem?" she persisted when I didn't reply and continued to stare. The night had only just begun but she was already drunk. It was a shame I wouldn't be there to witness the moment she wet herself, passed out on the street, and was felt up by a horny bouncer with low standards.

"I have many problems," I told her. "And clearly I'm not the only one."

"What's that supposed to mean?"

She was getting louder and shriller by the moment. She was with two friends, both the same age, with the same dress sense and the same level of drunkenness. She was clearly the outspoken one, the one likely to brand herself as the "crazy one," which to her was a good thing. She was the one who got drunk every weekend, vomited and shit on herself, and then proclaimed it to be a great night. In her eyes, she was the life and soul of the party, the optimistic and happy one; in the eyes of everyone else, she was a miserable, annoying tart, only devoid of self-loathing because she had yet to realize just how much the world hated her.

"Save your anger for tonight," I told her. "When the guy you suck off in the alleyway tells you that no, he doesn't want your phone number and no, he doesn't want to see you again. Save it for the bouncer who refuses to let you into the club because of the vomit and cum stains on your shirt. Save it for your reflection in the mirror tomorrow morning when you realize that your night on the town cost you half a month's rent, two friends, a brand new dress, and all the self-esteem you've ever managed to muster since you dragged your skanky ass out of high school."

Her mouth was agape, but her friends were smiling. I had either hit the nail on the head or they had been waiting for someone to put her in her place for a long time. She stuttered and stumbled and then, realizing that she was about to lose face, she increased the volume and the tempo of her voice. "What did you say?"

I laughed, shook my head, and walked away.

"Yeah, you better fucking run," I heard her shout before immediately bragging to her friends.

I thought about having a drink in one of the clubs, but failed to find one that wasn't filled with sweaty idiots. Instead I sat on a nearby bench and watched the hordes of revelers go about their business. I saw the worst of the worst, the shit scraped from the barrel of life and left to ferment in this country's small towns and cities. The vast majority of them were young, often no older than twenty, and a large number were in their early teens. I had no issue with underage drinking, far from it. If these kids were going to turn into their parents, and most of them did, then the sooner they killed themselves, the better.

One of those kids caught my eye, but for reasons that weren't entirely random. She was young, blonde, cute. She was naturally beautiful, that much was evident, but that beauty had been scarred and blemished by makeup an inch thick. It was obvious that her mother was either just as dimwitted as she was, or that she had passed away years ago and hadn't been there to tell her daughter the basics of how not to look like a whore.

She was with a couple of female friends and, although it seemed like everyone in the town shopped in the same budget store, she looked a little classier—her clothes matching the beauty that was hidden underneath the layers of powder. Her legs and breasts were showing—most of the latter seemed to be the result of some sort of stuffing, and this hadn't gone unnoticed by a group of men who were smoking outside one of the clubs. They began catcalling like drunken hyenas as soon as they saw them. The girls ignored them at first, but as they got closer, the calls intensified and the horny males became impatient. I sensed that something was afoot, possibly a show of aggression, or even violence, so my attention was piqued.

Although intimidated and disgusted, the females didn't stop showing off their plumage—their butts swinging as they walked, their hands stroking the curve of their hips or resting on the bulge of their breasts. The males grew increasingly horny as the females crossed their territory, then the battle began. The alpha male touched the alpha female's backside. It seemed harmless enough, but in the animal kingdom it is sly and backhanded moves like this that precipitate the biggest conflicts.

"Hey, bitch, it ain't my fault. If it's on show then it's mine to touch."

The dominant male misjudges the situation and instead of trying to resolve it, his youth and his inexperience only serve to exacerbate it.

"My ass is not a fucking toy!"

The fiery female stands her ground, backed by her clan.

"Come on, calm down, I'm only playing. What say we go around the back of the club and I show you just how sorry I am?"

And still, despite the impending violence, the male cannot stop thinking about his penis.

As I sat and grinned to myself, the girl whose ass was at the center of the debate swung for the man whose penis was trying to get inside it. He hadn't been expecting that. None of his friends had either. It seemed to come as a surprise even to *her* friends. I know her sort, though: motherless family, a dad in a position of authority, a lot of anger and resentment inside of her. It was only a matter of time. The punch floored the aggressor with the wandering hand and as the girl tended to her knuckles and her friends cheered her on, the boy's friends wondered if they were going to be next while trying to pretend that they didn't know the guy on the floor and that his proximity to them was pure coincidence.

I decided to step in, and just as the lad scrambled to his feet and attempted to launch into an attack, I grabbed him and pinned him to the wall with force. The air left his lungs on impact and a gasp erupted behind me as I took everyone by surprise.

"Now then, you weren't planning on hitting a girl there, were you?"

"She hit me first!" he screamed.

I turned to face the girl whose eyes seemed to twinkle when she saw me. She was impressed and that was just what I wanted. "Is that true?" I asked.

She nodded.

"Now now, you should know the rules, as well," I told her. "No hitting girls."

She laughed at that and as I turned to look for the aggressor's friends, I noticed they had already vanished. I let go of his collar and stepped back, knowing that wouldn't be the end of it. "Now, piss off and follow your friends to whatever rock they crawl under."

He paused, looked me over, and then immediately set upon the girl again. I heard her gasp, because even though I knew exactly what he was going to do, she didn't. I caught him on the jaw before he made it to her and he dropped like a sack of shit. He was out cold, and she was impressed. Job done.

The unconscious guy on the floor—several minutes away from pissing himself and an hour away from having penises drawn on his head by drunken revelers—could have learned a lot from me.

"Thank you," she said, beaming.

"Nah, you didn't need me," I told her. "I saw what you did, you clearly had him."

She blushed and I met her stare for a moment. I saw her play with her hair, avert her eyes, and generally look like an awkward girl lacking in self-confidence, all signs that she liked me and that my plan had worked. Attraction is a strange beast, but one that is very easy to manipulate. Love and lust cause an increased heart rate, perspiration, and general feelings of unease. These feelings are also stimulated through fear and, if you can scare a girl when she first meets you, then you can trick her mind into thinking she's in love with you. It's not quite as simple as that, otherwise rapists would have a very easy job, but those are the basics. The human brain is very stupid. Mine is not, but only because I'm not weakened by love or lust.

"Anyway, I have to go now," I told her.

"Oh." She seemed shocked and disappointed. "You're not coming inside?"

"I'm actually about to call it a night. I've been working all day. I just want to kick back, relax, have a few quiet drinks in a quiet environment." I gestured toward the noise roaring through the closed doors of the club behind us.

"Oh, well, maybe—"

"You can go back to her place," one of her friends butted in, doing what friends do best.

"No," she began, defending herself. "I couldn't ask him, I mean he wouldn't . . ."

"If there's free drink, some peace and quiet, and some company from a brave and beautiful woman, then it could be just what I need," I said.

She beamed, her eyes glinting. "My family will be there, but they won't mind if we're quiet. And I have some whiskey . . ."

"Perfect, and I'm as quiet as they come. Should I drive or do you want to?"

"You have a car?"

"Of course."

The smile on her face suggested that the deal was done.

"So, what's your name, anyway?" she asked as we left her friends to step over the idiot in the doorway and enter the club.

"Darren, you?"

"Anna."

"Ah, that's a beautiful name. It suits you."

"Thanks."

I was so sickly sweet that I thought I was going to choke on my own affability, but the job was done. She was just the right amount of sweet and naughty; innocent and tainted. And there was something else there, as well, all of which would ensure I would have my satisfaction.

3

—

nna took me to what I assumed was her bedroom, although it didn't have the fittings and fixtures you would expect of a teenage girl's room. There was a double bed, a set of powerful speakers fixed to an iPod dock, and an electronic contraption that provided a kaleidoscope of mood lighting. That was all we needed.

She was young, but she was definitely experienced. She gave me a whiskey and led me to the bedroom where we sat and talked. They were empty conversations and nothing was gained through them, but they served to put her at ease and to assure that we both wanted what came next. She kissed me and teased me on the bed, running her hand through my hair, down my chest, and then resting it on my thigh. Then she stood up, turned on some soft soul music, and began to slowly and sensually dance. I did taste some alcohol on her breath but she wasn't drunk. Her confidence was all natural.

She danced with her eyes closed, each of us in our separate worlds and yet linked together in one moment. She swayed to the music, her hips bouncing to the beats, her hands stroking her waist and her thighs to the rhythm.

She wasn't wearing much but she began to strip. First she kicked off her shoes, and then she peeled off her dress to expose the soft flesh underneath. She opened her eyes and looked at me, making sure I was paying attention, making sure I was enjoying myself. She continued to dance and move in her underwear, advancing on me, teasing me with her outstretched leg before pressing her breasts close to my face and then planting a soft kiss on my forehead.

When she stepped back, she removed her bra and then, watching me all the while, she took off her underwear.

"Are you ready for me, my hero?"

"Oh yes, I'm ready."

She climbed on top of me, her genitalia pressing against the crotch of my pants. She wrapped her arms around my neck and I saw that twinkle in her eye as she looked at me.

"Is that a gun in your pocket or are you just happy to see me?" She giggled and then pressed her hand against the bulge as she went in for a kiss.

She paused when her fingers brushed against something unexpected and she pulled back, the twinkle gone from her eyes.

"Actually, it's a knife."

Her eyes widened in horror and then, seconds later, she gasped, sucking in a breath through tightly pressed lips as the blade of the knife punctured her abdomen.

She made a move to climb off me and I helped by picking her up and tossing her on the bed. The blood had already soaked into my jeans, but it was more tolerable than the wetness from her vagina. I had been caught up in the moment and the thought of consenting to her nakedness had crossed my mind, but not for long.

She seemed too surprised to scream, and she merely lay on the bed, her widened eyes on her stomach as it gushed with blood. I climbed on top of her, straddling her as she had straddled me. There would be no kissing or fondling involved this time, though. I was there only to end her misery.

When Anna was dead, I switched off the radio and left the room in search of the other occupants. It had been a long time since I had enjoyed a kill so much—the buildup, the tension, the climax, everything was perfect. It reminded me of the night I had lost my virginity, the night I had entered Darren's house and killed his family, knowing he was out there and incapable of stopping me. Of course, Darren was more deserving than she could ever be, but as much as I enjoyed taking the lives of those who deserved death, those who served little purpose on this planet, murder was murder and I enjoyed it either way. This one was also personal, and the personal ones were infinitely more satisfying.

There was a younger boy in another one of the bedrooms. He had his back to the door, a set of headphones pressed to his head, his attention absorbed by an idiot box in the corner. He was talking to his friends through the headpiece, and with the sound of the game, and of his friends bellowing in his ear, he never heard me coming. The room was thick with smoke and as I crept up behind him, I saw the culprit on the floor next to him, a smoking bong. Like his sister the whore, he would die doing what he loved the most.

I didn't remove the headpiece when I slit his throat, knowing that his gurgling would be incorrectly interpreted by his dimwitted friends, who would probably assume he had taken a break to masturbate over one of his sister's friends.

I thought the adults in the house would be sleeping and was surprised when I walked in the master bedroom to see an elderly woman doing yoga on the floor. She was twisted into an odd position and saw me enter through a gap in her outstretched legs. She was confused at first, but she reacted more quickly than Anna, immediately springing to her feet.

She raced to the other side of the room and before she even uttered a word, she was throwing an assortment of objects at me, including a mobile phone and a remote control. The room was small and eventually she cornered herself between the bed and the window.

"Please, I have money, I have jewelry," she begged.

"I want neither."

I grabbed her throat with my free hand and then stuck the knife under her ribcage. I spent a little longer on her than I did the others, confident she was the last one in the house and that I had all the time in the world. I left my mark on her body and, when I had finished, I left something else in her room.

———

"... *local police have been assisted in their efforts by Lester Keats, the detective on The Masquerade case who was recently quoted as saying that The Masquerade is in fact a former local, pictured here just weeks before he killed eight people in town nearly fifteen years ago today. Herman, as you may recall, went to . . ."*

I stared at the image on the television screen above the bar, and then at my reflection in the glass behind it. There was a resemblance, there was no denying that, but not much. I had grown my hair, and as much as I despised having hair on my face, I also had a short beard and mustache. My eyes hadn't changed much, but that wasn't a lot to go on. Those who had known me back then would probably be able to recognize me, but I had no friends and I had killed what was left of my family. The pictures no longer did me justice, they never had. After the incident in Whitegate, I went into hiding. I wore a wig until my hair grew, I let my facial hair grow. I also lost weight, turning puppy fat into muscle, serving both to make me unrecognizable and to make me stronger, more agile, and more capable. The problem is—

"... *These images, which depict the killer as he is believed to look now, were given to us by the detective. He used pictures from Herman's childhood and family to piece together this photofit . . ."*

My face fell when I saw the image onscreen. It was luck and nothing more—they had given me a beard that didn't look too dissimilar to the one I had.

"You've got to be fucking kidding me," I mumbled.

I burned everything in the fire, there were no traces of my old life left. I had no friends, no family, no—

"Fuck." An image of an old and senile lady popped into my head. "How could I forget?"

"They say that's the first sign of craziness, you know."

I turned to see a red-faced, bulbous-nosed drunk staring at me with a friendly smile. He looked like a prune and stank like a brewery.

"Really? I thought that was drinking whiskey at three in the afternoon."

Rudolph chuckled. "No, that's the first sign of drunkenness. Name's Marcus, what's yours?" He held out a hand. I stared at him and wondered whether I really wanted to touch him. His face changed, a look of recollection swamped it, and I knew immediately that he had seen my eyes. He had seen the beard. He knew who I was.

"I know you." He withdrew his hand.

No. You don't.

I smiled faintly and turned back to the bar. The barman was now watching me, as was someone else who stood in an open doorway to the back room with a curious expression on his young face. Neither of them had seen the television above the bar, but it didn't matter, I was outnumbered. I wouldn't be able to kill the guy next to me and then make it over the bar in time to take down the two barmen. I had sufficiently vented my anger earlier in the day, but more people would need to die because of those television reports, because of Lester Keats.

"I really do," he pushed.

For your sake, I hope that you don't.

I wasn't convinced I could take them all down without creating a fuss, but I would certainly try. The one who couldn't keep his mouth shut would be the easiest, and once I took him down then—

"I've got it!" he barked.

I turned around to face him, my hand tightening around the knife in my pocket. The same blade that had, only hours before, glistened with the tainted blood of a young and promiscuous girl.

"You're Pamela Brown's son, right?"

A moment of silence followed, during which he gave me an open-mouthed, expectant stare. I could sense the same expression on the faces of the two men behind the bar as they all waited for my acknowledgment.

"Yeah, that's me," I said with a vague smile, finally allowing myself to shake his hand.

That's how these imbeciles' minds work. They recognize you as a familiar face, but in their search for the correct memory, their brain twists and turns through all of the failed ones until eventually it gets tired, stops, looks around, and picks the closest one. I went from "spree killer and potential serial killer" to "friend's son" in the time it took this imbecile to take a sip of whiskey.

"So, what are you doing back in town?" He looked infinitely more cheery now that he had a friendly face to gossip with.

I stood and drank what was left of my juice. "I was actually just leaving."

"Oh, okay." He looked genuinely disappointed, sensing the loneliness bearing down on him again. Back to the mindless television, the succession of watered-down whiskeys and the habitual self-loathing. "Are you in town for the holidays?

I frowned at him as I slipped my jacket on. "Holidays?"

He gave a short laugh, an utterance of disbelief. "Well, it *is* Christmas."

"Oh."

That went some way toward explaining the fact that the icy, bollock-biting wind that ripped through the country brought with it the sound of tuneless carols sung by hopeless cretins. It also explained the ads and the fact that everywhere I looked I saw posters, commercials, and flyers for children's toys, comedy DVDs, and cover albums sung by nameless celebrities with all the singing talent of a castrated Wookiee. Yes, of course, Christmas. How could I have forgotten?

Christmas also meant that the anniversary of my first kill was coming up, but that was something I knew, something I would never forget. The fact that it was due not long after I had been outed as The Masquerade only served to increase both my excitement and everyone else's fear.

"So, you here for long?"

"Maybe," I said.

"You going to see your mother?"

"Grandmother, actually."

"I thought she was dead," he said, looking a little confused.

"Give it time."

4

—

River Acres: a paradoxical piece of suburbia that should only be viewed from the outside.

Her rows and rows of detached bungalows look serene, silent, and strangely empty. Her well-manicured lawns glisten dewfully under a pre-morning shower; her cobbled driveways devoid of cars. Gnomes and flowers frolic in unhindered harmony on the lawns, watched from a single large window where a thin shroud of fabric shades the viewer like a ghostly bridal veil.

Her streets are silent. A juxtaposition from her neighbors, where the young, the uninhibited, and the jobless walk, talk, and play to while away their empty days. River Acres feels like a ghost town, a single street lost to the world. River Acres is where the old go to die.

At the middle house, down the empty driveway, and across an empty but surprisingly well-maintained lawn, I paused at a front door that looked built to suppress a medieval siege. It was a single thick block of unbreakable wood with a minuscule peephole in the center. I pressed a buzzer to its side, dropped my head toward a small speaker, and waited.

"Hello," a voice croaked as a static charge hissed through the intercom.

"Grandma," I said with my finger firmly pressed, feeding my flesh with a small static shock. "It's me. Herman." I cringed at that. It didn't feel real. I hadn't used that name in years.

There was a pause, as if she was trying to work out who Herman was and why he should know her. She coughed into the intercom, groaned something unappreciative, and then said: "Hold on."

I waited for a few minutes. Across the street, in one of the symmetrical houses, an elderly man watched me from his living room window. His hand pressed the net curtain against the wall, his spectacled eyes boring suspiciously into me. I gave him a friendly wave. He gave me an uncommitted nod and continued to stare.

The door clicked open and a small, frail face popped through the gap, smiling unsurely at me. I grinned back.

"You wanna let me in?"

She paused, weighing the question, then she stepped back, shifting her weight slowly out of the way before pulling the door open after her. I walked straight into the living room and took a seat on a sofa reserved for guests and therefore never used. A dust cloud popped into the air as I plonked onto the old and tattered leather.

She clawed her way across the floor after me, struggling with every methodical step. She lay down her cane by the side of a high-backed chair with all the necessary amenities—including a built-in chamber pot—placed around it. She gave me a big smile, her wrinkled face like a depressed bulldog.

"So . . ." her thin blue lips mouthed slowly. "What can I do you for?"

I gave her my warmest smile and then told her, "I'm here to kill you, Grandma."

"That's nice," she said genuinely.

I nodded. "I think I'll also take all your money."

She studied my face and my lips as I spoke, the smile still on her face. "Okay," she agreed.

"And then I'm going to cut up your corpse and post you bit by bit to every one of your nosy fucking neighbors."

She nodded and looked away. A wooden tray with more compartments than a stationery cupboard sat in front of the chair on a set of squeaky, silver wheels. On its top shelf rested an assortment of magazines, TV guides, and a large box of biscuits. She picked up the box and thrust it toward me.

I shook my head. "I prefer to murder on an empty stomach," I told her.

Her arm remained stretched; her eyes still studied me intently.

I sighed deeply, shifted forward on the edge of the sofa, and raised my voice as loud as I could. "No thank you, Grandma," I yelled.

She finally retracted her arm. I dropped backward into the comfort of the sofa.

She was hard work. She had been deaf most of her life. My father had bought her a hearing aid a few years before he died and she wore it when she saw fit, which was never. Since his death, it had been gathering dust in one of her many drawers along with keepsakes of a family long since dead and a life long since lost, and her vast collection of biscuits. It didn't really matter anymore; no one came to visit her. Except, of course, for nosy detectives who couldn't keep their opinions to themselves.

I shifted forward on my seat again, a thought suddenly occurring to me. "Who cuts your grass?" I asked her loudly.

She grinned back.

I rolled my eyes, lifted my voice higher. "Who cuts your grass?"

"Glass?" she said with a confused look at the window.

"*Grass!*"

"Grass, dear?"

"Yes," I said with an exaggerated nod. "Who cuts it?"

She looked from me to the window and then back again. She grinned, nodded, and then fell silent.

"Ah, for fuck's sake," I said, settling back into the chair and picking up a newspaper.

She owned the house, but I doubted she paid anyone to cut the grass. She didn't leave the house and I wasn't sure she was capable of using the phone since it didn't have an amplifier attached. There was a good chance she would assume it was broken or that people were constantly hanging up on her.

The council probably maintained the houses in the street at the expense of the government, but I didn't want to push for answers. It wasn't that important to me and I didn't know where the conversation would end up.

She slowly rose from her chair, groaning and heaving with every increment. I didn't make a move to help her; we both had too much pride for that.

"I'll put the kettle on," she told me with a meek smile.

I grinned back over the top of the newspaper. I had been reading a piece on politics that was topical three months ago and was now probably just as outdated as the milk she would pour into my tea.

She used to have home help, and she probably still did. They were nurses who were supposed to visit her on a regular basis, making sure she didn't choke to death on her own sense of self-loathing. But I doubted they bothered to visit and I was sure they didn't care. The newspaper would have been brought by one of them, right before they fished through her purse, pissed in her mouthwash, and shat in her kettle.

"Milk, two sugars, right?" she asked as she bumbled her way toward the kitchen.

"Not for me, Grandma. I'm good."

She mumbled something in reply. She probably hadn't heard me and had imagined her own answer. She would make the tea anyway.

At the edge of the living room lay a tattered old rug, as old as she was and just as weathered. She crossed onto its surface like a toddler on the first ominous step of a mighty staircase. When she moved across it, clumps of it moved with her, her bony legs and beaten cane kicking up the material like some miserable, malfunctioning, mechanical toy. When she had passed the rug, it looked like a tartan sand dune.

I rose to flatten it, leveling it out. She always looked where she was going. She took so long to move that her eyes never carelessly left her path, but if she noticed it and tried to rectify it herself she'd be there all day.

I imagined her not noticing the bumpy rug and envisioned her tripping over it on her way back, ending her life and my dilemma by splitting her head open on the sideboard, or simply crumbling to dust as she clattered against the solid floor, her bones capitulating inside her decrepit body.

That wasn't fair to her, though. I was there to kill her, but she deserved something a little less grotesque than that.

She gave me a steaming cup of tea, which had almost cooled and emptied by the time she hobbled over and lowered it toward me. I took it with both hands, gave her a smile, and then sipped as I watched her hobble back to the kitchen to fetch her own cup. Before she returned, I emptied the tepid tea into a flowerpot.

"What's wrong with the door?" I said at the top of my voice.

She mumbled something into her tea, took a sip, swallowed, and then pointed to the intercom system that rested on the arm of her chair. It was a normal-sized phone with a huge red flashing light, presumably to alert her when the buzzing tone inevitably failed.

"Knackered," she said with a dismal shrug.

"Isn't there someone who can fix it?" I shouted.

She grinned back.

"*Fix it!*" I clarified with a yell.

"I can't, dear," she told me. "I'm not very good with that sort of thing."

I glared at her for a while, mentally taking back my previous thoughts about her not deserving to die on the crumpled carpet.

"A man was here to see you a little while ago," she told me.

"I know."

"A policeman."

"I know. And you gave him all of my photographs, didn't you?"

"I gave him all the pictures of you as a little boy, I did. Odd that he wanted them, wasn't it?"

"It was, yes. And it was even more odd that you gave them to him. What if he was a pervert?" I said at the top of my lungs, making sure I was heard.

"Well," she said with a shrug. "It's not my place to judge, is it?"

She was an amusing woman, but she was on her last legs and she was going to become a nuisance. She had probably already done all that she could do to get in my way, but I was worried about my father, about what she knew and what she would give away. I doubted that she knew about him being The Butcher, but that didn't mean she wasn't holding onto some incriminating evidence that would implicate him.

My dad was dead and a small part of me wanted the world to know what a great man he was. I wanted them to know that he was the man who terrified a nation for a decade, but then they would also find out how he died. They would find out about his life. If they knew that the beast from their nightmares had wet the bed as a child, been involved in a difficult marriage, and then died of a heart attack, he would lose his edge somewhat.

"I was wondering," I said. "Are you scared of dying?"

She shook her head immediately. "I welcome it, son. My life isn't much of a life. No one comes to see me, no one treats me like a human being, no one cares anymore." I was rather impressed by that. Times had changed; in the past, a lot of what she said was tedious or obscene, she never did profound. "Also, I shit myself the other day and the stench was unbearable."

I sighed.

"When your guts start producing that sort of toxic waste," she continued, "and your ass doesn't have the power to keep it in, then you know you're not long for this world."

"Uh huh," I said, nodding slowly. "So, how would you like to die? Hypothetically."

"Hypothetically?" she said, twisting her face. "No, no, that sounds far too brutal for me. I'd much rather go in my sleep."

"What—"

"Or as I'm being ravaged by a big black man with a monstrous penis."

"Hmm."

"I could go either way."

I spent the next few hours with my grandmother and I actually enjoyed the time. My throat was a little hoarse from all the talking, and I was sure that half of what I shouted was missed, but she seemed to enjoy herself and I tolerated much of it. She reminded me of my father, her son-in-law, a man I hadn't thought too long and hard about over the years, but a man I respected.

We watched television together and she gave me a running commentary on the latest happenings in soap operas, before offering her opinions on the news. It seemed she had very little understanding of what was going on in the world, but as far as I could tell, she hated everyone in it. From minorities and immigrants, to musicians, celebrities, and even the entire southern hemisphere, which she insisted wasn't to be trusted because they couldn't even get their seasons in the right order. I hadn't seen the woman for years, but I found myself admiring her.

As soon as darkness fell, she drifted off to sleep and I made my move. She had plenty of strong narcotics in the house but most of them were in tablet form, and I didn't want her to spend her final few moments choking down a handful of tablets before waiting for them to kick in. I had a small vial of morphine I had taken from my homosexual fling that would be perfect for her.

I filled up a syringe, bought from a local pharmacy, and then searched for a vein on her arm. She looked so peaceful as she slept. I pricked her skin and injected the drug. I then apologized, said my final good-bye, and waited.

She never opened her eyes again. Within a matter of minutes, she had stopped breathing.

5

"appy holidays!" she called with a joyful wave. "Have a good Christmas!"

I hate that. There is nothing wrong with a simple goodbye, or even a smile to punctuate the end of the conversation and the point where the parties involved can respectfully move on. She doesn't want me to have a happy Christmas—a happy Christmas for me is one spent ripping her throat open and watching her peppy joy gush onto her cream carpets.

I grinned back, hiding a sneer. I instinctively looked to the case I carried. It looked nondescript, harmless. I could easily pass as a businessman, a smiling, caffeine-fueled solicitor off to ruin someone else's life and set another criminal free, or a teacher set to poison the minds of more hopeless future criminals. But it stocked a lot more than papers, books, and the pursuit of the capitalistic dream.

She beamed at me as I dragged my attention back to her Prozac smile. "See you soon!" she said.

Fuck you, bitch.

She didn't even know who I was and had interpreted my vacant smile as a friendly invitation to a brief conversation. I knew who she was, although it had been fifteen years since I had last seen her and a lot had happened since then. She was the vicar's wife, born in Stepford with a stick up her ass and a silver spoon between her smugly pursed lips. She was everything I resented about the holidays and religion. I watched her with a look of utter contempt as she greeted the next person to pass her on the street, a look of reciprocated joy on both of their faces, a glimmer of something else on his. He was probably sticking it to her when her husband was at church sticking it to all the little choir boys. I knew the little cunt when I was growing up. I had sought solace in his church when Darren and his cretinous cronies were chasing me. I tried to hide in the confessional as the bullies waited outside. Instead of providing refuge and doing the Christian thing, he had thrown me to the lions. I still held a grudge, but that wasn't why I was here.

I turned from his wife and her fling in disgust, catching a snippet about some odious fucking newsletter. These people disgusted me—more skeletons in their closets than most and not an ounce of irony about their twisted little secret lives. It was for people like this that I wanted there to be an afterlife; a God and a devil. Just to know that when they arrived at the pearly gates, he was wiping away their smug expressions and sending them down to hell, where I'd be waiting for them, preparing to spend eternity perpetually murdering them.

I made my way to the top of the street, into the backroads and onto the path that led to the church. The Old Lady was a three-hundred-year-old piece of architectural brilliance that had once been a beacon of light and hope in my hometown, but had since degraded into a place of bullshit and blasphemy. Easter egg hunts; weddings between airheads who should be barred from marriage, never mind encouraged to procreate; and christenings for lower-class fuckwits who should have gone the way of a worthless Spartan child, thrown into a pit and left to die.

The Old Lady was still a home for the local religious types, who were thankfully few and far between. If I had been christened then I would have been christened there, but my father was no man of God and he was no hypocrite.

My grandmother lived on the outskirts of town. River Acres was untouched by the hellhole that was Whitegate and unspoiled by the detritus that lived there. I spent the night in a local B&B not too far from where she lived, but ventured into the town in the morning for the first time since the night I lost my virginity. I had no fond memories of what I had left behind, but as I sat on the bus and watched the wilderness rush by my window, I remembered the journey I had taken fifteen years ago, following the demise of my unfortunate uncle, the somewhat-accidental deaths of Darren's father and brother, and the joyous deaths of those four imbeciles. I had taken everything that I could carry, everything that was important to me or my father, and I had destroyed the rest. At the epicenter of the fire that destroyed my home were all of the things that I didn't want anyone to see, the things that could implicate my father as The Butcher.

I had always intended to get away unseen after my first murders, to be a shadow as my father had been, but that night I had been too impulsive. I had made far too many mistakes. I got lucky, and after that, I vowed never to act on impulse again.

In the years that followed, I did my best to change my appearance. This was aided by my growth into adulthood, and despite my young face having been all over the news at the time, no one ever made the connection. I became a creature of the night after that, and I took to wearing hoods, hats, and anything else that could shadow my face when I was out and about. I honed my skills, realized my mistakes, and learned from them. I had done well to practice restraint in the past but had failed in the moment, acting on impulse, so I learned to restrain myself and to think about my actions even during the kill.

That fear of being recognized and that obsession with disguise also led to my new persona, although the mask was there for witnesses and for CCTV, as I knew my victims would never live to tell anyone who I was. The mask was a mottled gray, a diseased skull. I found it in the house of one of my first victims, someone who had provided refuge, someone I had killed for money after they had tried to exploit me for something else. It wasn't spotted with blood or guts, it wasn't your typical Halloween mask, but it was chilling. It was a prop for a play, a rendition of Edgar Allan Poe's "The Masque of the Red Death." It had been a story I knew little about when I was younger, but one I became fascinated with after discovering the mask. That was purely coincidental—although the connection had been made by a few journalists—but in time, when the plague came, laid a path of devastation, and then departed, it would be clear to everyone.

The Old Lady church was tucked away in a grim and uninspiring swath of woodland that enclosed an overgrown graveyard. No one had been buried there for two hundred years; the names that hadn't been covered by moss and dirt, or lost to the elements, were forgotten, dying along with the people buried there.

Death had always struck me as a bizarre ritual. Nobody wanted to die and nobody wanted their loved ones to die, so life was all about clinging on in desperation and then staying around for as long as possible, in one form or another. There were only so many graveyards in the world, only so much space. The world wasn't growing, but people didn't stop dying.

I left the bright, fresh afternoon and entered the cold, spacious confines of the church. A place big enough to hold a congregation of hundreds, when a small shed with a few benches would probably suffice for the number of locals that actually gave a shit about religion.

I didn't like the feel of church. I never had. If my life were a horror film, no doubt I would be naturally deterred by churches and would burst into flames or erupt with buboes of biblical proportions just by crossing the threshold. But in reality they just felt cold, empty, and dead.

I took a seat in the center of a middle pew and drank in the dead surroundings and the religious symbolism. At the foot of the church, down the aisle where many men and women had begun a journey on the long road to divorce, there stood a large statue of Jesus, looking like a holy Vitruvian Man.

The image of Christianity. A man who capitulated under the efforts of a malicious army and a malignant friend. The symbol of the ultimate sacrifice, enough to win the respect of future generations, yet if he'd have killed his captors by shooting spears out of his ass he would have won more respect and followers. Even I would follow a man capable of such heroics, although I'd still have a hard time believing it just by reading a two-thousand-year-old book.

I have no problem with religion, nor do I have an issue with the people who practice it. It keeps them out of my way, out of society's way. They usually hole themselves up in big empty buildings, singing, preaching, and following rules laid out for them hundreds of years ago by people they've never seen but who definitely existed.

I do have a problem with the people who sit on the fence. If you believe in God and an afterlife, then good for you, just keep it to yourself until the question arises. But if you don't go to church, don't follow any dogma, and don't count yourself as religious, don't continue to sit on that fence when faced with the question of your belief. These people don't want to refute His existence on the off chance that He does exist and will smite them for not believing. Where's the sense in that? As if He suspects you don't believe but is waiting for you to vocalize your doubts before He strikes you down. "It would be stupid to think an omnipotent being exists who controlled the world and made everything, but fuck me if I'm gonna say he doesn't in case he unmakes me." These people need to get a fucking opinion and learn how to use it. They piss me off. If ambiguity isn't the death of them, then I fucking will be.

A middle-aged woman with a solemn expression entered the church with two meandering teenagers in her wake—probably her sons—their faces grim enough to indicate a recent bereavement. They looked old enough to be thinking on their own and living on their own, yet they seemed to follow her every step and her every word, still under her thumb, still following her rules and her commands. Their father had probably been mown down in the middle of his life, no doubt his own doing—a heart attack brought on by years of stress, the annoyance of raising two ugly kids with an ugly wife he couldn't stand, and a diet of cigarettes, beer, and animal fat. Death had probably been an escape for him, a way of getting away from a controlling, obsessive, and neurotic woman who was always one misplaced text message away from making a broth from his pet rabbit or chopping off his penis while he slept.

The trio slumped down the aisle. One of the boys looked up at me as they passed, an attempted smile on his ugly little face. I smiled back, feigned a look of understanding and pity. He trudged on.

They settled at the front of the church, kneeling before the statue of Jesus. Their savior, their God; the man who gave his life as a symbolic gesture to the human race but couldn't stop their loved one from eating one bacon sandwich too many.

They say people are sheep; not true. Sheep are smart. Sheep follow a black and white dog that clearly exists. Humans follow an invisible man in the sky that does not. I think when I was a kid, I may have entertained the idea of God—until a certain age I'm confident I did believe in him, falling for the dogma taught to me through a Church of England education and the half-assed religious ideals preached by early era children's television presenters. I also believed in Santa Claus and the tooth fairy, but I grew out of those beliefs around the same time I realized religion was also a crock of shit. Maybe the rest of the world has yet to grow up.

The vicar appeared from one of the back rooms with a smile of spiritual contentment on his face. He flashed a sympathetic look at the woman and her ugly kids. They all smiled back, their smiles forced, hers genuine. His eyes crossed to the empty congregation, and his eyebrows raised slightly when he saw me. He smiled and nodded, and I pretended I hadn't seen him. He wouldn't recognize me, there was no chance of that. Although, maybe if my face were covered in blood and I was being pummeled by half-witted hooligans he would.

I watched him meander around the front of the building. He placed a book down on an altar, calmly walked up to the single-parent family, said a few hushed words and hugged them in turn, his eyes on the mother's flat backside as it waddled to the first row and plonked dully onto the wooden pew. The vicar watched as her children joined her and then he turned away.

He disappeared into the confessional, ducking behind the curtain. There was no one on the other side, the velvet fabric split to reveal an empty seat in the dusty box. I contemplated slipping in. I had plenty of sins to confess, and no doubt I would enjoy listening to his reaction while I did so, but life was too short.

I looked around the church. The mourning family sat slumped on the first row, their heads in their chests, their hands in the praying position. I could see tears streaming down the woman's face, silent expressions on the faces of her sons. At the back of the room, an elderly man cradling a cane had entered the church to collect a leaflet and leave some coins in the collection plate. He was already on his way back out.

I had been seen by the family, the kid in particular, but it wouldn't matter; he wouldn't recognize me. He had other things on his mind. Keeping one eye on the mourning family and one on the feet of the vicar below the curtain, I clasped my hands around the handle of a screwdriver in my pocket, a six-inch steel shank comforted by a rubber easy-grip handle. Easy to carry, excusable if discovered, and much more precise and clinical for what I had in mind. It wasn't the only weapon I carried. In the case was a set of chef's knives, sharp and strong enough to sever steel. They were a little less convenient, a little harder to carry in my pocket, but they would come in handy later on.

I sidled on my backside to the edge of the row and rested the case on the floor, kicking it underneath one of the pews and making a mental note of its location for later. I took one last look around the church—the mother now muttering between her sobs, her children bearing the burden of her whispered regrets—and walked down the aisle, toward the confessional.

I ripped open the curtain with enough nonchalance to imply innocence should the situation not immediately suit me. The vicar hopped to his feet with a broad smile. No doubt he was preparing to tell me I had the wrong end, or that the toilets were further down, but it didn't matter—the situation was perfect.

I pulled the screwdriver out of my pocket, clenched a tight fist around the cushioned handle, and then thrust it upward. He didn't see the flash of steel as it skimmed the tip of his hyoid, realizing what was happening only when the delicate flesh of his throat sliced open like a ripe tomato.

The first thrust took it through the edge of his throat, where it drilled through the back of his tongue before boring up into his skull, cracking and wedging in the bone. A gurgle of desperation and surprise escaped his mouth. A trickle of blood ran down from the corner of his lips, tainting and staining his white dog-collar. A bubble of saliva, infused with a frothy drop of blood, grew out of his mouth like cherry bubblegum, popping when he tried to talk.

He was incapable of speech, but I doubted he had anything useful to say anyway. I drove the screwdriver further, to the hilt, the tip of my thumb touching the wound that the weapon had created, my nail plunging into the open flesh. A torrent of blood had already snaked down my hand, painting my clenched fist and my forearm.

He slumped against the back wall of the confessional with a hollow thud, his eyes rolled into the back of his head. He was finished. He was with his God now.

The screwdriver made a sucking sound as it popped out of his flesh. The wound sprayed fresh blood and I just managed to duck out of the way, watching as it coated the inside of the curtain.

I pulled him off the bench and shoved him underneath it. His body tucked nicely into the space there. His head was already beginning to drown in a pool of blood. I removed a cover from the bench—a thick nylon sheet—and stuffed it up against his lifeless face. The blood immediately soaked in. It was enough to hold it for now, but before long the blood would begin to seep out and leak toward the bottom of the curtain.

I heard the curtain next door being pulled closed, followed by the sound of a body sinking into creaking wood. There was someone else in the confessional.

"Bless me father, for I have sinned."

I didn't want anyone to discover the body. Soon the church would empty; I would have the time and the room to do what I had gone there to do.

I sat down, my calves pressed up against the dead vicar. There was a small wooden shutter between the two rooms. I peeled this back, keeping my head pressed up against the wall, out of sight. Behind the shutter was a corrugated mesh, thick enough to obscure my face from whoever happened to be looking.

The ugly kid who had smiled at me a few minutes ago was staring forward. I could see the side of his face, his huge nose, pointed chin—the profile of a kid who'd had all his respect for life bullied out of him at primary school.

I hoped I wouldn't have to give the ugly little fucker any advice. He looked no older than sixteen, around the same age as me when my own father had died, but he clearly wasn't heading down the same path and wasn't anything like the person I became. I doubted I could tell him to do as I did. He barely looked capable of tying his shoelaces.

"It's been three years since my last confession," the voice beyond the mesh continued.

"That's a long time."

"Well, I, I have been busy."

"Too busy for God?"

It's not every day you get to judge someone through the eyes and actions of a respected authority figure.

"No, no. Of course not."

"How old are you?" I asked.

"I—I'm sixteen, sir."

"And you still live with your parents?"

"Just my mother, sir."

I grinned. "Of course. Silly me." I shifted in my seat and twisted my face as the stench of death tickled the hairs at the back of my nostrils. "Do you think it's normal to live with your mother at that age? Do you think it's normal that you still do everything for her, that she still has you running around like her little slave?"

He seemed confused. "What do—how do you know?"

"Doesn't the bible say that He knows everything."

"Well, yes, *God* knows everything, but—"

"Are you a faithful child, my son?"

"Yes, of course, of course I am."

"Do you touch yourself at night?"

"What?" The ugly kid shot a look across at the mesh. I had snuck a peek, but I ducked back out of sight when I saw him flinch.

"Well, *do* you?" I persisted.

"No more than normal."

"You consider *that* to be normal?"

"Well, I suppose. I mean, I guess other kids my age—"

"And if other kids your age jumped off a cliff would you follow?"

"No, God no."

"Please don't use the lord's name in vain."

"Sorry."

"So, would you jump off a cliff with your friends?"

"Of course not."

"But you'd happily indulge in mutual masturbation with them?"

"I don't under—" He popped his head closer to the mesh. I pinned my head against the wall. The stench of coppery blood and evacuated bowels was beginning to work its way up from my seat. I didn't have long before the kid figured something was wrong.

"What do you want to tell me, son?" I asked.

I felt his eyes flashing inquisitively through the mesh for a moment longer, then he settled back into his seat with a reflective sigh.

"It's my father," he said soberly. "I miss him."

"That's understandable."

"I feel so lonely. I mean, things were never great for me, ya know? But with him around, it helped. He put a smile on my face at the end of the day. He fought away the bullies and the tears, and now what? I'm never going to see him again, am I?"

I ducked forward, opening the curtain and peering down the church. As I suspected, the youngster's family had gone. He had snuck in unannounced, probably ashamed to let his mother know he was seeking help from someone other than her.

"The bible says that we will meet our loved ones in the afterlife, does it not?" I said, closing the curtain.

"I guess," he replied.

"And you believe that you will see your father again, right?"

"I suppose so. In time."

"You could always speed up the process."

"What do you mean?" I sensed his huge nose pushing up against the mesh. The smell was beginning to become overwhelming and with his huge snout poking around, he had to be able to smell it, as well.

I forced the steel end of the screwdriver through the mesh. It crunched the wire and punctured through, straight into the inquisitive teenager's eye. It popped like a fat grub, squirting opaque fluid onto the steel.

He recoiled with a croaking sound and tumbled backward. I sensed my heart quicken and my world momentarily slow. I had taken a risk; there was a chance he had been heard. A chance this would be seen.

I pulled the screwdriver out, darted out of the confessional, and turned toward the other side of the wooden death box. Bloodied hands were grasping at the curtain, pushing the material outwards like disembodied hands of velvet. I opened the curtain for him and stopped him from stumbling onto me by placing the sole of my foot onto his bloodied forehead and pressing him backward.

He was begging for his life. "Please, please, please." Repetition always suits the doomed and the frightened.

With his good eye, he sensed the daylight behind me and tried to dash through. I pushed him down again, watching him tumble into the corner where he promptly curled into the fetal position and began to pray to his God.

I closed the curtain behind me and silenced his prayers. His God wasn't going to help him. His God wasn't capable of stopping anyone, let alone me. God works in mysterious ways, and very few of those ways are helpful. God does have one thing going for him though: He is a vengeful, vindictive, brutal tyrant, and that God would have appreciated the work that I did in his house.

The scene I left in the church was a thing of beauty and one I knew would be appreciated and understood by the right people.

There was a storm coming and I was going to be at its center.

PART 4

1

Lester sensed the activity around him, that the world hadn't stopped turning and the chaos that fed through the hazy mesh in his mind came not from inside but from out. There was panic, shouting, questions. Nobody had ever seen anything like it. They were unlikely to see anything like it ever again and as Lester stared, lost inside his own thoughts, he couldn't help but think that he was to blame.

This was all his fault.

He hadn't been dumb enough to tell the press about his theory, but it was still *his* theory, and if not for that then this might not have happened. He didn't know who gave the information to the press, didn't know if it was one of the dimwits at Whitegate Police Station or one of his own back home, but it didn't matter. He had known they would find out, and he had been certain that someone somewhere would leak his theory.

"It's spectacular, isn't it?"

Lester angrily turned to face the police officer next to him. He was a local by the name of Tenant, a cocky little prick who Lester had had the displeasure of meeting earlier. He fancied himself, was always checking his hair, grinning into mirrors. The sort of man who hit on every woman he saw and assumed they were lesbians or frigid when they turned him down.

"Spectacular?" Lester spat. "Are you fucking shitting me? Two people are dead, in a church, their bodies strung up like meat in a fucking slaughterhouse. This is not *spectacular*."

The officer gave a nonchalant shrug. "To be fair, only one of them is strung up like meat." He chuckled at that and Lester felt like punching him. If he were a more violent man, a man more like the one who had done this, then he would have caved his smug face into the back of his skull and then stomped on it until the blood stopped pouring and the screams stopped curdling.

"It's not easy to do that," Tenant continued.

Lester frowned at him, for a moment wondering if he was talking about the images that had just been going through his head. "Excuse me?"

Tenant nodded toward the mess at the front of the church and Lester followed his gaze and nodded.

The vicar had been skinned, every inch of skin peeled away from his body, leaving nothing but muscle, blood, and bone. The crime had seemingly taken place in the confessional, because its floors were pooled with blood and spotted with chunks of flesh. He had been nailed to a large crucifix that had once belonged to a fiberglass model of Christ. It was positioned so that whoever entered the church, walked down the aisle, or sat in the congregation would face the figure of their lord, and that was what made this human replica so striking and so terrifying. They hadn't found the flesh yet, but they would, and Lester didn't really want to be around when they did.

At the vicar's feet, curled into the fetal position, was a young boy in his teens. He was naked and he looked vulnerable, almost infant-like. He had been positioned that way after death, that much was obvious, but why he had been posed like that wasn't clear. Lester hadn't walked down the aisle yet. He had tried, but the further he walked, the more his legs felt like they weren't going to support him. Walking toward the figure of the skinless vicar held aloft on the cross was one of the most terrifying things he had ever done. It activated a primal fear, a sense of foreboding he had never felt before and knew he would never feel again. This was a set, a piece of theater, one that had been orchestrated by the hand of the devil himself and one that succeeded in its mission to strike fear into the hearts of everyone who looked upon it, giving them a memory that would haunt them until their dying day.

He was stuck in the middle of the aisle, occasionally moving aside to let others through. At least a dozen police officers and forensic officers were in the church, with the majority swarming around the bodies on the altar and the blood in the confessional. At the back of the church, two officers kept guard at the door, keen to keep out the gathering crowd. The bodies had been discovered just a few hours ago by the mother of the boy beneath the cross. He had stayed behind after a family visit to church and when he was late, she got worried and returned. The church was locked and she assumed he had already left, but when she couldn't find him hours later, she spoke to the caretaker and asked him to open the doors. By then they were already open, the killer already gone, and what they saw was enough to put her in the hospital with shock and to turn the caretaker into a shaking, mumbling wreck.

"Are you not going to get a closer look?" Tenant asked, nudging Lester.

Lester simply glared at him and eventually Tenant left him, his hands stuffed casually in his pockets as he approached the dead bodies. This was no doubt the first time he had seen a corpse in person, but he was trying to play it cool to maintain whatever modicum of respect he thought his colleagues had for him. Lester knew that when Tenant finished work, he would rush home, cry into his pillow, and drown his sorrows in as much alcohol as he could find. Lester didn't blame him.

The Masquerade, whatever he was and whatever he would become, finally got the recognition that Lester always knew he had wanted. Whitegate would once again be filled with macabre tourists and terrified locals. For the next few weeks at least, Herman and the town of Whitegate would become the center of the universe, but there was something else, another reason. It felt like more than a stunt, more than an orchestrated nightmare, and the more Lester stared at the human destruction in front of him, the more he felt he wasn't seeing the whole picture.

There was something there. The way it was arranged made Lester confident Herman was trying to tell him something. This was grand and showy, and he had done that for effect, there was no doubt about it. Herman loved to make a scene; he loved to strike fear in the hearts of the people and to give them a memory that they would never forget, but this, this . . .

"I feel like I'm missing something," Lester said, half to himself.

"Me too," Matthews said. He face was pale and his lips were blue. He looked like he was about to projectile vomit a sugary breakfast all over the already desecrated ground.

"There's a message here."

"Yes. That this guy is fucking nuts."

Lester shook his head slowly.

"For He so loved his pathetic little world, that He gave his only begotten son."

Lester's face creased as he looked up to see a woman approach, decked out in the white uniform of the forensic team.

"Excuse me?"

"Your message," she said, holding up a bible. "That's it." Her finger was pointing to a passage, parts of which had been crossed out and rewritten.

He reached for the book but she pulled it away. "*Evidence*, I'm afraid. If you want to touch it, you'll have to dress up."

"What else does it say?" Lester asked.

"That's it," she told him. "It was open at that page when we found it. Oh, and there is this." She showed him again. He could just make out a faint word that had been scribbled onto the end of the edited line.

"And Devil?" he asked, a little concerned at the reference.

"Look again," she said.

He edged closer, close enough to get a whiff of the scent of old leather and ancient parchment. This book had probably been in the church's possession for more than a hundred years and yet in one instant it had been defaced.

"'And Daughter?'" He looked up into the eyes of the forensic officer and she nodded.

"We have no idea what it means," she confirmed.

Lester ran the phrase through his head a number of times and then spoke it out loud; it was nothing more than a mumble, but it was enough to drive the meaning home. "For He so loved his pathetic little world, that He gave his only begotten son and daughter." Lester felt every muscle in his body tense. He felt his heart stop and his lungs empty as the life in him froze.

"That can't be," he said softly, his voice breaking, grating out of his chest, barely making it past his lips, which had turned dry. Sticky. "He wouldn't. He couldn't."

The forensic officer gave him a concerned glance. "What are you talking about?" she asked.

When he raised his eyes to meet her, she became frightened. He had changed from disconsolate to terrified in an instant.

"I—I—" He shook his head and then pulled out his phone. They asked him questions, their voices growing louder and more concerned with each word, but he ignored them. He dialed the number he knew by heart, as if in that split second he didn't trust the validity of speed dial.

He waited, breathing heavily, beads of sweat popping on his forehead.

The phone rang once, twice, three times. There was no answer, and with every chime he felt his heart sink lower. Felt the life drain out of him.

How did he know?

By the fourth and fifth ring, his surprise and his fear began to evolve into anger—anger at himself and anger at the man who had caused those emotions to stir inside him.

By the seventh ring, he was prepared to hang up, but the sound of the voicemail message stopped him.

"I'm sorry, but no one is home right now."

It was a standard message, but it wasn't spoken by anyone who lived in the house. It wasn't his mother, his son, or his daughter. It was a man, a man whose voice he had never heard, but a man whose featureless face had haunted his nightmares many times.

"But if you would like to pay us a visit, then who knows, you might just get to see us. We haven't been feeling very well of late, so to avoid doing us any harm, please come alone." The voice changed at that point. Lester could almost picture the sadistic serial killer sneering as he finished. "I'll look forward to it."

2

—

L ester rushed out of the church, nearly knocking down the officers by the door when they tried to stop him. They yelled something at him, and he heard orders shouted from behind him as well, but he couldn't decipher them. He barely even heard them. It wasn't until he threw open the large doors leading into the church that he realized what they had been saying. As soon as the doors swung open, their ancient hinges screaming as the wood embraced the wind and parachuted backward, the crowd outside looked at him and at the scene they could now see behind him.

"Shit," Lester cursed under his breath.

He had entered through the same doors, as had a couple of others first on the scene, but after that they had shut them, guarded them, and stopped anyone from coming or going through them. Everyone had used a small side door that led into the back of the church, keen for the crowd not to see the image that The Masquerade had painted for them.

There were gasps, moans, squeals, myriad human vocal sounds, none of which produced coherent words. Then the flashes began. First from the dozens of photographers sensing their moment, then from the camera phones held by sickened but opportunistic locals. Before they had time to react and close the doors, social media was already gearing up to receive images of Herman's latest massacre.

It was just what he would have wanted, Lester knew that, and he knew it was his fault. Again. He tried to ignore those thoughts, to banish that guilt. He didn't have time to dwell. He didn't want to make it three catastrophic mistakes; he didn't want to lose what was left of his family to this monster. His kids hated him, he may as well have been a cardboard cutout with ears as far as his mother was concerned, and he didn't like any of them. But he did love them and knew that without them, he had nothing.

The journalists and the public hounded him as he pushed through, swatting them away like a celebrity on his way to a film premiere. The questions rang in his ears and boiled his blood. So mundane, so inane, so pathetic—didn't they know there were people's lives at stake? He was doing his best to ignore them and to swim through them, but then he hit a hurdle in the form of a six foot five, 240-pound iceberg.

"Just one question," the behemoth said.

Lester was grimacing by then, his face red, his ears practically steaming. He looked at the big man, so cool and composed, and instantly he felt angrier. He saw Herman in that man's body language. There he was, at a crime scene, surrounded by fear and death, yet he was calm, relaxed, only thinking about himself.

The big man seemed to think he had won, that he had manipulated someone into getting what he wanted, just like he probably did every other day of his working week.

"Can you tell us what is happening in there?" the behemoth said, a smug smile on his face as the other journalists stood and watched, reluctant to intrude on his prize catch.

He took out a notepad and a pen, both of which looked tiny in his hands.

"Smug, fucking sociopathic little prick," Lester said through gritted teeth.

"Excuse me?" Despite not being sure of what was said, the journalist scribbled on his notepad, at which point Lester reached forward and ripped it from his hand. The behemoth tilted his head to the side, a patronizing look on his face, as though someone were playing games, being mischievous. "Come on now, let's play—"

Lester put his hand under the notepad and pressed it up against the big man's hand. The behemoth immediately cut short his condescension to give Lester a curious glance.

Lester then drove the pen through the top of the behemoth's hand and grinned with satisfaction as it sank into his flesh and wedged halfway between his palm and his notepad. The big man opened his mouth to scream but nothing came out. Lester rubbed his hands together, gave a nod to the shocked and appalled onlookers, and then continued to his car, not failing to notice how quickly the throng parted in front of him.

It was a fairly short drive, but not a good one to make when angry. He needed a release, he needed something to cling to, something to stop the fear and the worry from overcoming him. He hoped the radio would help, turning it all the way up until it drowned out his ability to think, but then the music cut off and a breaking news story cut in. He didn't need to listen to it to know what it was. The world was about to be told about Herman all over again.

He practically punched the radio, turning it off and leaving the car in silence.

"Bastard!" he yelled, thumping the wheel. "Wait until I get my fucking hands on you."

The more he drove, the less anger he felt. The depression and the sadness crept in. He thought about his kids, about how hurt he had been when he lost his wife and how much more this was going to affect him. He also thought about how hurt they had been, about how Annabelle had tried to stay strong for her brother, who cried for two months straight, and that when she thought no one was around, she would break down herself. They had been through hell, and that, coupled with his inability to look after them, to stay strong and to be the father they needed, had turned them into the angry and rebellious children they were.

He was nearly in tears, close to being pushed over the edge by the sight of festive houses—decked out in Christmas cheer, ready for the season. Christmas was different now, but his kids loved it now as much as they did when they were younger. He could still remember their smiling faces, their squeals of joy. He could still remember the way his wife looked as she watched her children open their gifts.

"Please don't let this be," he whispered under his breath, his voice breaking. "Not them. Not now. Please."

———

Lester was a wreck by the time he arrived at his mother's house. That short journey had transformed him, adding years to his face, scars to his mind.

The sun had set so he killed the lights as he pulled into the driveway, not wanting to announce his arrival. The house was in darkness, none of the lights had been turned on, and as he clambered out of the car, he felt his knees going weak. He had to pause, resting on the hood, gathering himself, telling himself that he needed to be strong and reminding himself that if they were still alive in there, he was the only person who could save them.

This was the house he had grown up in, the house in which he'd drunk his first beer and, while his parents were away, the house in which he'd lost his virginity. It was also the house he had been in when, at age fourteen, he had learned about the death of his father following a road accident. There were good and bad memories, and he knew the next few minutes could create memories that would surpass all that had gone before.

As he gripped the door handle, he had flashbacks to his youth, to the times he had tried to sneak in or out when his mother was asleep. He remembered the time when he had crept out, stayed out for most of the night, and then returned, sedated with beer, only to find his mother waiting for him with a stern expression, a lecture, and anger that didn't subside for weeks. He wished he could open the door now and find her sitting in the living room like she had been all those years ago. He was happy to let her lecture him, to let her shout and bawl, if it meant she was alive and well enough to do so.

He breathed deeply, his hand sweaty on the cold metal handle. He opened the door and was both surprised and concerned to find it unlocked. There were no lights on in the hallway or in the rooms beyond, but if anyone could sneak into the house unannounced, then it was him. He knew every turn, every obstacle, and every squeak in the floorboards. If Herman was waiting for him then he would need to be paying attention, because Lester wasn't going to make a sound.

He doubted Herman would appreciate him sneaking around, but he had done what was asked of him. He had come alone. If he was caught, then he could worry about how to talk his way out of it; if he wasn't, then he was going to use whatever chance he had to take Herman down and save his family.

He went to the kitchen first, the closest room to the front door and one in which he could prepare himself. The old kitchen cupboards and drawers had been noisy. She had since refurnished, though, and the cutlery drawer didn't make a sound as he opened it and removed the biggest knife he could find before allowing it to roll shut on its magnetic rails.

He checked the living room and dining room, making sure the first floor was covered. But his search was quick, inattentive. Something within told him there was nothing to find here. And that something was dragging him away, toward the stairs and toward the bedrooms.

Something was worrying him, had startled him: it was the realization he was too late, that it didn't matter if he did or didn't make a noise; it didn't matter if he called the police, because Herman had already done what he had threatened to do.

Annabelle's room was first, but he froze as he reached out. He felt his heart sinking with every beat, felt a slimy film of sweat all over his body, gluing clothes to his skin, hair to his forehead.

"Please, no," he mouthed into the darkness. *"Please, don't be—"*

He opened the door and instantly it hit him. The smell that had irritated his nostrils on his ascent up the stairs, the smell that he had become familiar with throughout his career. His words choked in his throat.

It was dark in the room, but the curtains were open. Through the orange glow of the streetlights and the stark moonlight, he could see his daughter on the bed.

She was balled up, holding her stomach. It was the same position she had been in when she was seven and had suffered with a bout of gastroenteritis. She had been in agony for days and he had stayed by her side, stroking her hair, promising her everything was going to be okay. Back then everything *had* been okay, but he could no longer make those promises to her and she could no longer hear him if he did.

The bed was saturated with her blood, which had also spilled on the floor. In this light, it looked like a shadow had enveloped her room, spreading toward her before blanketing her in its dark embrace.

He stayed and stared for a moment. He wanted to cry, to let it all out, but he knew that he had to bite it down for the sake of his son and mother. He quietly closed the door, leaving his daughter to her peace, before heading for his son's room.

There was more light in there, spilling out from a television that showed the faded image of a video game menu screen. Damian loved his games, forever lost in a world of make-believe and graphic violence. He preferred the simulated worlds of gangsters and soldiers, people whose lives couldn't be further removed from his privileged teenage middle-class existence.

Lester moaned. It wasn't an intentional sound, but one that seemed to just spill out of him, coming from a deep, dark, terrified, and hopeless place. He covered his mouth, pressing his palm hard against his face until his fingers crushed his lips against his teeth, until the noise stopped and the physical pain took some of the mental pain away.

His son had been sitting on the bed playing a game. His final moments had been in virtual battle, before his life was lost for real. His throat had been slit, his blood showered on his clothes and on his bed. He was keeled over, looking like he had merely fallen asleep playing a game, as he so often did.

The stench of death was strong, ripened by the heavy and sweet stench of stale cigarettes and cannabis. Lester closed the door, blocking as much of that smell and that image as he could. With one hand still holding his mouth, he rested the other against the door and used it to support his weight. He remained like that for several moments, breathing deep, trying to clear his mind, to stop the emotions from coming.

His mother's room was next, but he had lost all hope already. He had also cast aside any hope of going unseen and unheard, no longer confident it would make a difference. It certainly hadn't done anything for Damian or Annabelle.

He staggered across the hallway, his laborious steps hitting every loose floorboard, every hollow spot. He switched on the hallway light as he moved, stretching out a long and forlorn shadow that reached his mother's bedroom door before he did. He didn't wait at the door, didn't pause to compose himself. Whatever was in there couldn't possibly be as bad as what he had already seen, and if Herman was in there waiting for him, ready to jump him and butcher him like he had done his kids, then he wished him luck.

Lester practically kicked open the door, slapping on the bedroom light. He took one look at his mother on the bed, one hard stare at the woman who had brought him into the world, loved him, looked after him and nagged him, and then he sank his chin into his chest.

Herman had taken everything.

3

—

L ester could have phoned for backup, bringing armed
response units to the door within moments, but he didn't
want their help. He wanted to do this alone.

The bodies had stiffened, rigor mortis had set in. He didn't
need to venture close, didn't need to touch them or look into their
glazed-over pupils to know they had probably been dead for some
time. There was a good chance Herman had killed them before he
had set up the spectacle at the church, which meant that all of this
was just a game.

He sat on the edge of his mother's bed. It felt strange to be
in the same room as her and to have the opportunity to talk. He
couldn't remember the last time he had been able to look at her
without hearing about her new foot fungus, how she suspected the
mailman was screwing her neighbor, or how every single one of
her friends had some form of terminal disease or knew someone
who had recently died.

"I'm sorry," Lester said softly, his chin still on his chest, his voice
sounding empty and hollow. "For this, for everything. I should
have never let the kids leave. I should have spoken to you more, I
should have—" He finally dragged his eyes to her and found that
he couldn't finish his sentence. He wanted to embrace her; she was
his mother and that's what mothers were for, but the person that

lay on the bed next to him, cold and pale, no longer had a strong shoulder for him to cry on or a warm embrace to envelop him. The last time she had done any of those things was when his wife died and she had been the only one to remain strong. She had been there when he needed her, but he wasn't there when she needed him.

He stood, facing the door and telling himself not to look, not to let himself see her in that way again.

And then there were the kids. When had he *ever* been there for them? He still loved them, he always had, but if he allowed himself to admit it, he had begun to despise them lately. He had grown bitter, resentful, taking their actions to heart and allowing it to affect his emotions, emotions that should have always remained true and should have *never* been altered by words spoken in anger. They loved him deep down, or so he believed, and he should have been there for them.

He walked back across the hallway, no longer worried about bumping into Herman. He had nothing to fear from him anymore. He paused outside of his daughter's door, his hand caught in transit as he reached for the handle. He had been in that situation so many times at home, hoping to talk to her after an argument, to calm her down and to put his mind at ease—contemplating knocking, contemplating walking in, contemplating walking away. More often than not he walked away. When he did knock, she rarely let him in, and when he walked in unannounced, she had never welcomed him or his chats. If anything, it had just led to more arguments.

He sighed, moved his hand away, and wiped the sweat from his palm onto the back of his pants. He did the same outside his son's door, his temporary bedroom and his haven for whenever he wanted to get away from his father. It had also been Lester's haven, as it had been his bedroom when he was a child, though he knew that Damian would have refused to sleep in there if he had known.

He left them both to it. For a moment, he felt a stab of déjà vu, remembering the countless times he had been in the same situation following an argument. There was often more shouting coming from Annabelle's room, and the noise of rock music or computer games from Damian's, but the setup was the same: anger, disappointment, and grief leading to emptiness and loneliness. Except this wasn't one of these moments. His kids weren't angry at him. They were dead.

He poured himself a large measure of gin in the kitchen. He hated the stuff; it tasted like perfume, but it was the strongest alcohol in the house. It got the job done. He refilled his glass and knocked back another before he carried a third glass into the living room. When he snapped on the light and raised the glass to his to lips, he got his fourth fright of the night and dropped his drink.

There was writing across the walls. Big, sweeping letters, arcing their shapes in vivid and intimidating forms. It was red, but he didn't know if it was actually blood, and if it was, he didn't want to speculate as to whose it was. He took a step back, standing in the doorway, and read what he saw.

THE CHORDS THAT PLAY IN THE HEARTS OF THE MOST RECKLESS.

He frowned. It sounded like a quote, but if it was then he had never heard the play, had never read the poem or the story. He moved forward—his legs had lost the anxious, jelly-like sensation they'd had upon entering the house, and it now felt like he was walking on air, as though his body was no longer connected to his mind. He was empty, devoid of life and of everything that had made him scared, anxious, and human.

He ran his finger over the words. It was blood. And it had been laid on thick, congealing on the walls before drying into a lumpy paste. He pulled his finger back when he realized, disgusted at the thought.

He read the words again and again, hoping to make some sense from them, but nothing clicked. He stared at them for a few minutes, waiting for something to jump out of his emotionless mind and to scream a realization at him, but nothing came.

Instead he headed back to the kitchen, decided that as disgusting as it was, the bottle of gin would help with his misery. It was then that he noted the other words, splashed across the opposing wall. These were smaller, yet somehow more sinister: LET US PLAY THOSE CHORDS TOGETHER, LESTER; LET US DANCE AND REVEL THIS NIGHT, AS TOMORROW ONE OF US WILL BE DEAD.

It struck a spot that Lester didn't know was still capable of feeling. He swallowed thickly. The writing was followed by a time-stamp, as big and bold as any of the letters behind and in front of him. It declared, MIDNIGHT, which seemed both apt and chilling.

Lester fumbled in his pocket for his phone, punching in his passkey on his way to the kitchen. He wanted the gin, but he also wanted to get out of that living room as quickly as he could. The letters were mocking him, towering over him and threatening him.

He typed the quote into Google on his phone and was immediately greeted with "The Masque of the Red Death," a story by Edgar Allan Poe, one that a few journalists had drawn comparisons to in the past. It had been paraphrased, of course, and Lester found that amusing. He had always seen Herman as a man who craved attention, someone who wanted people to be scared of him. The incident in the church was a one-off; he wasn't usually that showy, that grand, that obvious. As a boy, he had butchered eight people in a single night, striking fear into the hearts of generations. As a man, he had killed without preference, without spectacle, and he had been equally feared for it. But Lester couldn't help but feel that that was just a prelude, that the last few years were just the beginning and that something bigger was about to go down, something that would make the Whitegate massacre look like a picnic.

He read the quote again. "What the fuck does it mean?" he asked himself.

He took a swig from the bottle and cursed after the flowery alcohol burned its way down his throat. Already it was working its magic, burning a bigger hollow hole in his soul, digging at the edges of the one that was already there.

He searched for what he could find on the Poe story and he even read it. It was short, a quick read, but there was nothing in there that connected anything that had happened. He saw the connection with midnight and a man in a mask. It was the time the villain in the story struck, the time that he killed everyone at the party and—

"Shit," Lester cursed, his chaotic thoughts hitting a roadblock. "He couldn't . . ."

He quickly searched for local parties, doing his best to check social media and local online newspapers to scan for fancy dress parties, costume parties, events. Several were being held miles away, but they seemed irrelevant. He knew that the story had nothing to do with Herman or The Masquerade. If he had some sort of literary background, one that he was displaying with each subsequent kill, he would want the world to know. He would leave clues and references at every turn. The story was a clue to find him, a clue to lead Lester right to him.

Herman knew Lester would make the phone call; he knew he would make the journey and he knew he would find his family dead and then find the message. It was all prearranged. He could have waited, but one on one in a dark house with a grieving man wasn't his style. He would want something bigger, something grander, something that would live long in his and the public's memory.

It occurred to him that this *wasn't* the main event, that everything that had gone before wasn't the prelude. This was how he wanted to end it. Lester knew that the Whitegate massacre was more than a random spree killing, even if everyone else had ignored the clues. Herman was a killer; he had no intention of stopping after those murders, no intention of taking his life or going into hiding. It had always bugged Lester why Herman had been so open and so obvious, but what if that hadn't been his intention? What if he had wanted to kill quietly, to live in the shadows as he was doing now? What if something went wrong, he made a mistake, and he was forced to act on impulse?

Lester swallowed dryly, the moisture gone from his mouth, leaving a dry, flowery taste in its place.

He wondered if the same thing was about to happen again. Mistakes had been made, identities had been exposed. Herman couldn't go on killing as he had been, which meant he had two choices. He could put an end to it, go into hiding. Or he could do as he had done before, committing an act so violent, so catastrophic, that everyone would pay attention. The world would continue to fear him, and he would have a legacy like no other.

Lester knocked back half the bottle and ventured into the living room again. He scanned the quotes a few more times, running all of them through search engines. Nothing new came up. He flopped on the sofa, his eyes still on the walls and the huge bloody letters. He mouthed them, he whispered them, but the more he stared and the more he spoke, the less he understood and the more frustrated he became.

In his frustration, he tossed his phone at the wall, watching as it flew through the air before shattering. It did a good job of holding together, but the screen split and the battery broke free, landing on the coffee table in front of him. He stared at it vacantly, as if this detritus, this product of his anger and his frustrations, could hold the answer he needed. The longer he stared, the less he focused, and the less he focused the more he noticed the leaflet lying on the coffee table underneath the phone's battery.

He saw the red writing first, then the mask. His heart raced in his chest and all the muscles in his body seemed to spasm at once as he grabbed it, ripping the leaflet away and sending the battery crashing to the floor.

It was an advertisement for an adaptation of "The Masque of the Red Death." "A modern, twisted and surreal take on the Poe classic," the leaflet said. They were due to perform the opening night in over a week. It had nothing to do with midnight, certainly nothing to do with tonight.

The show was being performed at an old building in town and would no doubt be practiced over and over until it was ready, until all the actors knew their parts, until all of them were—

Lester felt his muscles turn rigid, his jaw tense, his eyes widen. He turned it back over and looked at the smiling faces of the cast. They were all young, all beautiful, all of them with their whole lives and careers ahead of them.

He checked his watch and saw he only had an hour and a half until midnight, ninety minutes to make it to where Herman wanted him to be. It would take him less than twenty minutes to drive to where the rehearsals were being held, but he knew he had to get there sooner.

He wasn't going to be responsible for any more deaths.

4

—

Lester drove with his foot down and his mind empty. Empty of the grief and the memories, both young and old; empty of the anger, the frustration, and the vengeance that had manifested as a bitter bile crawling its way up his throat. He was determined. He wanted to get to where he needed to be and to get there as quickly as he could. That was all that was important, that was all that mattered. Everything else, all those thoughts and emotions swimming erratically through his mind, pulling at his heart strings, poisoning his blood, only served to weaken his resolve, to stop him from concentrating on what was important.

He allowed himself to remember the faces he had seen on the leaflet. All of them happy, all of them young, all of them attractive. He knew they were Herman's type. He liked to take everything from the ones who had the most. He liked to take away what had made them superior, to eradicate what had made them special and expose them as the bland, boring individuals they were—the *humans* that they were. At least, that's the way he saw it. He knew there was no rhyme or reason to what Herman did. The people who wrote about him, and the sick bastards who praised him as a child, said that he was justified. He was killing his tormentors, after all. But they conveniently ignored the fact that he killed his uncle, as well as an innocent father and an innocent child. He wasn't on a mission to make the world a better place back then and it was no different now. Lester suspected that Herman probably thought otherwise, but it was clear Lester wasn't dealing with a sane individual.

And then there was his mother and his father. They were usually the ones to blame, but while his mother was relatively blameless, Lester suspected it was a different story for Herman's father. In the early days, there were those who suggested that Herman had been inspired by The Butcher, a killer who plied his trade across most of the country. It made sense, as Herman was just the sort of warped individual to take the lead of a serial killer. Those words, that statement, had never left Lester. It didn't leave him when The Butcher became inactive, and it didn't leave him when he began to notice similarities in the way The Masquerade killed his victims.

Lester could only take so much. He could only take so many vacant, empty faces, could only see so much chaos, so much bloodshed, and so much pointless destruction. Herman had turned him into a bitter, resentful, and disinterested prick, and then, when it seemed like there was nothing else to take, like there was no way he could make things worse, he took away his family.

Lester was just as empty and soulless as Herman's victims were, but at least he was still moving, at least he was still alive. He could use what he had left—whatever pathetic remnant of existence that was—to stop Herman and make sure he didn't hurt anyone else.

There was a theory that The Masquerade was a revamped version of The Butcher—the same man, with a slightly different appearance and a slightly different agenda. Lester didn't believe they were two and the same, but he had suspected there was a link and now his suspicions had gone into overdrive.

It was a murky night, as expected for the time of year, but the streets were dead, which wasn't as expected. As he paused at a set of traffic lights, he saw Christmas decorations hung in sporadic strings across nearby streetlights. Half of the bulbs were broken and the other half anemic, unable to give off enough light to penetrate the darkness. Lights in nearby houses were just as pathetic; few in number, tacky, weak, miserable. The spirit of the season failed to shine through in any of them; the darkness of the winter and the shadows of the night overcame each and every one, enveloping them in a blackness that seemed to intensify as he drove on.

The theater was located in an industrial area. It had once been home to booming businesses and factories, but they had decayed through the decades and the buildings were now dust and memories. It had been saved from demolition by an ambitious theater fan with a half-assed dream, little business sense, and a truckload of money. Its seats were never full and its shows didn't set the world on fire, but Lester knew that if he didn't make it on time, then tonight would be the night it went down in history, the night where the performance of a lifetime was played out for a sadistic audience of one.

The prince entertained his friends in the make-believe castle on the stage. A confident and showy actor, glad of his moment in the sun, both in fiction and in reality. He was the lead and he was playing an extroverted and powerful man, what more could he want? This was his shot at stardom, his chance to show his parents, his teachers, and his so-called "friends" that he could make it as an actor and that his career wouldn't be an assortment of television adverts and rejections.

He grabbed a fancifully dressed young maiden by the waist and spun her around. She did well not to spill the drink in her hand, but of course there was nothing in the glass, not now and not on the big night either. "Are you having fun, my dear?" he asked her as she pressed up against him.

"Why yes, Prince Prospero, I am."

He twirled her again, and as he did so the others clapped and reveled in the gaiety. There would be music playing on the night, but for now that music was just in his head. This was the dress rehearsal, but he was a capable method actor and he knew how to set the scene.

"Well, then, my dear, you can be thankful that the night has only just begun."

She giggled at that. It was all pompous, self-indulgent nonsense, but that was the director's cue. It was *his* self-indulgent nonsense.

"Then I say let the night begin!" she declared. She raised her glass and the others followed suit. Just as she prepared to announce something else, they would hear the clock strike as it hit midnight. But right now, the director's clap gave them the cue. At that point, they would turn to the audience, while from the aisle would walk the figure of the Red Death. He was an integral part of the story and everyone had been delighted with the idea to have him begin his walk through the audience. It was chilling, immersive.

The suit the actor wore was a little tacky and few of the others liked it, but as he approached, they noted this suit was different. It looked better, so much so that even the mediocre actor underneath—a product of nepotism and the director's extended family—looked more menacing. They were drawn to his face at first, and then to the axe that swung casually by his side. It took them a few moments to notice his other hand, and the bloodied head it carried.

There were gasps and screams, revulsion and terror, and all of it was real. A few thought it was a trick, another ploy by a sadistic director using Hitchcockian techniques to terrify his actors, to instill the horror that their characters faced.

The director, initially with his back to the newcomer, turned around to face him. His reaction convinced the unbelievers. As much as he liked his tricks and his games, he looked just as scared as they did, and he wasn't capable of faking it. "What is this?" he asked.

"This," the man in the mask began, "is my favorite part of the story."

PART 5

1

—

I dropped the head in my hand. It wore a cheap mask, nothing like mine, nothing like the legend he was trying to live up to. I knew the story well. "The Masque of the Red Death" was actually one of my favorites. My own career as The Masquerade had nothing to do with it; that—just like this night at the church—was just a delightful coincidence.

The arrival of the Red Death, dressed in a mask that I liked to think was similar to my own, instilling fear in all of the revelers, was the best part of the story. The pathetic costume worn by the actor whose head lay at my feet did not do it justice.

I killed the director first. He deserved it for ruining an integral part of a classic story and also for scripting the trite bullshit I had heard on stage. A blow to his temple did the job, opening up his cranium, severing the cords that kept him alive and dropping him where he stood. The actors on stage dispersed, with some of them running for me and the main doors and most of them heading backstage. It didn't matter where they ran because all of the doors were locked. I had already been backstage, I had already been outside. They were trapped like animals in a slaughterhouse, and they were about to become meat.

There was a good chance they would be scrambling for their phones, desperate for the little devices that held their world on five-inch screens, but when you rely so much on something so small, you're always going to be let down. I had disabled the Wi-Fi and placed a signal blocker by the door. No messages would be sent, no phone calls would be made. It's amazing what you can learn and what you can buy on the Internet.

"And now was acknowledged the presence of the Red Death," I told the woman by the door.

She fell to her knees and threw herself at my mercy. Pleading with me to spare her life, which I had zero intention of doing. I disposed of her quickly, the only form of mercy I was willing to grant.

I followed another as she darted for the backstage area. They were scrambling around backstage, trying the doors, trying their phones, their faces bleak, their voices shrill. They had their chance to band together and plot against me, they had their chance to find weapons and attack me, but such is the nature of the human race that they immediately sought help from others and refused to help themselves. I put pay to a timid stagehand who still bore the acne scars of youth and was probably only 110 pounds soaking wet. He was all skin and bones and the axe cut through him like a chicken carcass.

"He had come like a thief in the night," I continued, swinging again, this time planting the axe into the spine of someone who tried to flee. They twitched and convulsed like a merry bunny before flopping to the floor. The others ran away again, back into the main room, hopping over the recently deceased and rushing past me without making an effort to stop me. I followed them, enjoying my moment on life's biggest stage.

"And one by one dropped the revelers." The axe swung again, the tip of its deadly blade catching the edge of a young actress's skin, penetrating deep, bleeding instantly, and sweeping in an arc as it carved a red-raw smile on her terrified profile. "In the blood-bedewed halls of their revel, and died each in the despairing posture of their fall!"

The woman with the second smile dropped and clutched her face, her mouth open in a silent scream, her cheek open in a yawning bellow. I bent down until my face was inches from hers, until I caught the heat of the empty scream that tried to escape her mouth.

"Rather apt, don't you think?"

She looked at my face, at the blood-red mask, at the deep-black eyes set inside the sockets. She didn't reply, she just stared. I stood, ending her nightmare with another swing, this one across her neck.

Someone was waiting for me as I turned around, a cane held aloft above his head. He flinched when he saw me, when he realized his chance to strike unseen was gone.

He had seen the woman at my feet, no doubt a friend or a lover. He was shaking, his arms trembling, unable to move, unable to strike. He seemed to be seconds away from losing control entirely and releasing both his bowels and the blunt object.

"Well, are you going to hit me or not?"

He swung for me, but I knew it was coming and I moved quickly. With his arms held up, he couldn't protect his chest as I rammed the axe into it. It made an odd sucking sound as it penetrated his skin, breaking his ribs before wedging in place.

He dropped the cane, using his hands to grab the axe. The blood was gushing out of him at an extraordinary rate, the life leaving his eyes, yet a small part of him was fighting a final, pointless battle, desperately trying to pry the axe free. With what was probably his final exertion, he ripped the axe out of his chest. I thanked him, took it from his hands, and then left him to die.

"What was the next bit?" I wondered aloud. "Ah, that's right: and each died in the despairing posture of his fall." Another was trying to escape, clawing at the door, banging and kicking with all of his might. He didn't turn around as I approached, didn't see me as I drove the axe into the back of his skull, immediately silencing his wailing and his banging and leaving him propped against the door in a dull and rigid pose. "How fitting."

There were three others standing in the middle of the room. This was the moment for heroes, for macho men looking to impress, but the only man of the three was the one who looked the most reluctant, the most scared. He reminded me of Darren Henderson all those years ago, trying to use his female friends as human shields. This one hadn't resorted to that yet, but he was certainly thinking about it.

"Please," one of the women said. "Don't do this."

I stopped, opened my arms, and gestured to the room around me, a carnival of chaos. "But I have already begun. I can't stop now. The show must go on, right?"

She came at me and took me by surprise. I didn't have time to get the axe ready and she managed to land a disorienting punch, knocking me off guard. But I righted myself before she could do any more harm. I grabbed her by the throat with my free hand and held her there, my grip tightening as she tried to pry it free.

I turned to the other two, a man and a woman who were standing back, looking lost. Moments like these truly bring out the worst in people. When families and friends are not involved, there is no altruism, no sacrifice. They look after themselves and would happily see another die if it meant they could live for a few moments more.

"Are you not going to help her?" I asked them, squeezing tighter. "You can save her from this pestilence. You can be the heroes."

They looked at their friend, at me, and then back to her. She was kicking, desperate to break free but unable to do so. Her face was turning red, her eyes growing wider as I continued to tighten my grip.

I pointed the axe at her friends. "You can be the remedy!" I told them. "You can help her, help yourself, help the fucking world!"

And still, they didn't move.

Their friend's face turned blue, then purple. Her fingers, previously digging into my hand, loosened as she lost her strength. Her eyes began to roll back into her head, but she was doing her best to stop them, to retain consciousness and see out her demise.

"You disgust me," I told her friends.

The woman of the two turned and ran, but not before uttering a strangled scream. The man turned to watch her go and then turned back to me and his dying friend. He was clueless, lost, realizing that his death was imminent but unable or unwilling to do anything about it.

The woman grew limp in my hand and I let her go, watching as she flopped to the floor like a puppet on severed strings. The man tried to fight me. He held up his fists, realizing the only way to survive was to defeat me, but his fists were no match for my axe. I hacked at his hand first, removing it from his wrist but for a few strands of skin. He screamed, his eyes wide, staring in horror at his dangling hand. I aimed for his arm, hacking it off at the shoulder, before delivering several similar blows to his neck, decapitating him and showering myself in his blood.

The woman, the last one standing, had managed to break a small window at the back of the room and was trying to crawl out of it. It was a tight squeeze, and with pieces of jagged glass protruding out, it wasn't a comfortable one either. She winced and groaned as she tried to snake her way through, the glass puncturing her skin and ripping it open. She was doing most of the work for me. Realizing I didn't need the axe for this one, I stood behind her and waited.

When she got two thirds of the way through, with her legs dangling in front of me and her torso on the other side, I put the axe down and grabbed her by the feet. She had been relatively quiet until that point, no mean feat considering how much blood she had lost, but as soon as she felt my hands on her ankles, she screamed and she kicked.

I battled with her for a few moments before finding a grip. Then I pulled, dragging her back through the window. The screams were long and tortuous, and with each incremental movement, they increased and intensified. When she had finished and when I had dragged her back into the room, there was very little of her left. Many of the broken shards had been ripped out of the window frame and were now embedded in her, but the ones that had remained had done the most damage. They had torn deep into her body and were decorated with chunks of her flesh, colored with her blood.

Her screams softened when she looked herself over and realized how close to death she was. She was bleeding out, incapable of moving, incapable of breathing for longer than a few moments. I picked up my axe and headed backstage, grinning and mumbling to myself as I went. "And the flames of the tripods expired. And darkness and decay and the Red Death held illimitable dominion over all."

The show was over but the encore would follow.

2

—

I'd had my fun, but the real excitement was only just beginning. As I sat backstage, I took in my surroundings—the cos-
tumes, the props, the blood, the bodies—and awaited my big
moment. I had no doubt that Keats would show. I had faith in him
and I had faith in my plan. On the surface, it didn't look like he
had much love for his children, and they certainly had no respect
for him, but he was human, he had weaknesses. That love did exist
deep down and it would trigger the anger, the hatred, and the
impulsivity that I wanted to see.

My father had not expressed an interest in toying with the
police and I had no desire to do so either. It was far too risky, far
too stupid. But the more I saw Lester on the evening news, reporting on my latest victim, the more I liked him. I could see something in him that I hadn't seen anywhere else. He didn't remind me
of myself. He was far too normal, far too accepting of the world for
that. But he reminded me of my father.

He had the same hatred, bitterness, and resentment that
I knew that my father had possessed. They were traits that had
always existed in me and had always been on the surface, but like
my father, Lester had hidden them away, tucking them beneath a
veil of normality. He wanted the world—his boss, his children—
to think that everything was okay, that he was functioning as a

normal human being should. On social media he interacted with his friends and acquaintances; at work, he acted with professionalism, even when the press jammed cameras and microphones in his face. My father had done the same in his own way. It had probably contributed to his early death and the end of his legacy.

My fascination with Lester had grown since the death of his wife. That tested the barrier that separated the angry Lester from the Lester that he wanted the rest of the world to see. Eventually, as I studied his movements online, watched the interviews he gave, and generally kept a close eye on him and his family, I saw that barrier break. I had always hoped that the same would happen to my father, that he would become more like me, like the person I knew he was and not the one he wanted to be. I never had the chance to see that, but I had seen it in Lester.

The death of his kids would make sure the barrier was completely obliterated, but that wasn't why I did it. This was my moment, my final act as The Masquerade, and I wanted Lester to be in attendance. My adversary, my comrade, and in many ways, my father. Those murders would have accessed a primal part of him, and that's exactly what I wanted to happen. I wanted an angry and feral man to come for me, not a calculating cop.

Of course, if I were wrong, then I would be caught. The police would swoop on the building like vultures on a carcass and there would be little hope of escape, little hope of getting out alive. That was a risk I was prepared to take. If I were arrested or shot, then at least I had gone out in style, at least my legend would be given a fitting end, one that was never bestowed upon my father. And that was what this was all about: my legend, my legacy. My attempts at taking on the name of The Butcher had ended in a cataclysm of violence and bloodshed, with my name and face plastered all over the media. Now that The Masquerade had also been discovered, it required another fitting end. Regardless of what happened from this moment on, I was one of the most brutal and prolific killers in history. My name would be spoken, remembered, and revered throughout the world for many years to come. My father had gone out with a pathetic whimper, but the person I was many years ago had gone out with a bang, and the same would apply to the person I had become. As for the next step, the next legend, the person I would become next. That was anyone's guess.

"Please . . . help . . . me."

The noise was weak but it was enough to interrupt my thinking. I looked down to see a woman in period costume crawling on the floor, a trail of blood behind her like sticky slime emanating from a slug's behind. She hadn't made it far, but in her state, even a few inches was commendable. After what I had done to her, just the fact that she was still breathing was enough to win my respect.

"And why would I do that?" I asked her.

She stared at me, her pleading eyes doing their best to see the human in me.

"You can stare all you want. I'm not going to help you."

"Please, I—"

"You realize I was the one who put you in that situation, right?" I leaned over in my seat, my elbows resting on my thighs. "What makes you think I won't just torture you and make your last seconds even more miserable?"

"Please, if you help me, I won't tell anyone."

That made me laugh.

"Please, I need . . . ambulance."

I shook my head and straightened up. "You need a fucking miracle, that's what you need."

She reached out but her arms didn't possess the strength to remain upright for long and she eventually flopped to the floor.

"Then . . . kill me," she said, her face now pointed downward, her words muffled. "End this."

I picked up the axe and stood over her. "Now that, I can do."

The axe embedded in her skull. She was dead and out of her misery, but I didn't care about that. As much as I tried to yank the axe free, even standing on her skull to get some leverage, it wouldn't move.

"Ah, the irony," I said, shaking my head with disbelief. "You keep it."

As I searched around for another weapon, I heard the heavy doors to the building open and shut. My guest had arrived—the encore was ready to begin. There was no axe, no sword, nothing that could make my job easier, but I did carry a switchblade in my pocket, which was going to have to do.

I headed for the stage, took my spot at its center, and then waited for my audience to walk through the side door that had been unlocked in anticipation of his arrival.

3

—

I didn't need to say anything as he entered. I let the surroundings do the talking for me. He couldn't fail to notice the pools of blood, or the arcs of crimson where the axe had swooped on its deadly curves. He also couldn't fail to notice the bodies or the stench. The young men and women were strewn around the room, left where they had been killed. They had only been deceased for an hour or so, but the stench of drying blood, of emptied bowels and exposed organs, was prominent.

He seemed agitated, almost desperate when he entered, but he immediately deflated when he looked around and realized he was too late.

"You expected something else?" I projected from the center of the stage, my arms spread.

In my mask and my bloodied clothes, I expected him to fear me just like the young actors and actresses had done, but despite the distance between us, I could see there was no emotion in his eyes, no terror, no apprehension, no respect. That disappointed me. I hated it when things didn't go as planned, but I continued regardless.

"I should have waited for you," I told him. "And for that I apologize. But I was so eager to start. I mean, look at this!" I threw my arms open. "Isn't it fucking beautiful?"

I could tell by the look on his face that he didn't think so, but he didn't say anything. He walked up to the stage, doing his best to slalom through the bodies, but not seeming to care about the blood. He trod in a sticky patch left by the director and left singular crimson footprints as he approached the stage.

"And your kids," I said. "I guess I have to apologize for lying on that one, as well. I jumped the gun a bit."

"I did what you asked." His voice was barely audible. It was gravelly, tired. "I went there alone, and yet you killed them anyway. Why?"

"Why did I kill?" I asked. "That's what I do. You know that better than anyone."

He shook his head. "My kids were different. You did that to get at me. This was vengeance, this was a game. But why them and why not me?"

"Ah." I pointed at him. "But why not *both*?"

"They did nothing wrong. The people you killed, they had their faults. Darren Henderson bullied you, the priest, well, you knew him, so I'm guessing he had a *hand* in making your youth a misery, as well."

That amused me. There was a twinkle in his eye. He was trying to get to me. He wasn't intimidated by the mask, by the knife in my hand, or by the bloodshed around him.

"But my kids," he continued. "They did nothing wrong. Neither did any of these." He gestured around him.

"And what about Darren's brother? What about the boy in the church? What about all the others I killed that did fuck-all wrong? This isn't a mission of vengeance or righteousness, Lester. I'm not a fucking vigilante. If people wrong me, they die, but that doesn't mean that everyone else gets off the hook. Stop looking for reason in this, because you won't find it."

He nodded slowly and then he turned away, gazing around the room. "So that's what this is all about?" he asked. "You brought me here so you could kill me? Why the pomp, why the flair, why not just wait for me at home and kill me then?"

"Ah, Lester, you disappoint me." I shook my head, showing my disappointment. "I mean, where's the fun in that? As you said, this is a game, and games should be fun. If you make them too easy then they stop being fun. Am I right?"

He didn't answer and continued to look up at me. I felt powerful on the stage. It gave me such a thrill to be above others, to be looking down on them and to be leading the show. It was a shame I had no interest in acting or singing. I was a great performer, of course, but although my performances would soon be famous in all four corners of the world, it wasn't the sort of thing people paid money to see. At least not the normal ones.

"Why me?" he asked eventually.

"You exposed me and my past. You gave the media a taste of my true self and you dug up old bones that should have remained buried. I wanted to show you that you're not the only one who can excite the press or toy with the public."

"That wasn't my intention," he said.

I shrugged. "That's all irrelevant now anyway. What's done is done, and what I did was *fucking* fantastic, so I would never take that back." I had a bright smile on my face and although it didn't show through the mask, it did carry in my voice.

"You're fucking sick."

"You've only just realized?"

He stood still, staring at me, unmoving, unblinking. Eventually he asked, "So what are we going to do now?"

"You tell me."

He shook his head defiantly. "This is your show, this is your setup. You decide."

I put my hands behind my back and waited patiently, not saying a word.

"Are you going to stay up there?" he asked.

"I belong here."

"You belong in an asylum."

"I beg to differ."

"This is what all of this is about, isn't it?" he asked, a cheeky smile spreading across his face. "Delusions of grandeur. You want to get back at the world for bullying you, for calling you ugly and weird, that's why you kill, that's why you destroy families, that's why you wear a mask."

I couldn't help but laugh at that. "Don't underestimate me, Lester. I'm not one of your pathetic criminals that you can manipulate with a few emotional tricks. I kill them because I like it, pure and simple."

"It's sickening."

"Again, I beg to differ. As a race, we humans kill for food on a mass scale. We torture intelligent beings who feel pain just as much as we do, and we do it so we can buy ten hamburgers for a dollar, or have something to jam in our mouths when we get bored between TV programs. We torture them for cosmetics, just to make sure the shit that's killing them doesn't turn our eyebrows green or make our hair fall out. At least what I'm doing makes sense. I kill for pleasure, for a feeling that is unrivaled and cannot be achieved by any other means."

He didn't seem to agree. "We kill for food, to survive; you kill for fun."

"To survive?" I laughed. "You're telling me that an overweight Westerner with his Big Mac, his bacon sandwiches, and his heart clogged with ten pounds of animal fat, needs to kill an animal to live? Fuck off, Lester, I thought you were more intelligent than that."

"So what are you, some sort of radical vegetarian?"

"Again, stop fucking around. I like meat just as much as the next man. I was making a point. This thing that you and society deem as unforgivable is no different from what man has been doing for centuries, no different from what we've been doing as a race since we crawled out of the ocean, developed brains, and then spent thousands of years trying not to use them."

"So if you kill at random, then why my kids?" he begged to know. "You didn't need to do this. You got the fame that you wanted, the world is paying attention to you now. Why me, why my children?"

I shrugged. "This was personal. I wanted to test you. To take away everything, to bring you to your knees. The great men are the ones that make their own way in life, the ones that drag themselves from the bottom and make it to the top. I did that and—"

"Bullshit," he spat, interrupting and infuriating me. "What bottom? You were a middle-class white boy with clothes on his back, a bed to sleep in, and a roof over his head."

"How dare—"

"Let's be honest, you're just some puny little twit with maternal issues. A pathetic kid who was bullied all his life. There's no two ways about it, that's why you do what you do."

"That's nonsense and you know it," I said, trying to keep my cool but getting increasingly annoyed.

"I beg to differ."

That, along with the smug smile on his face, was what tipped me over the edge. I jumped down from the stage and grabbed him by the throat. He was still smiling and didn't seem to care when I tightened my grip. His expression also didn't change when I pulled the switchblade out of my pocket and opened it close to his throat.

"This is my show, Lester, stop trying to spoil it."

"But aren't I part of the show, as well?" he asked. "Otherwise, why haven't you killed me already?"

We locked stares for a moment and then I stepped back, ripping off the mask. "You know what I look like, so there's no point in hiding it."

Lester nodded and instinctively rubbed the spot on his throat where my hand had been. "The whole world has seen you, or at least a representation of you. And once this is over, everyone everywhere will be doing their best to find you. How do you plan on staying hidden?"

"I have my ways," I told him confidently. "But mostly I will be relying on others, because believe me, people are not as smart as you're giving them credit for."

"Killing will be impossible. If there's a murder in your area then someone will see you, they'll put two and two together. Hell, they might even check CCTV. That didn't exactly work out for you last time, did it?"

I shook my head, maintaining a smile. He was trying to mess with my moment, to cast doubts on my future and throw me off guard, but I knew exactly what he was doing and was happy to play along.

"You see, that's the issue with England, and with smaller countries. They don't cater to the serial killers who truly want to make a name for themselves. They're too small, too claustrophobic. The cities are the lifeblood of any country and the excitement that lures any killer, but here the cities are wrapped in cotton wool, mollycoddled by a paranoid government intent on making sure that every burglar, every mugger, every rapist, and every pickpocket is accounted for. Whether you're strolling to the shops in your pajamas to buy some bread and milk, fucking some local fancy down some piss-stained alley, or relieving yourself against a lamppost in the dead of night, you're watched and studied all hours of the day."

Lester shrugged. "I don't know about that. You did well as The Masquerade."

I grinned. "Thank you for noticing, but that's different and it bores me. These shitty little towns have nothing for me. I want something bigger, something more exciting." I paused to allow myself a laugh. "That is, unless you stop me."

He didn't find it as funny as I did.

"It's places like America where I can truly shine," I continued for my one-man audience. "A country so vast and so grand that hundreds of people are murdered every day without anyone knowing and without anyone caring. There are probably hundreds of serial killers that have been unaccounted for, people without rhyme or reason who drive from state to state, ticking off prostitutes and hitchhikers to rack up a high score. With a bit of invention and the balls to own up to your crimes, a prolific killer could really make a name for himself there, cementing his place in history."

"And is that what you want?" Lester asked. "A place in history? Is that why you do what you do?"

I could see that he didn't have a genuine interest in what I had to say. He was playing my game, trying to lure me into a false sense of security, be my friend, but it wasn't going to work. I was, however, willing to play dumb, but only because he intrigued me, because these were the moments that I longed for, the moments that I dreamed about. Here I was, face to face with my adversary, my equal in many ways, albeit to a much lesser extent. He was an adversary like Darren Henderson, a comrade like my father. He was both and neither, and he was the only non-blood-related person I had enjoyed speaking to since the cold December night I had ended Darren's life.

"That's not the only reason," I told him. "I enjoy what I do. And most of them have done something to deserve it anyway."

He shook his head. "Many of them were young girls. Innocent girls. They don't deserve that; what could they have possibly done to deserve *that*?"

I laughed and shook my head. "No one gets it, no one truly understands. It hasn't changed and it never does. These people are locked away in their pathetic little lives, completely oblivious to the outside world, to all the little demons that scurry about and threaten their perfect families, their perfect careers, their perfect selves." I stamped my foot and expected Lester to jump. He didn't even flinch. "I'm the threat, I'm the demon, I'm the one who disrupts, causes chaos. These people do nothing wrong on the face of it. They're not killers, they're not abusers, but they deserve to die, because ignorance and stupidity is just as bad as all of those things."

"I get it," Lester said, nodding. "I really do, and I believe you. I've walked in your shoes, I know how you think. I know how your brain operates."

I laughed at him, giving his pathetic response the reply that it warranted. "You don't have a clue what I do or why I do it. I'm not on a mission for the greater good, I'm not a whack-job who thinks that by stripping away the rust of civilization the foundation will thrive. I do what I do for myself and no one else. I do what I do because I like it."

"And why the women?" he asked. "Why, if there is no sexual motive, did you kill so many young girls?"

"Ah!" I put my hands together and squeezed, allowing him to see my face light up as if I were recalling a fond memory. "Back to this. Why indeed? I have no idea. Maybe it just feels right, maybe it's just easier, maybe—"

"Maybe they remind you of your mother?"

I thrust the knife at him, the point of the blade just a few inches from his throat. "Don't you dare talk about my fucking mother!" I ordered.

"But that's it, isn't it? That's what all this is about. That's certainly what Irene Henderson was all about."

I kept the knife pressed to his throat, lifting the blade up and down as he swallowed, tracing the movement of his Adam's apple. "Believe me, Lester, I have killed many men. Maybe not wearing that mask, maybe not under the guise of The Masquerade, but many men and boys have died by my hand. Your son included."

He flinched at that.

I grinned, eased off. "Irene Henderson. Now, that's a name I haven't heard in a long time."

"You ruined her life."

"That may be so, but I didn't kill her."

"She would have been better off dead. You scared the life out of her and left nothing but an empty shell." Lester spoke without emotion, without the crippling fear or the capitulating emotional anxiety that I could forgive him for expressing. This lack of emotion had nothing to do with the fact that he was a policeman. I had encountered plenty of them, both experienced and naive, and they hadn't shared this apathetic facade, this vacant stare. It was something else entirely and it intrigued me.

"And what about you, Lester Keats? Why are you an empty shell, as you so eloquently put it? What or who scared the life out of you?"

Lester continued to stare, not flinching. "That's none of your fucking business," he said slowly.

"You realize I have a knife pointed at your throat, right?"

"Do you think that scares me?"

"Evidently not."

We locked stares again.

"I like you, Lester."

"I want to kill you, Herman."

"You're not the first."

"But I *will* be the last."

I pulled back, keeping the knife close. "The truth is, I know why you broke, Lester. I know about your wife. I know your kids grew to resent you for her death."

"That had nothing to do with it."

I shrugged. "You're right, maybe they just thought you were a useless cunt. But either way, they hated you."

I could see the anger flare behind his eyes as he recalled everything they had put him through and everything he regretted saying and doing to them.

"I know about the incident with the drug dealer. In fact, that's when I really started to like you. You see, you're a lot like me, Lester. You may not realize it, but we're very similar. In a different time, a different place, we could have been good friends. Brothers."

I could see the anger increasing; his lips were instinctively curling in distaste as I spoke those words.

"You're not as pure as I am. You're not as honest with yourself as you need to be. But . . . you remind me of someone I respected once."

His demeanor changed in an instant. He grinned. "The Butcher?"

My face dropped. I gave him a curious, shocked stare. "What did you say?"

"You're not always the most intelligent person in the room, Herman. You don't always know more than everyone else. I figured it all out. Your father was The Butcher and you tried to follow in his footsteps, but you failed."

His grin was bigger, his confidence had increased. I was speechless.

"He died, so you tried to take on his legend, didn't you? That's what all of this is about. You want to do what your father didn't, you want to become the person he failed to be. The person you failed to be when you let your anger get the better of you fifteen years ago."

"Anger had nothing to do with it," I said. "They weren't where they should have been. That was their fault, not mine."

Lester laughed. "Well then, I guess they paid for that mistake, didn't they?"

"How do you know about my father?"

Lester was enjoying this. I could tell. He shifted forward, but I reacted quickly, pressing the knife back to his throat. He didn't seem to mind and spoke like nothing had happened. "If you really want to know, it occurred to me a number of years ago. A woman I was looking into was reported missing around the start of The Butcher's reign. I wondered if the two were connected. Your father always fit the profile and as soon as I realized that she couldn't possibly still be alive, I made that connection."

"What the fuck are you talking about?"

"That woman was your mother, Herman. I know your father killed her."

I didn't speak a word, but I watched his face change as he stared at me, and I realized that my expression spoke for itself.

"You didn't know? Come on, you must have." I could feel his breath on my face. "Did you know the police investigated your father after your mother went missing? Did you know they suspected he had killed her, but couldn't find any proof? There were at least half a dozen reports of assault, none of which she followed through with. He beat the shit out of her, Herman, but every time he convinced her not to press charges. He manipulated her like only a true sociopath can."

"You seem to know a lot about common assault, Lester. Did you beat your wife, as well?" He laughed again. I knew he could sense the unease in my voice. "It must have been hard to grow up around all of that violence," he said. "Witnessing all of that anger and then losing your mother . . ." He shook his head slowly, the point of the knife tickling the skin on his neck. "God knows what that would have done to a child's mind. That's why you kill, isn't it? That's what turned you into a monster. Your mother was the only person you loved and having to watch her suffer before losing her completely, that fucked you up."

That amused me immensely and I laughed to express this amusement, but in doing so I gave him the opportunity that he had been waiting for. He swung his arm and caught me on the wrist, not enough to knock the knife out of my hand, but enough to direct it away from his throat. Then, with his free hand, he punched me in the face. I was still taken aback, still a little fazed, so I didn't see the punch coming until it landed.

I felt my nose buckle under the impact, felt one of my back teeth chip as my jaw clenched and then shifted, my molars grating against each other. I had taken plenty of beatings in my life; I knew how to maintain composure. While fazed, I managed to drag the knife back to him, to thrust forward with the blade. But he was too quick. He moved out of the way, swiveled until the back of my hand pressed against his chest, and then he clawed at my fingers.

He was a dirty fighter, doing what he needed to get the job done, which, even as it was about to cost me my life, I respected him for. At first he dug his nails into the fleshy part of my hand, and when that didn't work, he bit me. When that still didn't work, he peeled my forefinger away from the handle of the blade and continued to peel it back until he heard it snap. That was enough to cause me to drop the knife, enough to give him the edge that he needed.

As soon as the knife was pried out of my grasp, I fell to my knees and realized that the end was nigh. I'd had a good run, and although being stabbed in the back by a policeman wasn't my first choice as a way to go, it certainly had a nice ring to it.

I waited for the thrust to come, to end the agony that soared through my body, but it didn't come. Eventually I looked up, craning my neck, blinking through the pain and the haze to see Lester standing over me. The vacant expression had gone from his face and was replaced by a crude smile, a smile I was sure had been on my own face a number of times over the years.

"It's better than you could ever imagine," I told him.

"What are you talking about?"

"Killing. It's everything that you imagine it to be and so much more."

"I'm not a murderer, Herman. I'm not even a violent man."

"Says the guy who just broke my fucking finger."

He laughed and I couldn't help but join him, but when I did, he seemed to take offense. He swung for me and his boot caught me on the chin, spinning me over and causing me to land in a heap, the back of my head clattering against the solid floor.

"What the fuck was that for?" I spat, thrusting my neck up just enough for me to spit a colorful concoction of my own blood and mucus onto the dusty floor beside me.

"You're a filthy fucking murderer, you have no right to laugh, no right to smile. I don't care why you did what you did. I don't care if you had a bad childhood. You're scum." He dropped to his knees and hovered above me, the knife held tightly in both hands, experienced enough not to make the same stupid mistake I had made. "Did your victims ever smile, did they ever laugh?"

"You'd be surprised."

He kicked me again, a toe-poke into my ribs, but that wasn't enough to sate my sense of humor.

"Does this take you back, Herman? Does this remind you of your schooldays? All of the times those kids beat you up? If only they knew what you would turn into, hell, if only the *teachers* knew, they would have given them medals. You got exactly what you deserved."

I laughed. "Ironic, really, because so did they."

He hit me, another crunching strike with his boot, this time into my waist. It sucked the air out of my lungs, caused me to crunch into a ball. He seemed to enjoy that more than the others, but when I stopped hissing, when I stopped moaning, I laughed again.

He gave me a blank stare. "Do I amuse you?" he asked.

"You? God no, you're hardly a bundle of fucking laughs, are you?" I scrambled up until I was leaning on my elbows, moving slowly. "I was just thinking how the roles seem to have been reversed. I'm the psycho killer here, yet you're the one standing over me with a knife, taunting me."

"Now you know how it feels to be one of your victims."

I shook my head. "You know as well as I do that I can never know that. These people are weak, they don't feel or think the same as I do. As *we* do."

He didn't say anything to that but I could see that I had gotten through to him.

"You and me are alike, and I know you see that. Only, it's got nothing to do with Whitegate and it's got nothing to do with being miserable. It's about being disillusioned with life, about being fed up with the human race on the whole."

Lester nodded, it was faint and it might have been instinctive, but it was definitely a nod.

"Take your kids, for example—"

"Leave my kids out of this!"

I held up my hands as best I could, grunting through the pain that the movement caused. "I'm just saying. Do you feel the love that all parents feel? Do you feel enlightened and enlivened that you have spread your seed?"

He shook his head, another faint and almost invisible movement.

"And why is that?"

"I loved my kids."

"That's not what I asked."

He shrugged and as he did so, I saw his grip on the knife loosen. He was a professional man, an experienced officer, but he was letting his guard down, letting his emotion get in the way.

"My kids lost respect for me. After their mother died . . ." He trailed off with a shrug. "They stopped caring."

"And eventually you stopped caring as well?"

"I still loved them," he said, his voice picking up, fluctuating as emotion took hold. "But I didn't *like* them."

"I'm sure the feeling was mutual."

He nodded in agreement and I clambered to my knees, grunting, groaning and hissing through clenched teeth, showing him I was no threat—I wasn't capable of doing anything. He didn't stop me, seemingly lost in his own thoughts as he idly watched.

"Life has been cruel to you, but that's the way things are," I told him. "Most people suck it up and move on. But there are those who refuse to let it wash over them, the ones who decide to fight back, to kick life in the balls every time it threatens to do the same to them." I was closer to him now, just inches from the loosening blade and from his defeated posture. "So why don't you quit your job, ignore your kids, and join me?"

"You're a murderer."

"I'm more than just a murderer. I'm one of the most prolific murderers there has ever been," I informed him. "The fear and the respect I get is unparalleled, and that fear and that respect will continue long after I'm dead."

He looked me in the eyes and I sensed a great deal of emotion. He wasn't a murderer, I knew that and he knew that, but he was fed up with his lot in life. He was angry, bitter, and although he would never take that first step, he wanted the satisfaction of vengeance.

"You can't tell me that murder has never appealed to you." I locked him into eye contact and moved closer, until he couldn't see my hand edging for the knife. "You can't—"

"You're right." He backed away. "I *do* want revenge, I *do* want to hurt those who have hurt me."

Just when I thought I had him, I realized that he had been fucking with me.

"But you're the one who has made my life a misery these last few years; the one who has given me sleepless nights because I can't get the faces of your victims out of my mind; the one I have to thank for losing my appetite because I couldn't get the smell of rotting flesh out of my nose. Yes, my kids hated me, and no, that wasn't entirely my fault. Maybe it had something to do with the fact that I couldn't look at my daughter without knowing that her face could be the face of one of your victims, without realizing that all the love I had for her could be exploited and taken away with one thrust of a knife. Maybe it's got something to do with the fact that I couldn't look at my son without seeing Darren Henderson or Barry Barlow, the ones you butchered, cutting short their young lives and the lives of their parents, their brothers and their sisters."

"They deserved everything they got!" I spat, feeling a surge of anger at the mere mention of those names.

He ignored me. "And in the end, my worries about my children weren't unfounded, because my nightmares came true, and that was your fault." His expression twisted, a menacing look spreading thickly across his face. "They were kids!" he roared. A veil of spittle flew from his mouth. Strands of saliva stuck to his chin and he wiped them away with the back of his hand. "How could you even think for a moment that I would want to end up like you? You disgust me."

"I'm so much more than you could ever be," I said, growing increasingly incensed.

Lester shook his head. "You're nothing. And as for your legacy and your *legend*, let's just see what happens when the world learns that the *most prolific* serial killer in the country was taken down by a depressed cop."

I knew how things were going to play out and I knew I was at a disadvantage. I was weak, nearly keeled over and vulnerable to attack. I had no weapons, nothing but my own fists, but I did have the element of surprise. The last thing he was expecting was for me to charge at him with little regard for my own safety. After all, no one in their right mind would run at a man holding a knife. But that's exactly what I did.

The charge was effective—he didn't have time to prepare the weapon. I felt it stick into my waist, rip through my clothes and dig into my flesh, but his grip was weak and before it penetrated much further, he dropped it. He grunted upon the impact, the air knocked out of his lungs, and then he fell backward with me on top of him.

He was surprised and fearful, I saw it in his face—the same expression that had been on all of their faces. He was stronger, more experienced, but when it came down to it, they were all the same.

I ignored the pain in my stomach and the blood that soaked my shirt, and I pummeled my fists into his face, relishing the sound my knuckles made as they crushed against his jaw bone, his cheek bones, and his temples. I broke his nose, crushing it against his face and decorating his flesh with its crimson innards. I broke some of his teeth, the crushed enamel collecting at the back of his throat along with blood and mucus, threatening to choke him on his own body fluids. I also broke his jaw, leaving his mouth a twisted mess. I gave it every last ounce of energy that I had, gritting my teeth like a marathon runner on the final sprint as I pushed through the pain.

He tried to stop me, and he was strong enough to land a few powerful punches, but I had more experience than anyone when it came to being hit. I could deflect those punches like I had deflected Darren Henderson's punches. Back then I had dissociated, gone to my special place, a beautiful place where I killed Darren in so many beautiful ways, but now I was already in my special place. And no punches and no pain could stop it from being so beautiful.

Lester Keats was a bigger and better nemesis than Darren Henderson had ever been. He took a lot more to catch and a lot more to defeat. I had been terrified of Darren, overcoming my fear using sheer determination alone. I hadn't been as scared of Lester, but only because I was a man now. Much more than that, in fact.

"You know," I said, stopping, breathless. "I actually thought about avoiding you," I told him, grinning at his mangled face as he tried to breathe, tried to spit out the blood collecting at the back of his throat. "I thought you were a worthy match, that you might actually put an end to everything I had worked so hard to create, but . . ." I shook my head. "I couldn't have been more wrong."

I stood up, kneeing him in the groin for good measure. He tried to scramble to his feet, but he was punch drunk, barely conscious.

"If this were a film, this would be the point where someone would burst in and save you." I walked over to the knife, and as I bent down to pick it up, I felt a sharp pain in my torso. The blood was pouring heavily now and the pain was increasing, but I would live. It would be a reminder of our battle, a scar fittingly deeper and bigger than anything Darren had left. "Do you have anyone lined up?"

I held the knife above him. His eyes were open and seemed to be looking at me, but his face was so swollen and so bloodied it was hard to tell.

"A partner that you argue a lot with but really, deep down, you're best buddies with?"

He choked out an inaudible reply.

"I'll take that as a no. What about someone who you thought was dead or missing?"

Another choke. There was also some movement, a wriggle or a spasm, but I didn't know if it was intentional.

"Again, that's a no. It's not looking good for you, is it?" I rested a finger thoughtfully on my chin. "Okay then, what about your kids? You used to love them and I'm sure they felt the same way about you at one point. Years of arguments and hatred later, I think it would be rather apt for them to show up, save your life, and make your happily-ever-after come true—what do you say?"

I was silent then, waiting—only the sound of his moaning, grunting, coughing, and spluttering breaking through the silence. I checked my watch, tapped the top of the timepiece, and then I raised a finger, remembering something. "Ah right, they can't, can they? Because I killed them."

"I. Will. Not. Play!"

I frowned at the bloodied mess before me. "Excuse me?"

He was trying and failing to pry himself up. "I. Will. Not. Play. Your. Games."

"Who said anything about games?"

"This. This is what you enjoy," he said, breathless from the struggle, the words grating and bubbling out of his throat as if spoken under water. "And I want no . . . no part in it. Kill me. You fuck."

"Well then, there's no need for that."

He summoned some energy from somewhere and used it to throw out his arms and legs, like a wounded animal kicking its last kick. He caught me in the shin and threw me off balance, but I retained my footing before falling over.

"Kill me!" he yelled, his voice screeching. "You fucking piece of shit. Kill me!"

"You're not—"

"Shut up and kill me!"

"Well I—"

He lashed out again and this time he managed to sweep my feet out from under me. I toppled forward, landing next to him, at which point he threw himself on top of me. We fought again, but there was little strength left in him and I managed to get to my feet, with him on his knees as he tried and failed to follow me up.

"What is wrong with you?" I asked him. "I just wanted a—"

"What is wrong with me?" He spat. "That's rich coming from you!" He laughed maniacally and I felt the excitement drain out of me. This was supposed to be my moment, my crowning glory, but he seemed to be having more fun than I was. I had been dreaming of such a kill for a long time, a worthy adversary, a long and drawn-out vengeance, but he—

"Well!" he spat again. "Get it over with!"

In his anger, he managed to scramble to his feet, looking like a sleep-deprived zombie as he rocked back and forth, seemingly unaware of where I was or where he was, or so I thought. He reached out and grabbed the knife in my hands. His bloodied and soppy appendages clasping around the blade and my flesh.

He looked at me and I could just about see two small pupils poking through a swamp of blood and swollen flesh. "I. Will. Not. Play. Your. FUCKING. GAMES!"

He drove forward, his hands still holding the knife. I felt it sink into his waist and, with his face inches from mine, I saw the smile slowly develop and I felt his final breaths leave his body. I tried to rip the knife free. This wasn't how I wanted it to be, this wasn't how I wanted him to die. It was supposed to be my kill, my time to shine, but this, this was barely even murder. As weak as he had been before, once the knife was inside him, there was little I could do to pry it free. His body was reluctant to let it go, desperate to die, clinging onto the steel blade as it sucked the remnants of life from him.

When I finally ripped it out, it was already too late.

Lester was still smiling when he fell to his knees, his hands cupping the blood gushing out of his torso. "You're not a legend," he said, almost giggling despite his imminent demise. "You're just a lost child." He fell backward, hitting the floor with a thump and a moan. He laughed as he made contact and then, as the last of his laughter and the last of his life drained away, he added, "And a fucking prick."

I watched him breathe his final breath. I did not smile. I did not enjoy it.

I bent down over him and checked his pulse, making sure he was gone and sighing in disappointment when I realized he was. Not that it mattered—if he were still clinging to life, there would have been very little I could have done to prolong it, very little I could have done to make it enjoyable for me.

I was annoyed. He was my greatest adversary and yet had delivered me no satisfaction. He had been better to me alive, and that was a thought I had never had about anyone else. It was almost enough to make me want to give up killing, to pack my knives away, settle down, and try to live the normal life.

I chuckled to myself.

As if that were ever going to happen.

EPILOGUE

". . . And what about Herman, Keats believed that he and The Masquerade were one and the same, do you think it was Herman who got to him?"

"I don't—"

"—Surely you see that this has to be more than a coincidence?"

"Look, I really—"

"What about the town of Whitegate? Should they be worried? Do you think he wants to seek revenge?"

"Forget about them, what about the general public! This guy is nuts and he's still out there, what are you doing to protect us?"

I grinned to myself as I watched the press conference unfold on television. I had never seen Chief Inspector Atwood before, but I liked him. He was Lester's boss and he had been put in charge of the investigation, struggling to field a barrage of questions from journalists who refused to let him answer one before moving on to the next. He looked strong, defiant, like he took no shit from anyone. He reminded me of the big, hairy, cigar-chomping detectives of old, the ones who had probably only existed on eighties television shows but whose images had been imprinted onto the minds of an impressionable generation.

"Is everything okay, sir?"

I looked up to see a pretty waitress standing over me. She looked a little tired and more than a little dumb, but she had striking blue eyes and a comforting smile. She was like a lot of attractive young women around Whitegate in that with a bit of poise, makeup, and attention, they could make it to the front pages of many magazines. But instead they were resigned to a life of customer service in some greasy diner while their drug-addled boyfriend waited to steal their meager earnings, force them into depraved sex acts, and then threaten to leave them or kill them if they refused.

I returned her question with a tired smile, still feeling the effects of my battle with Lester. Two days had passed, but I had avoided hospitals and doctors and had been forced to see to my own wounds. It didn't require a lot of stitches, but I needed a great deal of whiskey and morphine to get me through and it was that combination of drugs that had left me worse for wear. I had been staying in a bed and breakfast at the time and only when I heard the sound of a police officer knocking at my door did I wake from my sedated slumber.

They were local officers, thick as shit. They were there to do what amounted to the most serious thing they had ever done, and they did it with all the style and competency of a drunk at a poker game. They didn't ask me who I was or why I was there, nothing that could have raised suspicions. They were just doing the rounds, knocking on doors, asking questions, going through the motions so they could finish sooner and leave earlier. It didn't matter that there was major manhunt on, it didn't matter that there was, potentially, a serial killer staying somewhere in town, what mattered was that they could go home early.

Ironically, one of those officers was in the café with me, sitting on the other side with a bright and cocky expression on his young face. He had evidently been given his wish and was on his break, but his partner wasn't with him. I didn't worry when I saw him; I had already met him and I had met his type many times before. It would take more than a feckless idiot to stop me, even though I had been incredibly feckless myself.

The officer looked over at me, but he seemed more interested in the waitress. He had been watching her the entire time. She seemed to be the reason he was there, the one thing that occupied his mind when he should have been thinking of protecting the public and doing his job. That's the weird thing about love and lust: it gets in the way of everything else. On the promise of sex, human society can collapse in the blink of an eye. I am not bound by the laws of attraction, certainly not in the same way. I have no room for love and lust, but I am still drawn to beauty and I do still desire to take attractive young girls home. It is what I do with them when I get them there that differs from the rest of society.

"What's your name?" I asked her.

She seemed shy, but then again they all are. It's the country life, the seclusion, the ignorance; true confidence is rare in these parts. "Cassie," she said, pointing to a name plate that sat perched upon her perky bosom.

I tried to catch the eye of the young officer in the corner, but he seemed too concerned with staring at the back of Cassie's head, as if willing her to turn around, to pay attention to him.

In another town, somewhere less deprived and less washed-up, she could have had an army of suitors, from businessmen to professional sports stars. But in this town, where few people of merit ever venture, her choices were limited to the same brainless simpletons who had hit on her in high school and tried to coax her into the library so they could finger her behind the reference section. A talentless local cop was probably the best that she could do for herself. In another place, she could have maintained her looks into middle age, using them to climb the career ladder one way or another, but in this town, they would be gone before she hit thirty, dried up thanks to poor nutrition, poor living standards, and one too many beatings.

"That's a beautiful name, it suits you well."

"Thank you," she beamed. "What about you, what's your name?"

"Lester," I said without hesitation.

"Oh, like the man who was murdered?"

We both looked toward the television, sitting on a grime and dust-encrusted stand behind the counter—too high up to clean and too far away to care. Atwood looked tired as the questions continued; he was also getting incredibly annoyed and looked like he was ready to blow. I didn't want to miss that.

"Yes, I suppose so."

"Terrible news, isn't it. You know, I went to the same school as this Herman fellow." She seemed proud of the fact. That was her claim to fame.

"Really?" I feigned surprise and intrigue, which I knew is what she expected.

She nodded slowly and sternly, her hands on her hips in a ponderous manner. "You would have never have guessed it by looking at him."

I barely managed to suppress a smile. This girl might have gone to the same school—she worked in the area so it wouldn't have surprised me—but she was also a good few years younger than me and probably only had fleeting glances at best. I was nothing to her and wouldn't have warranted a second thought, let alone a second glance.

"Did you ever talk to him?" I asked her.

She shook her head. "But my cousin's friend once sat next to him in the lunchroom. She said she could sense the evil, she said that she knew he was planning something like that."

Again, I had to stop myself from laughing. It was intriguing to know these conversations were going on, that I'd had such an impact on the lives of those I had hated so much, but the idea that any of these idiots had an idea of what I was going to do was pathetic.

"She should have said something then," I told her. "Could have saved a few people."

She shrugged. "I think she was talking out of her ass."

This time I did laugh. I was beginning to like this girl.

She smiled and I saw her eyes flicker as she checked me out. It was brief, but it was enough to show me her intentions. "So, you're not from around here?" she asked.

I shook my head and saw her intrigue increase. It wasn't like I was from another country, but to a small-town girl in a small town such as Whitegate, anyone of the same age who didn't go to her school, and anyone older who didn't know her parents by name and couldn't remember her when she was "just *this* tall," was exotic.

She lost my attention as I concentrated on the television above the bar; Atwood was about to snap and although he was far less attractive, he had many things that this silly little girl didn't have.

She said something else but I ignored her, and a few seconds later, her disappointed voice chirped up again. "So, is everything okay with your coffee and sandwich?"

I diverted my attention from the television long enough to give her a smile—committed enough to tell her that she should leave me alone, warm enough to keep her hanging on.

"Should the people of Whitegate be fearing more murders?"

"No, I—"

"How can you be so sure? How do you know he—"

It finally happened. Atwood snapped. The little vein that had been throbbing in his temple for the entirety of the interview finally popped. His face, which had been growing redder and redder by the second, turned a vicious shade of crimson as he rose to his feet and slammed his fists down angrily on the table. Several people in the room gasped, several of them jumped, but all of them continued to train their cameras and recorders on him. This was journalistic gold and they didn't want to miss a second of it.

"*Will you fucking let me speak!?*" he barked. "*I am a busy man, a grieving man, I came here to give you some answers but if you don't let me speak then I can't fucking give you those answers, can I?*"

His heavy breathing was the only sound heard over the click and flash of cameras and the murmurings of hushed phone calls.

"*Herman is not an idiot,*" Atwood continued, putting a smile on my face. "*The people of Whitegate are safe! Right now it happens to be one of the most heavily guarded towns in the country, with what amounts to half of the county's police force in and around it. If he was lingering around, I'm sure we would catch him.*"

That seemed to settle a few of the murmurings, and it also went some way to settling Atwood. "*Lester Keats was a good man and a great detective, one that was killed by a very evil and corrupt mind, but you have my word that we are working night and day to stop the man that did this.*"

"*And what about—*"

"*Yes!*" Atwood snapped, playing them at their own game. "*I am not forgetting the young men and women in the theater. We have lost one of our own, but we are not taking sides. Many lives were lost and we will do our best to ensure that justice is served.*"

He settled down after that, releasing a long and tired sigh that seemed to expel some of the fatigue emanating from his very soul. The questions started again and Atwood sat back down, the life and the anger drained out of him.

Atwood was probably right; Lester Keats was a good man. An intelligent man, as well, much more than I gave him credit for. His words had been playing over and over in my head. His accusations. His theories. Not to mention the calm, sadistic way he had delivered them. He had surprised me, but I had surprised myself, too.

I took out my wallet. It was brand new, leather, barely creased. There was a smiling, square-faced man in a Polo shirt grinning at me through the little transparent sleeve. It was a placeholder, a stock image of a man who was probably unbearable to be around. I kept it there to remind me why I hated people so much.

In one of the other compartments, hidden away, was a crumpled photograph. I took it out, opened it, and Irene Henderson stared up at me. This was one of the few possessions that had survived the fire, one of the ones I had purposefully taken with me. It was technically one of my first souvenirs, but as Lester had suggested, it was much more than that.

She didn't really look like my mother. She wasn't as beautiful, as elegant. But there was something in her smile that reminded me of her, something that activated a deep, internal part of me that was usually silent, a part I didn't understand and didn't like.

I had spared her life all those years ago and, truth be told, I had no idea why. She was the only one to have gotten away. If Lester was right and Irene Henderson was some representation of my mother, someone I had spared out of love, out of humanity, then I had made a mistake. This was about me—not my father, not my mother. It was my legend, my legacy, my fucking life.

I felt the anger rise inside me as I recalled Lester's words and when I turned back to the photograph, that feeling, that humanity, was gone. Replaced by bitterness, hatred. I had thought about revisiting Irene in the past. I had no idea where she lived, but I knew that her family—who still lived nearby—would, and with the right persuasion, I was sure they would tell me.

I jammed the image back in my wallet.

I looked around the café and noted that everyone else had already stopped paying attention, even the two officers in the back. The one who had been staring at me earlier had now moved his focus entirely to Cassie and was trying his best to win her affections. He called her over and fed her his best chat-up lines, seemingly derived from an anthology on how to be a dickhead. He was the same age as me and he was also probably better looking, but he was an idiot with all the maturity of a ten-year-old and even Cassie could see that. It pained me to realize these were the people who were supposed to be catching me; Atwood had just reassured the country they were safe because people like this were protecting them. It was laughable—if Lester hadn't stood a chance, then what hope did these idiots have? What hope did *anyone* have?

I caught the look of distaste on Cassie's face when she stopped flirting, gave the copper his tea, and headed back to the kitchen. He stared at me, a long and lingering stare. He was weighing me up and I realized that I might have underestimated him, that he had been watching me and was onto me.

He then pointed to Cassie and made a sexual gesture with his hands. He wasn't telling me that he knew who I was, he wasn't telling me that he knew there was anything suspicious about me, he was telling me that Cassie was his and that he had won.

It made me laugh, and he took that laugh as a sign that I was admitting defeat.

Atwood had called me evil, he had said that I would get what was coming to me, but that wasn't the way the world worked. This guy was clearly terrible at his job; he was clearly a sexist pig with little use to the human race. But who would complain if he didn't get what was coming to him? Who would complain if he wasn't murdered, maimed, or at least dragged back to reality with a vicious beating? There is no karma, but there are people like me—people who make their own karma. In a different time and a different place, I would have killed this cocky little prick, doing the female population a favor and creating a job opening that could be taken by someone who was competent. If someone had provided their own form of karmic justice before today, killing this nitwit and thus creating a space for someone else to fill, then my reign might have come to an end. Someone who was good at his job might have sussed me out and made me pay for my own cockiness.

My time may come, and my end may be unpleasant and karmic, but in the meantime I am a free man; free to murder; free to assault; free to maim; and most importantly, free of any remorse and regret. What I told Lester was right: there is no means or motive to what I do. I do it because I enjoy killing and because it feels right, but that isn't all strictly true. There is a drive within me that guides me toward these crimes. It is not a voice; I am not insane. In fact, I believe I am saner than many people and may be one of the sanest people alive. No, this drive, this inner guide, is something bigger than even I can comprehend.

Atwood would have made a nice adversary, but I preferred Lester. If anything, Atwood reminded me of Darren. He had a thuggish and brutish approach, lacking in the subtlety and darkness Lester possessed. As outwardly monstrous as Darren was, and as stern and forceful as Atwood is, the deepest darkness is in those who hide their true selves from the world. External evils like Atwood and Darren Henderson are limited to what they can express, because their minds are too small and their intentions are too meager for them to contemplate hiding those feelings. If they had any true darkness within themselves then they would hide it from the world and from there they would either do as I do, unleashing it in sporadic outbursts, timed for maximum effect and release, or they would hold it back and take the resulting frustration out on themselves, as Lester did.

Atwood certainly had some anguish inside of him, but the fact that he showed it all to the world, the fact that he unleashed it in such an uncouth manner, told me he wasn't the right man for me. He would be too easy to defeat and I would gain very little satisfaction from doing so.

"Can I get you a refill?"

Cassie was standing above me with a coffee pot. I smiled at her and then directed that to the other side of the café where the cocky copper's smile had faded, replaced by an irritated grimace.

"Sure," I let her bend over and refill my cup and when my face was out of her eye-line I winked at the cop. It didn't matter what the context was; toying with someone in authority was always fun.

"He giving you any trouble?" I asked.

She gave me a half-smile, indicating the answer was most definitely a yes, but that she was too timid and too nice to say anything.

"Just ignore him. He's new to the force, probably just got his badge," I told her. "Give him a couple weeks or so, a grisly murder or two, and he'll change. Hell, if we're lucky, then maybe Herman will get him."

She giggled and put a hand to her mouth. "That's horrible," she said with a smile that said otherwise. She paused for a moment, looking like she wanted to say something but wasn't sure what.

Finally she looked down at my feet, at the suitcase that was resting up against them. "Are you going away?" she asked.

"Holiday," I said with a nod.

"Oh, really, anywhere nice?"

Small talk was a baffling beast. After all, few people would go on holiday to the pits of hell, few people would dig out the travel brochures and search for the worst destination they could possible find. *"You know what, fuck the beach, I want to go to some hellhole in the middle of the desert where strange men with stranger urges will probe every available orifice while slathering my testicles in honey and pointing me toward a wasps' nest."*

"Yes. America."

"Ohh." The sound she made said she had surprised herself by being genuinely interested in what I had to say. "I always wanted to go to America. Which part?"

I shrugged. "I don't know. I figured I'd hit the road, try and see as much of it as I can."

"Great idea." She was besotted, lingering a little longer on the stare than she needed to, her interest in me suddenly extending beyond her desire to get a tip that I had no intention of leaving. "I wish I could do that."

"You're welcome to join me."

The officer rose to his feet. He hadn't finished his coffee, but his morning had clearly been ruined. He stormed out of the café, brushing past us as he did so. I could see that he was hoping to catch Cassie's attention, that a small part of him still hoped he had a chance, but she barely even noticed him. He locked eyes with me on his way out; it was not the first time a police officer had me in their sights and within their grasp, and it wouldn't be the last.

When the door swung shut, I turned back to Cassie.

Her jaw was open in disbelief, but then reality kicked in and she looked coy, almost embarrassed. "We've only just met. I couldn't do that."

"Well." I checked my watch. "I don't fly for another three hours, so what do you say you join me for a cup of coffee and we can get to know each other. After that you can walk me back to my house and if you think you know me well enough, then you can come along."

"Are you serious?"

I nodded. "Come on, it'll be fun. What do you say?"

She beamed a bright and happy smile. I picked up my wallet from the table. Irene's picture was poking out, the edges of her smile revealed.

I thought back to that night, to her house, to the bloodshed. I thought about her sons, her husband. I thought about her parents and then I thought about my mother.

"Is everything okay?" Cassie asked, a concerned expression on her face as she noted how quickly my smile had faded. "You're not changing your mind already, are you?"

I forced a smile, handed her some money, and then closed the wallet. "Of course not. I just remembered that I have some business to attend to before I go. Just an old friend. You know how it is." I winked at her. "Don't worry, I won't be long. And who knows, maybe I'll bump into your old friend from school on the way."

ACKNOWLEDGMENTS

This book is dedicated to my father, whose love of reading rubbed off on me at a very young age. If not for him turning a blind eye when I chose to read his Stephen King novels at a time I should have been reading Roald Dahl, my life may have taken a different course. I would also like to thank my mother, who has done more than I can ever repay, and my brother, Gary, who was always there to fight my battles, even though I was always trying to fight him. I extend the same gratitude to my sister-in-law, niece and nephews, to my second family in Greece and Cyprus and, of course, to my partner, whose love and support has made life more bearable over the last decade.

I owe a lot to the team at Skyhorse Publishing, who have made this process a lot easier than I ever thought it would be. Most of that is down to my editor, Nicole Frail, who goes above and beyond the call of duty and is always there to field my endless questions and to ease my—equally endless—concerns. I also want to thank Nicole Mele, who has the unenviable duty of reading my novels in their unedited form, and my agent Peter Beren, who has been brilliant throughout.

I would like to thank Lilith_C of lilithcgraphics, an incredibly gifted designer who is responsible for this cover and some of my others. I would also like to thank Alan Fraser, Gary Neil, and Carl Ridge. I thanked them in the last acknowledgments but no matter how many times I express my gratitude, I still can't repay them for the help they gave me.

Steve Kelly, Anthony Harvison, and Jon Kirk also deserve my gratitude for helping me to promote my work. They took some of the burden off my shoulders and made my life easier. The same goes for Steve Rutley, who has an unrivaled knack for numbers and a huge heart.